FRENCHIE

Lewis Cox

FRENCHIE

Published by Sapere Books.

20 Windermere Drive, Leeds, England, LS17 7UZ,
United Kingdom

saperebooks.com

ISBN: 978-1-80055-033-9

This book is dedicated with all my love to Tam, Johnny and Priscilla.

CHAPTER 1

When the season at Le Touquet, Deauville, Evian-les-Bains, and other Continental pleasure resorts ends, the Cosmopolitan crowd turns South to Biarritz, the pearl of the Basque Coast. The boutiques of the great fashion houses in Paris open their brightly painted doors to show amusing clothes, fantastic playsuits, droll millinery, exotic flowers, glamorous scents and fabulous jewels suitable for the plage by day and the Casino and numerous exciting night-clubs and restaurants by night.

Here come the English honeymooners, the French models, the Spanish lovers and the rich Argentines from the pampas. Here, at the gaming tables of the Casino Bellevue, or La Roseraie at Ilbarritz, come the gamblers, rich farmers and businessmen from South America and their elegant womenfolk, mysterious white Russians and chic Frenchwomen. All the finest brains seem to collect to cater for those looking for fresh amusements. The best chefs are employed to excite seasoned appetites; the finest cellars in Europe are visited and ransacked for enjoyment by the connoisseur — at a price.

Along the plages, in the famous restaurants, the hotels and the Casino is a polyglot crowd from all corners of the earth — the rich and poor, the greedy, the seekers of pleasure, the lovely and ugly. Here is a cross view of life, a means of escape from life, if only for a while. At one end of the plage is the Hôtel du Palais, its ugly red and white facade dominating the scene. It was once the seaside home of the Empress Eugenie, and has changed little since that day. It is still overpowering and richly ornate, even to the gilded lifts that speed up and down throughout the day and night, filled with beautiful chic women wearing fortunes in clothes and jewels, and their handsome, sleek and wealthy escorts.

In her bedroom in a suite on the first floor of the Palais, and known as the Royal suite, was Olive de Witt, a wealthy American lady. She was large in body and spirit, with a calm expression on her beautiful face, and a quietness in her steady brown eyes which could only be found in any person through prolonged physical suffering. She was sitting up in a great wide four-poster bed. Four carved rosewood pillars supported the canopy, at the corners of which were black plumes frothing from gilt cornucopias. The headboard and valances of the bed were of deep rose brocade.

Olive de Witt had a lace cap perched on her head, and a dressing-jacket of peach-coloured crepe-de-Chine trimmed with swansdown covered her ample shoulders. With her tranquil expression, she made a ravishing picture.

On first seeing this heavy, ornate room, Olive had laughingly said that she felt like a royalty of yesterday. She did her best to lighten the atmosphere with masses of flowers, and by letting in all the light and sun she could.

Her secretary, Emma Ferrer, a slim, dark figure with tragic eyes and a pretty mouth, was plainly but elegantly dressed in black and white taffetas. She sat at an Empire period table close to Olive de Witt's bed. Her manner, as she worked, was sweetly serious, and, noticing this, Olive had a sudden wish to see the girl laugh. Everything about Olive de Witt was generous, like her heart, that wonderful organ which had held its own through countless operations to the hip which had given her so much trouble over many years.

The two women were going through the morning's mail, or rather Emma had already sorted it out, and now passed over the 'personal cream' to her employer. The mail was larger than usual, for the long list of charities to which Olive de Witt contributed so generously was beginning afresh. Donations, subscriptions and those private pensions which Olive took a personal pride and joy in giving annually, were falling due.

Olive and her secretary were on a friendly footing. Each thought a great deal of the other. The post was discussed in high spirits. One would have thought from the way they talked that business was a pleasure — and in a way it was.

Olive was gay and she had an apt wit. Emma was a demure foil. Except for their voices, the one a soft, rich contralto, and the other a light soprano, and the rustle of paper, the large room was quiet. Through the open windows, above the thin sound of children's voices from the beach, and the occasional note of the lifeguard's tinny trumpet warning the more venturesome bathers to keep nearer the shore, was the noise of the great green ocean that leapt and danced in the sunlight and broke with a roar against the rocks below the lighthouse at the end of the bay. Here were immense purple-shadowed troughs, as the grey-green surface of the sea heaved light-heartedly against the solid rock, broke in white frothing spray high into the air, then fell back as feathery spume into the restless sea.

At last, having disposed of the various charitable problems, and gone through some accounts, Olive picked up one of her letters from the pile marked 'personal'. The envelope had been slit so that the letter could be taken out easily. Olive looked at the address on the envelope, then glanced covertly at Emma.

"You know whose writing this is?" she asked.

Emma replied at once. "It is Arthur de Witt's."

"Yes, and I see the postmark is Cherbourg."

"The *United States* called there yesterday."

"It is a safe bet to say that Arthur writes inviting himself here. He will say he wants to see me, but actually Arthur wishes to see you."

Emma flushed, but the eyes that met Olive's were steady.

"Is that a warning?" she inquired.

"I am just telling you."

Olive smiled, but no answering smile broke the quiet repose of Emma's face. There was a short silence. Olive's smile faded. She pushed the lace cap half off her head as though she found even its feather-weight irksome. It sat at a rakish angle on her dark hair.

She spoke energetically, and with that directness of manner which she sometimes used. "Well, I shall be glad to see Arthur, if only for your sake," she said. "He will cheer you up. You are inclined to mope, my dear, if you are left too much to yourself."

Emma, perversely, did not wish to be cheered up. Her one fear in returning to her former employer, while she was stricken with grief after Geoff's tragic death, had been that Arthur, who had been so kind to her at the time, and then left for America, would re-join his aunt's party, travel around with them, and possibly renew the attentions which she, Emma, had once refused and which she did not want.

Arthur de Witt was a cheerful and charming companion, but under his light, irresponsible manner there was a layer of stubbornness. He did not like giving up what he wanted. If he achieved nothing else with her, Arthur de Witt could be depended upon to monopolize Emma's time, insisting upon her attention.

Though the two women were sincere friends, and each had proved herself to the other in time of need, Olive as the employer, the elder, and indeed the reason for Emma's presence in her entourage, had the final word. Emma never forgot this.

There was a soft knock at the door.

Emma looked towards it with relief. She was still rattled by Olive de Witt's words. She guessed who it was.

"*Entrez, s'il vous plaît*," she called out.

The door opened, and a Frenchman, tall, slim and debonair, in a navy blue double-breasted suit, entered. With his eyes seeking his mistress, he said, smilingly:

"*Bonjour*, Madame." Then with a fine touch of irony because Emma had bidden him enter in French, Alphonse looked at Emma, bowed slightly, and said with a pronounced English accent, "Good morning, Mees Ferrer."

Emma thought vexedly, 'Will Alphonse never learn to speak English like an Englishman?' Almost at once, she thought: 'My French accent is awful, I know, but after all it was Alphonse who taught me. It is his fault.' Then Emma smiled at herself, because it struck her as funny that she was not in the position to think Alphonse's English bad.

"*Bonjour*, M'sieur Alphonse," she teased demurely.

The chauffeur's arms were full, and he had to close the door with his shoulder. He brought books, and more flowers, a box of candies, a gaily coloured sunshade, a sheaf of papers, and a small dog, a French poodle which was a present from Olive's old friend, the Comte de la Tremblay, to replace the delicate little chihuahua dog which had been given to Olive over a year ago in Mexico by the Duque de Veragas, and which had pined and died.

Alphonse walked with easy grace and assurance across the big room. He would have done the same on a theatre stage, or in a hall full of people. It was his natural manner, this kind of swagger, and either irritated, amused or fascinated the onlooker.

Emma, seeing how laden he was, rose quietly to meet him and relieved him of some of the burdens. Firstly, she took the flowers because they were white, appealing and fragile, and if Alphonse should drop them they would be broken or wilt.

The poodle clawed at the brocaded bedspread, and Olive encouraged him to spring onto the bed via a chair covered in Genoese velvet. She liked the dog's gay and frivolous spirit, his intelligence, and his affected mincing walk. He had just been clipped and washed, and Olive tied some bows of ribbon on his head so that he looked sillier but more amusing than before.

Emma took the flowers out of the room and put them in a pail of water in a dark cupboard for arrangement later.

Alphonse put the sunshade on Emma's chair. "The bathing attendant from Chambre d'Amour returned it to the reception office this morning," he said. "You left it in a tent on the plage yesterday."

"I remember," Olive nodded. "I had complained that my tent was too far from the sea. The attendant changed me to a front-row tent. He and Suzette moved my things. I am glad to have it back." Olive seldom complained about anything, but she was well aware that her figure was ungainly and liked to bathe in as much privacy as possible on one of the less-frequented plages.

Olive went on reading Arthur's letter which Alphonse had interrupted. He had posted the letter at Cherbourg before leaving for his aunt's flat in Paris. He intended joining them next day at Biarritz.

'That will be today,' thought Olive.

She looked up from the letter, her face alive with excitement.

Emma was already aware of the news, but Alphonse did not know.

She said to him, "Mr. Arthur is coming to see us today, Alphonse."

It was a week since Alphonse had heard that Arthur de Witt was in New York and likely to remain there until Christmas. Not that he was surprised at any change of plans in the de Witt household. As courier-chauffeur to Olive de Witt, who was a renowned globe-trotter, and whose name was well known and respected throughout that knowledgeable world of those who deal in exotic foods and exquisite wines, Alphonse was accustomed to flitting here and there in any country of the world at practically a moment's notice. Though he was ostensibly Olive de Witt's right-hand man, he looked after the interests of her entourage — Emma, the secretary, Suzette, the French maid, and the several friends who made up Olive's party. Alphonse drove the front car, but often he was Captain of a fleet of cars, all filled with Olive de Witt's friends. Alphonse used to like Arthur de Witt, but that was before Emma came on the scene. There had been times when he could scarcely conceal his jealousy of Arthur, and others when there was a kind of brotherhood between them because they had both been rejected by Emma for Geoff. Now, at the mention of Arthur's name, and the fact that he was coming to Biarritz, Alphonse's jealousy flamed anew. It said much for Alphonse that he heard Olive de Witt's news about her nephew without fluttering an eyelid. Yet there was a something in his manner that he could not quite hide as he replied impassively: "That is good. Mr. Arthur will make us laugh again."

Olive looked at Emma, saying gaily, "There, you see, Alphonse considers us dull and stupid."

Thus goaded, Alphonse looked reproachfully at his mistress and said: "Not dull or stupid, Madame, nevaire. But just a little quiet, perhaps."

Alphonse spoke in English because his remark was meant for Emma.

The girl flushed deeply. First Olive, and now Alphonse! It was like a conspiracy against her.

Mrs. de Witt began a lively conversation in French with Alphonse. "Please tell the Comte de la Tremblay that Mr. Arthur is coming," she said at length. When Alphonse had left the room, Olive said to Emma: "We must celebrate Arthur's arrival. He would not consider it a welcome unless we had a few friends to greet him."

"It is not Mr. Arthur's birthday," Emma ventured to object. She had nothing against the 'little' dinner of fifty or sixty friends of Olive de Witt's that must be chosen from the long list of friends or acquaintances that had gathered around this remarkable woman since she arrived in Biarritz some weeks ago, but Olive would expect *her* to be at the dinner. That was an ordeal which Emma felt was beyond her as yet.

"Oh no, not his birthday; but we haven't seen Arthur for six months, ever since —"

Emma, startled, breathed: "Say it. I've got to hear it said soon. Perhaps it would be better to get it over. I shall feel better afterwards."

"Then I will say it," decided Olive. "It is wiser to talk about these sad things. We have made a mistake in not doing so freely, long ago. One bottles them up and broods over them." Then Olive said in a softer tone, a little apologetic in case she was administering Emma's medicine too roughly, "Ever since your fiancé was lost over the sea in a plane accident."

Emma's swan-like neck drooped forward. She looked down at her hands, which were clasped tightly in her lap. On the third finger of her left hand was the diamond and sapphire engagement ring that Geoff had put there under a year ago. She had never removed it. The ring was a vivid reminder of Geoff.

Emma did not cry. All tears over Geoff had been shed long since, but the memory of him, and the way of his going, would be a lasting and poignant memory. There was a void in her heart which nothing and nobody could ever fill.

Olive went on: "I shall not speak of this again. I would not have done so now, but you are growing too introspective. It will make you a dull companion, and that will never do."

Emma's feelings were mixed. She did not want Olive, who was her idol, to think she was dull. Since Geoff's loss, Emma, after the first terrible shock, had attuned herself to a quieter and calmer life, attending more to business and studying a new language, than to pleasure. She had no wish now to be disturbed. The coming of Arthur de Witt filled Emma with dismay. It meant a return to a life of gaiety for which her taste had gone. Arthur would draw her into his amusements. He was that kind, and could never change his light-hearted outlook on life. If boredom threatened or Arthur considered he was not extracting his full enjoyment out of life, Emma would be expected to amuse him. Already Olive was aiding him by suggesting she was dull.

Emma looked straight at Olive, but her employer's expression was guileless. The brown eyes as they met hers were soft, tender and healing to Emma's spirit.

She said, "It was you who invited Arthur to come here now."

"Did I? I write so many letters to him. I love him like a son, and naturally I like to see him happy. I know, too, that it will do Arthur all the good in the world to settle down with the right girl. I am aware of his many faults, but I also know that at heart Arthur is good and kind."

Their eyes held. Emma was not a fool. She knew what was in Olive's mind.

Presently Emma, staring out of the window, said in a shaky voice: "You did this for me as well as Arthur, because you wanted to rouse me from my silliness in continuing to mourn over something that is past. That is like you. You have sympathized and helped me, but you haven't been able to cure me, and so you wrote to Arthur, who is naturally gay at heart, not actually asking him to come, but mentioning my name casually, and saying that I was still with you, and thinking far too much of — Geoff, for my good." Emma spoke bravely, then her voice died away into silence.

Olive, too, was staring out of the big windows at the sunshine making a sparkling carpet of the restless sea.

"You are too penetrating, Emma," she laughed. "When I first met you, I thought what a mousey little creature you were. And though you have a beautiful polish now, and can speak several languages, hold your own, and have cultivated a dress sense, you are still a mouse at heart — but a mouse with a fine brain." Then Olive continued in a deeper tone. "Seriously, Emma, I am often worried about you. The time has come when I cannot let you mope any longer. I could not rouse you, and I wondered if Arthur might do the trick where I failed. If he succeeds in doing nothing more than dragging you out of that torpor of spirit into which you have fallen, then I shall be content."

Emma defended herself. "I like it this way," she told Olive. "I am not so unhappy as I seem."

"But *I* am not happy, dear Emma. I hate seeing you like this. You cannot deny that you were wretched when you first came to me. There was an interlude when Arthur and Alphonse played their parts in teaching you to laugh at life and be gay, to be witty and light-hearted, to wear clothes with chic, and to know what to eat and drink. Yet all this might never have been to look at you now, for you have gone back to your wretchedness. You are wallowing in depression and apathy. You seldom laugh or joke. It won't do, I shall not allow it."

"But you don't understand," protested Emma, flushing with mortification at such a true analysis of her condition.

Olive grew indignant. "How can you be so silly? I don't understand? You know I do. I have been through all you have and more. Like you, I once was foolish enough to think that for me no other tide could rise like the one that fate had just blighted, but I recovered. The tide swelled up again — and yet again."

Olive could have reminded Emma that she had never enjoyed such health as her secretary, that she had endured many serious operations to her hip, the result having left her with one leg shorter than the other, and that she was often in grievous pain, but self-commiseration was not Olive's line. She would have scorned such weakness.

But Emma understood. She said: "I am not clever like you. I have not your capacity for living."

"It is your life, and you must make your own capacity. Arthur is coming to help you. That is why I am overjoyed that he is coming."

Late in the afternoon, after Emma had invited nearly fifty guests to dinner to greet Arthur de Witt; and the manager of the Hotel du Palais and the head waiter had been summoned to Olive's suite and consulted about the food and wines, the flower decorations, and where each guest should sit, everything arranged expertly to the smallest detail; and when Olive was in her maid, Suzette's, capable hands, Emma was free until dinnertime. She went out, walking slowly along the plage. She climbed the rocky hillside path among the tamarisk trees, and at the top met Alphonse.

He seemed pleased to see her.

"I was hoping we should meet," Alphonse said in French, for though he spoke many tongues fluently, he was a Frenchman and fond of his country, and it was the language of his thoughts. "Shall we have a drink at the Bar Basque?" he suggested. "Or would you rather we took an auto over to Juan les Pins? We might be disturbed here."

Emma knew by these words that Alphonse had something special to say to her.

"There isn't time," she said, shaking her head. "We must risk people seeing us."

Both realized that for the time being, in a world where for a while unimportant people are made to feel important, provided they know the right people, they were marked. For Olive was a famous figure, and as part of her entourage they could bask in her reflected glory — if they liked.

They sat at a table outside the Bar Basque, and while Alphonse drank an iced beer, Emma sipped a *sirop groseille* of which she was very fond. She looked young tonight, more like a schoolgirl than a sophisticated miss. Alphonse seemed to be tongue-tied. With his elbows resting on the table, his clasped hands supporting his chin, he gazed gloomily across at Emma for a long time.

Then meeting Emma's dreaming blue eyes which held a note of inquiry in them, he smiled gently, saying, "This is a bad day for me."

"Oh, what has happened?" Emma asked. She had been too busy all day to examine the wound which Olive had given her this morning, but now Emma thought that this should have been a bad day for her, too. She looked away from Alphonse's tanned face and nice eyes, and pretended to be interested in the passing pageant of colour and noise, in the gleaming cars that seemed to glide by like great ships on smooth seas, and in the smart white dresses and fashionable footwear of the crowd sauntering along on the pavement.

"Arthur de Witt is on his way here — is already here, I suppose, and staying at the Palais."

"Yes: well?"

"When Madame told me this morning I felt terrible."

"Why?"

Alphonse appeared to be struggling with some emotion. He did not speak for a few moments, then he said: "You can ask me that! Oh, dar-r-rling Emma, how cruel you are!"

Emma smiled, but she coloured too. This was the first time for many months that Alphonse had called her darling, in that special intimate tone, and with that rolling of the r's which was his own peculiar and enchanting way of saying it. The endearment told Emma more clearly than anything else that Alphonse considered she was 'in circulation' again.

There had been moments in the past, before she became engaged to Geoff, when Alphonse had let an endearment escape his guarded lips, for he had a fine sense of the fitness of things. Emma was Olive's secretary, and he the courier-chauffeur, and they were thrown together a great deal. Olive, for all her friendliness, was dignified, and both Emma and

Alphonse knew she would be hurt if they were familiar with each other. As neither wished to hurt Olive, they were careful how they behaved when on duty. Alphonse went a step further, and was most circumspect *off* duty. Yet there were occasions when he had called Emma 'dar-r-rling'. But when she became engaged to Geoff, Alphonse had retreated at once behind an impenetrable barrier of reserve. Now, tonight, he had broken down the barrier.

To hide the sudden emotion that memory brought, Emma took refuge in lightness.

She said practically, in that silvery voice which could seem so light, but which hid so much, "Well, Arthur has as much right to be here as you or me."

"I know. That is the worst of it. You are the magnet. I do not expect de Witt has changed, and so he will do what he quickly continued to do before — demand all your attention."

"Oh, I don't mind. Madame thinks I need to go out and about more."

"I do, and just when I expected to be busy with you."

Emma remembered the papers Alphonse had brought to the suite this morning. When he heard about Arthur's coming, Alphonse was so upset that he forgot his precious plans of a new tour. Emma had been too occupied to open them. She had put them in her desk and forgotten them.

She asked now, "You have worked out a new tour?"

"Yes. I wanted to talk it over with you. It is a Christmas tour."

"Where?" Last Christmas Geoff was here — Emma caught herself up. 'I mustn't pity myself,' she told herself severely. Madame was right. It was stupid to worry over the past. Nothing could alter that. It was madness for her to allow what had happened to colour and spoil her whole life.

"You would never guess," teased Alphonse, seeing that he had not her whole interest.

"Tell me."

"It is to give Madame a surprise. I would take her back home to New York. Then, in January, we could go north to Canada, to the winter sports in the Laurentians." Talking in a mixture of English and French, Alphonse described the tour. He painted an attractive picture like an artist. New York might be Olive de Witt's home town, but Alphonse was born and bred in France and had a Frenchman's outlook on things.

Emma smiled suddenly. As usual, when Alphonse launched an idea for a new tour it struck an adventurous and ambitious chord within Emma, and she was at once enthusiastic. Her thirst for adventure and knowledge was insatiable. The smile of appreciation was like a brilliant flash, lasting a few seconds, and in spite of the fears which filled his mind with foreboding at the thought of young de Witt monopolizing this special girl's society, Alphonse smiled too.

It seemed to him rather in the nature of a personal triumph for any man to bring a genuine smile to Emma's face these days. They had been here, there and everywhere all over the world these last few months. Alphonse appeared to be possessed of a demon of restlessness. He had been indefatigable in suggesting new and exciting tours. Emma had gone through them as in a dream, following Olive about from this historic city to that. Olive had long ago guessed that Alphonse was trying to help Emma get over her grief for Geoff's loss. She had encouraged his zest. It was Emma who remembered, and said soberly: "Madame isn't ready to go home, Alphonse. She is enjoying herself here. There are visits in the country until Christmas. She is arranging to be at Versailles *for* Christmas."

"She will be homesick by then."

"So many of her friends at the American Army Headquarters are in the neighbourhood. They can make a Christmas together."

"And afterwards she will want sunshine — the Riviera, Morocco. It will be summertime in New Zealand."

Emma waited while Alphonse let his mind dwell on these places.

He said, "Do you want to go south of the Equator, Emma?"

If she had said yes, then no doubt Alphonse would have tried to please her. He was still very much in love with Emma. Though he had lost her once to Geoff White, that episode was closed. Alphonse had waited quietly in the background, helping where he could to heal her wound, hoping that soon a fresh chance would come to him. It was natural to hope, for Emma was young and lovely and much sought-after. Alphonse was a normal man, practical yet with the sentimentality of the French. He hid his heart within the blue serge suit of, what Olive dubbed him, the perfect courier-chauffeur.

"I shouldn't mind," replied Emma.

"You still have a wanderlust?" Alphonse spoke wistfully.

"Oh, I wasn't thinking of myself," Emma said with more energy than she had shown of late. "Madame needs sunshine and she must have it, or we shall have her ill again."

"*Certainement*, and she shall, our dar-r-rling Madame. But where would *you* like to go? If I can please one person I can please two. It is no effort."

"Madame comes first," said Emma firmly.

That was understood. It was Alphonse who had first taught Emma the essence of service. She had learned the lesson well.

Many beautiful and unforgettable places in various parts of the earth were photographed on Emma's mind, passing in lightning-like flashes across her brain. She shook her head a little helplessly. "I don't know, I haven't thought much about it." Emma could have added with truth, "I haven't cared much." But that might have seemed like dramatizing her loss, something she did not wish to do.

"Please, do so now."

"Can't you let Madame decide?"

"That need not stop your suggesting. I am no fool, Emma. You can be so clever at arousing in Madame a nostalgia for some place that you would like to visit."

Emma was startled. Alphonse's remark implied that she had some power over Olive. She cried, "How can you say such a dreadful thing, Alphonse!" The idea was pleasing because Emma had faithfully copied Olive de Witt's mannerisms, hoping to attach to herself a little of that enchantment which was so attractive in the older woman.

She said suddenly, "Then make it Paris, Alphonse."

The reply was unexpected and welcome coming after the tireless flitting about from place to place of the last few months, so that even Alphonse felt nerve-racked. He smiled readily now.

"You have always loved Paris, Emma."

"You taught me to. It was you who showed me what was worthwhile and why. I shall always love Paris."

"Yet you have not always been happy there?"

"I have known great joy and tragedy in Paris, but it makes no difference."

"Then I promise you we shall spend Christmas there. As you say, Versailles is nearly as much American as French." Then Alphonse added gloomily: "I suppose de Witt will stick. Now that he is over here, he will be in no hurry to go back to America. He may be as unstable as quicksand over most things, and gives a feeling of insecurity — but he will never change his mind about you."

Emma shrugged. "Does it matter?" she asked indifferently.

"Yes," snapped Alphonse.

"Arthur gets quite a kick from following the pleasure crowd. He would be lost without his holiday routine of bathing, drinks, lunch with friends, golf, dances, drinks, dinner, gambling, night-club and dance again. He is amicable and easily amused."

"So he should be," snorted Alphonse. "Biarritz boasts of the finest night-clubs in the world." He looked at Emma. "But I wonder," he said, then stopped. He could have added:

"These things used to satisfy Arthur, before he met you, but now he only enjoys them if you are there too. One of these days you will wake up, Emma, and find out that you are no longer employed as Madame's secretary but as a friend for Arthur de Witt."

It was Emma who broke the silence that followed Alphonse's exclamation.

"Arthur has worked hard for nearly a year, and deserves a holiday. Besides, he puts in quite a lot of useful work making the right kind of contacts for his firm."

"In the bars of every place we visit."

"Even if it is in bars, what then? Men must drink; and I've never seen Arthur drunk. Have you?"

"No — only noisy. But he is always noisy."

Emma laughed. "You are looking at him through the wrong end of your glasses," she said.

Alphonse was puzzled. "I do not follow."

"It isn't important."

Alphonse did not dwell on the subject. He could not imitate Arthur de Witt even if he wished to do so. He sought to hold

Emma's interest in other ways. He was not only a first-class courier and chauffeur, but was singularly well informed about most things. What Alphonse did not know natural curiosity made him try to find out.

So they talked uninterruptedly for a while. The lighthouse looked cold and lonely. Its intermittent beam of light shone brightly amid the lights of the town. The tamarisk trees were dark shadows beneath the stars. The procession of gleaming cars had eased a little, for the afternoon rush was over, and the evening amusements had not yet begun. The café tables were emptying in a kind of lull before filling again for the evening.

Then Emma said, "I must go back to the hotel and change for dinner."

"You are to join the party?"

The question was perfunctory, for some months had gone by since Olive had allowed Emma to dine alone in her room on the pretext of work or study. She had insisted on the girl taking some interest in social affairs to keep her thoughts turning outwards instead of inwards.

"Madame wishes it."

Alphonse nodded. What Madame wished must be done without argument. It was good for Emma, too. Jealous as Alphonse was of Emma's imminent meeting with Arthur de Witt, he knew that it was better for her to meet as many of her older friends as possible.

Alphonse sighed. Then he asked, because he was French, and thought clothes important, "What dress are you wearing tonight?" There was nothing odd about such a question, for Alphonse had always taken, from the first, an interest in Emma's clothes.

Glad to leave the subject of Arthur, which fascinated Alphonse while it irked him, Emma answered, "My favourite black." Then as she saw the quick frown of annoyance on Alphonse's face: "What's wrong with that? It is my best dress — one of Conrad's models. You remember Madame insisted on making me a present of one of Conrad's dresses at Easter?"

"Yes, I recall that and it suited you well, but at that time your spirits were low, and Conrad foolishly dressed you for a funeral. He forgot that in time even the darkest clouds roll by."

"Alphonse!"

"He did. I never liked the dress. He gave in to your mood, and he should not have done so. You are too young to wear black, Emma."

Alphonse paused effectively and Emma said, "You are sour tonight, M'sieur Alphonse."

She gathered up her bag and gloves and rose.

Alphonse said quickly, "You are annoyed."

"No, I'm not."

"Then why the 'M'sieur'?"

Alphonse was touchy, a sure sign that something was upsetting him.

"Because everything I do or say tonight is wrong, and I do not think you have the right to speak to me like this."

Alphonse said at once, "Pardon, Emma," but he spoke stiffly. Then with one of those quick changes of which only his volatile nature was capable, he said, "I remember when I first knew you and tried to get fresh, and you did not know what to do about it. I advised you to slap my face."

Emma recalled that time. She had slapped Alphonse's face and been sorry immediately.

She laughed. "I cannot imagine you getting fresh with any girl, Alphonse."

CHAPTER 2

Arthur De Witt arrived at Biarritz just in time to dress hastily for dinner, which was at ten o'clock. Leaving a *valet de chambre* to unpack for him he ran briskly downstairs, not waiting for the gilded lift, and went into the great *salon* in search of his aunt's party — or so he told himself. Actually, Arthur's eyes were avid for one face — Emma's. He was young and eager, virile and restless, broad-shouldered and narrow-hipped. Everything about him was cut to an American pattern. His knife-pleated, well-cut trousers, his 'built-up' tuxedo, worn a little longer than Englishmen wear theirs, but fitting snugly about his hips, proclaimed that he was a product of the States. His was a pleasant, tanned round face, with roundish eyes and dark cropped head. Usually, even at the risk of keeping dinner waiting, Arthur would have made for the bar of the hotel, meeting old friends and acquiring new ones. He had his aunt's genius for 'mixing well' with his fellow men. But tonight, no thought of wasting time entered Arthur's head. Something more important attracted his interest — Emma.

He spotted her at once. She was standing in the centre of a group of men, dressed in white. Emma had put on the Conrad model, but Olive had asked her to change it. Arthur saw that Emma had changed the style of her hair. It was cut short and curled close to her head, revealing the slender line of her lovely neck.

Arthur paused for a while, caught up by a strange emotion that welled up from somewhere deep within him and brought a lump to his throat. During that time, he recalled Emma as she was when they had first met — pathetically young, unformed and gauche, dressed badly, without poise, and lonely. Her youthfulness had appealed to Arthur, for she was eager to please, frank about her ambitions to get on in the world, and anxious to succeed. At that time, too, Emma was emotionally upset. Arthur's aunt had said it was to do with a boyfriend. He learned later that it was Geoff, a brilliant young member of the British Embassy's staff in Paris, who had made Emma unhappy. Arthur had plunged in to cheer Emma up, not realizing that soon he, too, would suffer because of her. He had been a looker-on, later, at Emma's happiness with Geoff. Then he had gone away, to be recalled within two months by Aunt Olive. News had come through that Geoff had been lost in a plane accident at sea, and Emma had gone to pieces. He would have stayed to see Emma through her trouble, but went away because Emma seemed to turn against all men. Now, Aunt Olive had written that Emma's old vitality and zest were showing signs of a revival, and Arthur had read this as a hint he should return.

The pictures of Emma, then and now, did not seem to fit.

Olive spotted Arthur. She had been on the lookout for him. She, too, was holding court, but the crowd that milled about her were older and more sophisticated people, and most of them bore honoured and great names in their own countries. There were women in Olive's circle renowned for their beauty, wit and chic, for Olive de Witt adored anyone who was intelligent and joyous, whether they were men or women.

As she waved her hand, when the diamonds on her fingers and wrist sparkled wickedly, and smiled beautifully at Arthur, who grinned back a delighted welcome, he was aware of a shadow behind her shoulder.

It was Alphonse, in faultless evening dress. Indeed, the Frenchman was better dressed than most of the men, who were in dinner-jackets. He had a good figure and went to an expensive London tailor for his clothes, as Arthur had long since found out. Alphonse was standing quietly, his manner one of becoming deference, but with no humility, and ready, at a moment's notice, to be of physical and mental assistance to his employer. He was holding her sticks in one of his hands, without which Olive could not move far.

A flame of jealousy shot through Arthur. All this time, while he had been working hard in America, trying to forget Emma, and to please his aunt, sure that Emma was in no state of mind to look at another man yet, Alphonse had been on the spot, making himself indispensable not only to his aunt, but to Emma. Curse him!

Arthur went forward. He took his aunt by the shoulders and kissed her enthusiastically on both cheeks. His manner was even boisterous, for suddenly he realized that he was close to Emma, and he would soon speak to her and touch her.

Then, having greeted Olive, and impelled by an emotion far stronger than his will-power, Arthur turned sharply to the group of black-jacketed men who seemed to close around Emma's white figure as though guarding a jewel, and called over someone's shoulder, "Hi! Emma!"

Quickly but calmly, as though she guessed he had come and would soon be calling for her, Emma looked towards Arthur, who was grinning broadly. For a second he saw the girl's spirit, which flamed occasionally in her dark blue eyes. Someone moved sharply aside. Arthur may have pushed him; or perhaps Emma may have unconsciously made some movement. Anyhow the crowd parted miraculously, and Arthur was holding Emma's hands in his.

"Well, what do you know about that?" was all he could think of to say.

The meeting had all the emotion and shock of a violent impact. Still holding Emma's hands in his own warm flexible fingers, Arthur said: "It's good to see you again, Emma. I didn't realize how good until a moment ago."

There were people looking on, everyone talking and laughing at once.

Emma was smiling. "The same old Arthur," she teased.

"You haven't changed a bit either," he retorted, but even as he spoke Arthur had an uncomfortable feeling that Emma had changed. Everything about her, the smile and the few words she said struck a hollow note, and he thought: 'She doesn't mean a word of what she says. Emma does not care whether I am here or not,' and a resentment against his aunt filled Arthur's heart for bringing him here under false pretences. Emma's heart was closed to men. He saw it at once, in those first short moments of greeting. It struck him forcibly from time to time during dinner that though outwardly Emma had never seemed so *soignée* or attractive, so gay and amusing and young, inwardly she was still suffering.

Without thinking he asked, "What have you been doing with yourself since I last saw you?"

It was an ordinary enough question, but he saw at once how his careless words had stirred up an unfortunate memory. Emma's breast heaved with sudden violent feeling.

She said quickly, withdrawing her hands from his, almost snatching them away: "It is nearly half a year since we met, a year of incessant change. Of course, I have changed. All I hope is that I haven't gone back. I should hate that." She took a step towards him, and as though her friends understood, the two were left alone.

"Even if you have — aha!" Arthur broke off to say: "I said 'even'. You who have so much can surely give away a little."

"No, I can't. I prize every little thing I've learned. I should loathe to lose anything I have worked so hard to gain." Emma caught her under-lip in her teeth to hold back the torrent of words that ached to be said, damming the weariness, the aching yearning that longed to pour out. It would have been a physical relief if she had let them out. But that, of course, was impossible in such a company as this, while Olive would never forgive her for making a scene and ruining her party.

Arthur's eyes were troubled. Emma had grown hard. There was no sign of the softness he associated with her.

"Isn't that selfish?" he rebuked, and then he laughed, aware suddenly that they were not alone in the world, that several people were about them, wanting to talk to Emma and lure her away from him.

The Comte de la Tremblay was at Arthur's elbow. He was small and agile as a monkey, older than Arthur though they had shared many of Olive de Witt's journeyings. For when Olive was ill and in pain, it was the Comte whom she thought of asking to sit with her. He had a beautiful voice, understanding, smooth and gentle, and even when she was too ill to take in what he was reading to her, the sound of his voice flowing melodiously close to her seemed to soothe the pain so that she slept and forgot for a while her hip, which had been like a blight on her life.

He said now, "How are you, Arthur?" The two men shook hands solemnly, and Arthur knew by the Comte's clasp that the latter would do anything for him.

By that time, Emma had recovered. It would be a mean trick to take it out on Arthur, who had never made any secret of his liking for her, and could be counted on to help her always, because Geoff, whom she loved, was dead, and happiness with him denied to her. Also, Emma wanted to stand well in

31

Arthur's eyes, for he had been infinitely kind to her in her time of trouble. Emma could be natural with Arthur. She did not mind what she said. He was a man of many faults, for few people say anything good of a man who likes pleasure as Arthur did. Yet he seemed to understand her and to make allowances, and took her bad moods lightly, so that her sharp barbs fell away from him.

She said soberly: "You are right, Arthur. I am selfish. But that seems to be my nature now. I seem to enjoy being unfair, catty and nasty."

"It's not the real you," said Arthur sympathetically. Then tritely, because it expressed just what he thought of her: "Even I know that the leopard can't change his spots. One of these days you'll recover and be your old self again."

They sat next to each other at dinner. That, of course, was Olive's idea, and Arthur was blissfully content. There was a certain lightness and zest in their talk at first, a little reckless, but none the less enjoyable, as if each were trying to find a weak spot in the other's armour, for that kind of talk covers awkward moments gracefully.

Over the *tasse* of iced consommé, Arthur said quietly, "We invariably meet at dinner in front of a forest of flowers or a mountain of fruit." He indicated with a gesture the profusion of flowers in the centre of the table which appeared to be specially arranged to hide them from the other diners.

"I think that is a very nice arrangement," replied Emma, who had long ago mastered the outward signs of shyness, but had never succeeded in doing so inside.

"I thought you would not be content to sit forever at the side of the table in lowly state, on the bottom rung of Aunt Olive's social ladder," twitted Arthur.

"You don't seem to mind it."

"Oh, I'm used to being pushed around to suit Aunt Olive's convenience," said Arthur easily. "I am a man, and I have few ambitions."

"Because you started life with all within reason being satisfied," replied Emma composedly.

"You are a dissatisfied little creature."

"I wasn't always. I was content enough until I realized that I hadn't the faintest idea how to enjoy life. Mrs. de Witt showed me how."

"Yet you don't aspire to sit in Aunt Olive's chair at the head of the table."

That high spot was beyond Emma's dreams. She said:

"I enjoy my dinner this way. At one side, and sheltered by flowers and tazzas of luscious fruit, I can relax and be myself. There is too much limelight at the top. I have still so much to learn. A duke, or a marquis, especially a foreign one, still has the power to terrify me if only with his important-sounding name."

"Take a tip from me: treat 'em rough. They expect it these days; and secretly, I think they like it," advised Arthur. "It makes them feel democratic, and everyone likes to be called democratic."

"I couldn't do that. I haven't acquired Mrs. de Witt's genius for making the right kind of friend, or her knack of drawing the best out of people. Indeed, I often manage to rouse the worst in them, and they take a delight in behaving badly."

Arthur turned his head and looked at her keenly, observing the clear, beautiful line of her profile and throat. His heart beat fast.

"Exactly what do you mean by that?" he demanded.

"Well, they get fresh."

Silly little innocent! 'Aunt Olive keeps Emma too close. She doesn't look after her properly,' Arthur thought. He said aloud, "Does Aunt Olive know that?"

"Of course not. I shouldn't dream of telling her."

"Why not?"

"I can look after myself."

"Can you? I shall make it my business to put her wise."

Emma laughed lightly. "Don't be silly. Mrs. de Witt is not my guardian. I am her secretary. You seem to forget that."

"I forget nothing." Then Arthur said, "What is Alphonse doing that he can't look after you better?"

"Alphonse looks after me too well for my liking. He would like to put me on a pedestal with a red museum cord around me, and keep me like an exhibit. Or he would like to put me under a glass case — only that would kill me. Besides, moving about as we do, and meeting so many different kinds of people, we must expect a few surprises."

They drank champagne, and Arthur said, "You still love champagne?"

"Oh yes. I have always liked the word 'champagne'. When I was very young, I used to think how nice it would be to have enough money to drink champagne every day of my life. I do have it fairly often, though I never buy it myself." She laughed. "But it makes me feel rich — especially if it is dry and cold."

"And clear in the head, I hope," added Arthur.

They talked of many things in light vein, not because Emma felt particularly light at heart, or because she wanted especially to amuse Arthur, but because seeing him again had reopened her mind to that grief which she was doing her best to stifle. Today Emma had definitely decided to put a stop to any more self-pity.

Arthur drank little, as was usual at meals. Mostly he drank only iced aerated water. He took his drinks in the bar before lunch and dinner — a few cocktails or some light beer. He had no palate for fine wines such as his Aunt Olive had, or as Emma had learned to cultivate.

"I came down from Paris on the train with a chap I want you to meet," Arthur said towards the end of dinner, when they were eating ice-cream over candied sponge soaked in brandy from nut toffee baskets.

"Who is he?"

"Except that he is British and his name is Tim Crake, I know little about him. His father was a shipyard foreman and invented watertight bulkheads for ships, and Crake works with his father's firm."

Emma laughed. "What is the betting that this Mr. Crake knows everything about you?"

"Well, I told him. I always tell everybody. It is a good thing to do. A chap knows where he is with me. But I kind of cottoned on to this chap. He has heard of Aunt Olive, of course."

"Most people have. Though we try to keep it from the Press, Mrs. de Witt's good deeds are well known."

"While Aunt Olive's fabulous parties are bound to be talked about."

"Did you mention my name — or Alphonse's?"

"Yes," Arthur said shortly and thrust out his chin. "Alphonse is a remarkable man. There are not two Alphonses in the world. Anything wrong in speaking about the people who make up my world?"

"Nothing."

"You mean everything. I guess that's the difference between your country and mine. Your people are kind of reserved, while mine are too frank. Anyhow, I'll bring Crake along in the morning to be vetted. If you and Aunt Olive don't like him, you can freeze him off. He's staying at the Carlton for a couple of weeks. Even if you don't take to Crake, it's a safe bet that he'll like you. By this time tomorrow, I may be chewing my nails and wondering whether it is better for your girlfriend to go off with your new friend or the chap you are so jealous of that at times you would like to shoot him."

"Either way you would lose her, so why worry?" laughed Emma.

After the last guest had gone and Suzette was looking after Olive de Witt, massaging her hip so that she might get a little rest for the remainder of the night, Emma returned to the *salon* of the suite to look up Madame's engagements for tomorrow. She was tired and yawned wearily. The windows were closed and the air was stuffy, but dawn was already filling the windows with grey light.

Alphonse was there. He had come to get his list from Emma's desk, to find out when the Rolls-Bentley was wanted, and where he was expected to go.

Emma in her white dress, looking lovely in spite of her tiredness, exclaimed when she saw him.

"I thought everyone had gone to bed — except the army of night workers in the hotel," she said.

"So did I. That is why I came to get my order list for tomorrow."

Emma opened a drawer and took out a slip of paper.

"Guests were using this room," she said, "so I put away the list. Here it is."

"I suppose it is the usual?"

Alphonse guessed what was written, but he wanted to enjoy five minutes of Emma's company. He had seen her at dinner. She appeared to be enjoying herself with Arthur de Witt. Alphonse wanted her to enjoy herself, but not with Arthur.

Emma read the list aloud. "Bathing at Chambre d'Amour plage in the morning, cocktails at the Bar Basque, lunch with some Argentines at the golf-house at Chiberta, a visit to a new specialist over at St. Jean de Luz at four o'clock — a party at La Roseraie at Ilbarritz at six. At nine-thirty a dinner party at the Château Basque, where the Russian ex-duke will provide an exquisite menu for Madame."

Alphonse nodded grimly.

"I know. He will tempt Madame with caviar pancakes served with lots of cream."

"She will only taste it to please him."

"Even a taste is poison to her."

"You would make life very dull for Madame," Emma objected.

"But think how she has to pay for it afterwards. I do not like to see her suffer, even if you do."

"You know I can't bear it," she cried almost passionately.

Alphonse looked at Emma. She looked so sweet and young in the white dress that foamed and frothed about her that he quickly relented.

He smiled crookedly. "Dear Emma!" He felt better already.

Emma did not respond. She had not finished the list. She said: "There is a *fête des chrysanthèmes* in the hotel tomorrow night — or rather," with a glance at the twilit dawn, "tonight. It should be amusing. I wonder what souvenirs they will give. I have quite a collection of them waiting to be sent to my goddaughters in London."

"The little twin girls of Mrs. Jennifer and Mr. George?"

"Yes: Lila and Emma."

"Lila! That is a pretty name."

"Isn't it?" Emma spoke without enthusiasm. She stared out of the window at the heaving grey expanse of sea. She recalled Jennifer, with whom she had shared a flat when Jennifer was a sales assistant and she was a typist in an East End biscuit factory, writing apologetically to ask whether she minded one of the babies being called Lila. 'I hope you don't mind,' said Jennifer's letter, 'because George and I want our little girls to be prosperous. Lila is clever and rich, and you are one of the luckiest girls I have ever met. You are both on Easy Street.'

The letter had come just after Geoff had — gone. There was a time when Lila, the lovely predatory blonde, had stolen Geoff's affections from her, Emma. But he had not enough money for Lila and she had cast him aside; Geoff had become bitter for a long time.

Emma had made no objection to the children's names. Jennifer was never moved by sentiment. She was practical. It was characteristic of her that she had not suggested happiness for her children, only riches and what she called luck. Perhaps she thought riches and luck synonymous with happiness.

She turned towards Alphonse, and put down the list. "That is all."

"That is all!" echoed Alphonse. "So I should think. What a feverish rhythm of life it is here. It would seem almost as though everyone in Biarritz must be unhappy, trying to drown their sorrows in amusement."

Emma smiled. "It is a busy day," she agreed. "But Madame isn't unhappy. Every day is one of pleasant anticipation for her. She adores meeting people, new faces to look at, clothes to admire, new minds to explore. Think what pleasure her parties give to others. And now that Mr. Arthur is here, she is more than content."

"Oh, Mr. Arthur!" exclaimed Alphonse offhandedly. Then he asked, "Did you have an enjoyable evening?"

"It was delightful — and something like old times. Everybody was so friendly."

"I noticed you and Mr. Arthur had much to say to each other."

"I loved seeing him again. But it was rather harrowing too. Last time —" Emma could not go on. She waved her hand in a futile gesture. Meeting Arthur had recalled to her mind vividly the last time she saw him. For Arthur had been with her when she had been summoned to the British Embassy in Paris to hear details of how Geoff had been lost. She had felt numb with grief, like a person moving in a nightmare. Geoff's was only a minor post at the Embassy, though his career already showed promise of being a distinguished one. The Ambassador had spoken to her kindly about Geoff, praising the brilliancy of his mind and saying that this was a loss that could never be replaced.

Emma remained silent, fighting for that self-control she had promised herself over the past. Alphonse took her hand and crushed it between both of his. She could feel the strength in his flexible fingers. She knew that his distress at seeing her so moved was nearly as great as hers.

"Is it so bad?" he whispered.

"I shall always feel it," Emma said abruptly.

"Oh, Emma, what a lucky fellow he was to have such a love."

The words rang in Emma's ears for days, long after Alphonse had forgotten them. They haunted her because love had kept her humble, and she knew how insignificant her love was. There were times lately when it had occurred to Emma to wonder whether she could ever have been the right helpmate for the brilliant, nerve-ridden and impatient Geoff. He had so many complexes, and he made masses of complications about everything he did or said, and he was worried about his income which he thought was too small for one, so how could two people possibly manage on it? Emma had offered to work, but Geoff would not hear of the idea. He expected her to manage as Olive de Witt did, yet without the American's experience or money. They had many arguments and often squabbled because Emma had taken a firm stand with Geoff. It was so bad for him always to get his own way.

Emma resolutely shut the door on all such thoughts, for they sapped the self-confidence she had taken such pains to build up, and made her feel a failure.

She smiled at Alphonse, and gently loosened her hand from his grasp. She replaced the list in the drawer and closed it.

"I will try to make Madame rest tomorrow," she said unemotionally.

But they were accustomed to a full pad of dates, for Olive de Witt was a popular woman. Their combined aim was to see that Olive could carry out her programme with the least possible fatigue. It was useless to protest, to say that Olive was wearing herself out, and ruining the health she should be conserving. This had grown to be Olive's way of life. Friends seemed to go out of their way to aid and abet her, for they clamoured to have her at their parties, and to go to hers. They sought her out, doing their best to interest and amuse her. She was known to be clever and amusing, and generous to a degree. The roving life, seeing new places and fresh faces, seemed to suit Olive best.

At Chambre d'Amour, on the plage d'Anglet next morning, in the brilliant sunshine, when the dark emerald sea broke and frothed against the rocks, where each wave curled, then dashed madly in a foam of cream along the shore, Arthur brought Tim Crake to Olive's tent. Both men were in loose-collared shirts and bathing trunks and wore basket shoes.

Olive was sitting in a camp-chair in front of her large gaily striped tent, which was in a conspicuous position at the head of the front line of bathing tents. She wore an enormous Mexican beach hat decorated with coloured tassels. It shaded her face and shoulders, and was as big as an umbrella. She wore a voluminous yellow beach robe which, while it obviously hid the clumsy figure of a large woman, also concealed Olive's infirmity. A huge plastic bag, with an applique of bright flowers on it, was by her side.

The devoted Comte de la Tremblay sat close to Olive. He looked more wizened and monkey-like than ever in a scarlet robe which was thrown back to reveal his brown sticks of arms and legs. He wore dark glasses which hid his alert eyes.

Emma was there, dressed in a simple white cotton dress. It was one which Suzette's clever fingers had fashioned out of one of Olive's old dresses, and cost Emma five hundred francs as a tip.

There were several American girls in the circle about Olive. They were in colourful bathing dresses and lay about on the sand in the sunshine, determined to acquire that lovely tan which so many women of the southern countries seem to get without much effort. They were 'doing Europe', and taking a look at Biarritz in their stride. There were, too, young Armand de la Tremblay who had lately graduated from St. Cyr and was now a lieutenant in the French Army, and a brother-officer.

Both men were polite and shy, with brown eyes and little dark moustaches which their fingers caressed continuously.

At sight of Olive de Witt seated in the midst of her friends, Arthur paused momentarily and said to his new friend:

"There's my aunt."

"Where?" Tim looked about him for the smartest woman on the beach.

"You can't miss her, Crake. The one in the yellow beach robe."

"Oh, that!" Crake dismissed Olive from his mind. He did not mean to be disparaging, but that type of woman had no appeal for him. His roving eye had seen someone else — a slim dark girl, not dressed like the others, who was standing behind Olive de Witt's chair.

"Who is the lovely girl standing by your aunt?" he asked with enthusiasm.

"Which one?" Arthur quickly followed Tim's glance. "Oh! — well, that's Emma," admitted Arthur unwillingly.

"And who is Emma?"

"Aunt Olive's secretary."

"An English girl?"

"She *was*. Emma is fast becoming a cosmopolitan. Her recreation is learning new languages; but she's not a bluestocking."

"She looks too pretty and intelligent to be that," commented Tim. "Your aunt may want to keep her in the background, but she can't hide the obvious."

"I don't get you," said Arthur roughly.

Tim laughed disbelievingly. "Then you're not so quick as I thought you were," he said.

By that time, the two men had reached Olive.

She did not see them at first, for her head was turned towards one of the American girls who was talking to her. Crake's eyes strayed to where Emma, silent and dreamy, was standing aloof. He thought she was even lovelier close to than he had at first thought. She wore a rush broad-brimmed sun-hat to shade her eyes. Though it had not the eye-catching size of Olive's, it suited Emma very well, framing her face and protecting her from the sun. She was watching the sea, which had never seemed more beautiful in the sunshine. Her quietness gave no clue to her thoughts. If anyone had asked Emma what she was doing, she would have answered, "Watching the bathers."

At that moment something strange entered Tim's consciousness, and his eyes wavered. Olive's voice, a rich, thrilling contralto, had caught his sensitive ear, and in spite of himself, forgetting for a while Emma's loveliness, Crake listened. He enjoyed its soft pitch, and recognized its controlled power. He knew at once that here was a woman out of the ordinary, one who was wise about many things, one to whom he would be compelled to listen. He looked at Olive's profile, and noticed the clear skin of her cheek. He could not see her eyes or smooth brow for they were hidden under the brim of her hat, but from what he saw and heard, Crake realized dimly why people spoke of Olive de Witt almost with bated breath.

Arthur jogged his elbow, and mentally Crake pulled himself together, anxious for the first time in his life to make a good impression upon a woman old enough to be his mother.

Olive sensed that someone had come to join the party, and she turned her head, leaning back in her chair so that she could look up to smile at Arthur, who was bending under her hat brim to kiss her soft cheek. At the same time she saw Tim and held out her hand to him, almost before she heard Arthur say his name.

Tim was accepted at once as a friend of Arthur's. How or when the two men met did not seem to matter.

Squinting a little in the brilliant sunshine, Olive said, "Do you bathe, Mr. Crake?"

"I have already been in this morning, Mrs. de Witt."

"Then take a chair over there and sunbathe before we go back for drinks." It was then that Olive saw Emma. The latter had come from behind her employer's chair. She was standing in Olive's direct vision. Olive looked up at Emma and saw that she was staring at Tim with round eyes. It occurred to her that Emma's face was pale and a little tense. She introduced them at once, then, puzzled by something in Emma's manner, she added:

"Do you know Mr. Crake, Emma?"

"No, Mrs. de Witt — we have not met before," said Emma. She invariably treated her employer formally in public. It was only in private that they were Olive and Emma to each other. Not that Olive was a stickler for what was proper. It was Emma who decided their position.

Emma bowed to Tim who at once moved to her side, and together for some minutes they stood watching the animated scene of bathers in the sea in silence.

Then Tim said, "Is there anything odd about me?" He sounded puzzled.

"No. Why?"

"Is there a smut on my nose?"

"No."

"I have scarcely looked at you, but I know you have some freckles on *your* nose."

"Oh!"

"Why do you stare at me like that?"

"Am I? I'm sorry." Emma spoke breathlessly. "It's only that you reminded me of someone I used to know."

"I hope he was a nice fellow," Tim said lightly.

"Oh yes."

"And that he treated you well?"

"Very well." But she seemed agitated, and Tim continued:

"Because if he didn't, and you tell me where to find him, I'll seek him out and sock him on the jaw."

"It is kind of you to say that, but I'm afraid you'd have to go a long way to do it, Mr. Crake."

Emma hoped she did not sound so confused as she felt. Actually Crake found her ready answers well composed.

"How far?" he demanded. "I am used to running about at my father's beck and call to all the ports of the world, selling his bulkheads to shipbuilders. Distances don't mean so much to me as they do to some people."

Emma shook her head. She was still rather white.

"He is dead," she said in a flat voice.

"Oh dear. I wish I hadn't said that. It was silly. Now you'll hate me forever."

"No, I couldn't do that ever, if only…"

Emma stopped, stuck for words.

"Yes? Do go on." Tim's voice was impatient, and once more Emma was reminded of her lost fiancé who was so often impatient, especially if he had to wait for anything.

"You are very like him. You have the same colour eyes and mannerisms." Though she would not say so to this stranger, the word 'arrogant' occurred to Emma. He might misunderstand if she were to speak of Geoff's faults. Yet she had loved him in spite of them, or because of them.

"He was a special friend?" persisted Tim, and wondered if he could use this similarity to further his friendship with her.

"We were to have been married," Emma said, so simply that Tim did not catch the anguish behind the words. "So if I seem to stare, you will know that I do not mean to be rude."

"I shall try to remember," said Tim seriously. "But I am made the way that I do not mind how much I am stared at by you, so I give you leave to look at me when and how you like."

Then Arthur joined them, and presently the three sat down in the sunshine. The American girls spoke to Tim, and before long he was a part of that magic circle which had Olive de Witt as its centre. It was a new pleasure for Tim, who had never had such an experience before — meeting many important people whose names he had often seen in the Press, talking amiably and simply to them on the beach in the sunshine, not about anything in particular, for they were not exerting themselves to be witty or clever. It was the pleasantest way of idling away an hour. There was nothing in it. Yet next day, a roving reporter made them all front-page news, and a photograph was splashed across the daily paper, under the caption 'Olive de Witt's beach party'. Underneath was a paragraph of all their names.

Alphonse disturbed them. He came down to the beach and walked along to the group. Looking at the two watches he was in the habit of wearing on his wrist, Alphonse came to a stop behind Olive's chair.

He bent to speak to her.

Olive nodded and picked up her beach-bag. It was a signal for Suzette, who had been sewing, seated within the beach tent, to appear with two sticks. With Alphonse's help, Suzette assisted Olive to rise.

Arthur did not help. He went on talking, rising presently to give his aunt extra room to pass. Tim saw then what he had not known before, that one of Olive de Witt's legs was shorter than the other, and that she moved forward with difficulty, making full use of her sticks.

He said impulsively in an undertone to Arthur, "You didn't tell me your aunt was lame."

"I never thought to. I often forget she is," was the careless answer. "But I bet if you'd had half as many operations as she has, you'd want to be shoved around in a chair for the rest of your life."

Olive turned to say to Tim, "No, please don't get up," as he attempted to rise. "We are dining at the Château Basque tonight. Do join us if you have nothing better to do."

In case she should go without knowing his intentions, and perhaps snub him as an interloper if he turned up, Tim made sure of his invitation. He said quickly: "Oh, thank you so much, Mrs. de Witt. I shall love to dine with you."

Olive smiled and nodded and passed on.

Tim caught Emma's arm. "What time?" he asked her urgently.

"At nine-thirty, but they won't sit down until ten." She drew away from his touch.

"Aren't you going to be there?" Tim asked, aware that he was disappointed.

"I hardly think so."

"It's a shame!"

"What is?" interrupted Arthur.

"That Miss Ferrer won't be dining at the Château Basque."

"It's Emma's fault if she doesn't."

"Mrs. de Witt may not permit it."

Arthur laughed. He hailed the Comte de la Tremblay, who was hurrying after Olive de Witt, and spoke to him for a few moments. Then he said:

"Listen, Crake: my aunt and Emma are friends. Emma may draw a fat salary from her each week or month, whatever the arrangement is between them, but Aunt Olive treats Emma like a daughter. She loves her. See?"

Tim nodded. He was duly impressed. He felt rather foolish taking up the cudgels on Emma's behalf when there was no battle to fight. In spite of a certain youthful sophistication Emma had seemed rather a mousy little thing, pretty enough to warrant his sticking up for her... It was unnecessary, it seemed.

Emma left them smilingly.

Tim and Arthur looked after her in silence. Tim watched Alphonse helping Olive de Witt up some steps, then he asked in a puzzled tone: "Who is that man with Mrs. de Witt? I mean, the chauffeur?"

"That is Alphonse."

"A Frenchie?"

"Yes. But like Emma, Alphonse can speak several languages, far more than Emma really. It was Alphonse who started Emma on the craze."

Tim looked blank. The more he heard about Mrs. de Witt and her ménage, the more puzzled and astonished he felt. He remarked, "Mrs. de Witt seems to like him."

"So she should," was the hearty reply. "Alphonse has been with Aunt Olive for years, ever since she took to globe-trotting. He thinks there is no one like her, and of course there isn't. But just as Emma isn't an ordinary secretary, or Suzette a commonplace French maid, so Alphonse is an exception among chauffeurs. He is a courier-chauffeur."

"Same thing, isn't it?" And for some unexplainable reason, Tim was suddenly jealous of all those people who lived so close to Olive de Witt and meant so much to her.

"Aha! You are wrong there. Alphonse combines the knowledge of Cook's with the ability to organize a personal tour for Aunt Olive — and by organization, I mean that he leaves nothing to chance. Everything is arranged down to the smallest detail. Alphonse even makes allowances for the human element which can contrive somehow to smash the finest plan. He extracts every ounce of enjoyment out of each pleasure he arranges, not for himself, or because he wants that particular pleasure, but to please and delight Aunt Olive. It is service *par excellence.*"

"I expect she pays him well," said Tim, who would not concede Alphonse any honours.

"I daresay, but payment thought of as dollars can only buy their approximate worth. What Alphonse gives in service and loyalty is something that money cannot buy."

"It sounds ridiculous to me — rather farfetched."

"Perhaps, because you have never come across it before," said Arthur shrewdly; and he advised: "For pity's sake, don't call Alphonse a glorified chauffeur to Aunt Olive. You'd be outcast forever if you dared to criticize Alphonse — unless," and here Arthur laughed wickedly, "you want to hand him the palm for glamour. I hear that he has been approached by film magnates who want him to go to Hollywood and make pictures, but Alphonse, instead of being pleased at the idea of being a star and a dollar millionaire, is furious. He has personality, good looks in a Latin way, and is certainly idolized by the girls. I've heard them. I know."

Tim listened in sour silence.

By that time, Olive had reached the top step.

The group on the beach had fallen silent. Without Olive's presence to encourage and spread interest among them, they were lost.

"Where do we go from here?" Tim asked flatly of Arthur.

"We'll join Aunt Olive at the Bar Basque in about an hour's time," was the reply.

He hailed some people sauntering along the promenade. He had spoken to them in the sea earlier in the morning. They stopped to speak to him.

"Come and have a drink," Arthur invited cheerily.

They were nothing loth, and shouted, "Where?"

"The Bar Basque."

"Right-o. We'll be there."

Tim said, "Will Mrs. de Witt mind?" Someone had to put the brake on Arthur's impulsiveness.

"Aunt Olive mind! Say, why should she?"

"Must she have an audience?"

"She's big enough to have one — but I can tell you they'd be lost without her in the centre of the stage. It would be a tame party."

"But you don't know these people."

"I do — not so well as I know you, but that makes them interesting because there is more to find out," laughed Arthur.

"You'll be filling the bar with *your* friends."

"Then the management will be glad. Anyway, they always welcome Aunt Olive with open arms. She brings the customers in."

"It is extraordinary," repeated Tim. "It is like a snowball rolling, this gathering together of people for drinks." He was dazed and felt out of his depth. He said to Arthur: "I'm not used to such hospitality. As a matter of fact, I can't really afford it."

"Then don't. Come and enjoy ours. I promise you we are amusing, and I know the drinks will be good." Arthur flung his arm across Tim's shoulders in a boyish gesture that was meant

50

to be reassuring. "After dinner tonight," he prophesied, "I will take any bet that you will be one of us."

Emma did not go to the bar; but Olive, who was dressed ready for her lunch with her Argentine friends at Chiberta, came in for half an hour, during which she drank a little iced tonic water, and was the centre of attraction in the crowded bar.

Again Tim Crake was surprised. Olive wore trailing skirts.

She did not look fashionable. She was remarkable for her clear skin and the calmness of her broad brow which showed beneath her hat brim. What astonished Tim was that when she made her appearance it was the signal for everyone to rush towards her. Even Tim, who thought Olive's entrance theatrical and effective, found himself, glass in hand, edging towards her. He was caught up in other groups of people. He heard himself making dates with comparative strangers. He thought: 'This time yesterday I did not know such a world existed. If anyone had told me I should be invited to parties and accepting them, I should refuse to believe them. Yet here I am talking glibly of attending fêtes and cabarets, dinners and gambling, picnics and rounds of golf at Chiberta.'

He felt strangely excited, not only because of the prospect of many pleasures crowding his life, but because he had just met a lovely girl who intrigued him as no other girl had ever done. Tim was nonplussed what to do about it, for Emma was a part of this new strange existence which had opened golden doors of fun in his life, yet she stood apart from it. Though she seemed amenable enough, and he had the extra pull with her of being like the fiancé who was dead, Tim did not know how to approach Emma. He knew instinctively that Arthur liked her. It would be difficult to overcome that barrier and push himself forward, because it was through Arthur that he had met her at all.

Then Olive spoke to him, and Tim forgot Emma and the problems that were worrying him.

He was pleased and proud when Olive singled him out to talk to him. She made him feel somebody, and as though someone had crowned him with a laurel wreath for something worthwhile that he had done. Tim never knew that Olive had learned the secret of raising the insignificant to an art.

CHAPTER 3

The Château Basque is perched on a rock which juts out into the sea. It was owned by a Russian who had fled from his country at the time of the Revolution and taken refuge in France, where he became a French citizen. He bought the Château Basque and turned it into a famous restaurant, where fine wines and perfect food were to be had. His personality succeeded in making it the hub of night-club life in Biarritz. It was a high distinction, for Biarritz has many wonderful night-clubs. In the garden of the Château there are many deal tables standing about under the dark tamarisk trees, where people come for *apéritifs* about lunchtime, and to watch over iron railings the heavy seas pounding against the rocks below.

The old Russian, now dead, had cultivated a flowing red beard, and his son who succeeded him in this unique business did the same.

Here, behind the little green-painted gate, looking so innocuous, all the smart world of Biarritz gathers nightly to eat and drink and to watch some of the most daring cabaret shows known. Behind the gate which leads on to the Corniche road, life seems to sleep all day, except for an hour before lunch, or when the weather is rough. But in the evening, when the fairy lights are lit in the dark trees, and the windows of the ugly turreted Château are ablaze with light, things wake up.

The Château, with its fine cellar and world-renowned chef, its *maître d'hôtel* who hand-picks his staff so that the service is smooth as velvet, is known far and wide. Not to have dined or supped at the Château while in Biarritz is proof that one is of no importance; while to be a privileged member of one of Olive de Witt's parties is to set the seal to one's social success.

In immaculate dinner-jacket and neat black tie, the accepted dress of any man dining abroad — immaculate because it happened to be new and cost him a packet of money at a Savile Row tailor's — Tim walked along to the Château Basque for dinner. He was hungry because at home in England he had finished his evening meal at this hour. He looked forward with some excitement to a pleasant evening.

During the day, after a round of golf at Chiberta among the pines and sand dunes with Arthur, and a drink at the clubhouse, Tim was at a loose end until the evening. He bathed again, and made some inquiries about Olive de Witt — not in a spirit of curiosity, but because he was genuinely anxious to hear more about this American widow with her fabulous wealth, who was both so lavish in her hospitality, and so generous in her charities — a woman who intrigued him because she knew how!

Emma came to dinner after all. Arthur had made a special point of it. He said to his aunt, "Make Emma come tonight."

"My dear boy, if Emma does not wish to go I cannot force her."

"You must. Crake thinks you are holding her back."

"Why should he think that?" asked Olive.

"He's got a complex about employers and employees. He thinks you are a tyrant, and Emma is a poor downtrodden thing."

Olive laughed.

Later, when Olive made a point of inviting Emma to dinner, the latter pleaded her usual excuse of work.

Olive would not listen. "That is nonsense. If the work is too much, we must get extra help," she said.

Emma did not need much persuasion. She was glad to go. She could not get Tim out of her mind. If Tim had not been so like Geoff, she would not have given him a second thought. As it was she longed to see him again, wondering how far the similarity went, and to feed her inward grief upon Tim's face and mannerisms.

Emma wore a black dress, partly because it was her newest one, but also because her coloured ones were months old and dated. She had worn the white one last night. Arthur had sent a shoulder spray of stephanotis to her room earlier in the evening, which she wore. It brightened the sombre dress and gave it a new lease of life, and made Emma feel festive.

They were greeted at the gate by the Russian. He looked wild, mournful and happy all at once. The party was slow to sit down. First of all they had drinks in the *salon*, which was crowded and noisy. It gave latecomers time to arrive before going in to dinner.

Olive's table was decorated as for an occasion. The tablecloth was sewn with gold stars, and there were yellow candles in filigree gold candlesticks on the table, and red roses in flat gold dishes. It was a dinner to dream about. The rich clear soup that caressed the palate when drunk was served from a golden bratinka encrusted with barbaric semi-precious stones. With slow ceremony the *maître d'hôtel*, attended by two waiters, dipped the kofchick into the bowl and poured a little of the amber fluid into each plate. There was a mousse of lobster, and wild duck garni with the sauce of bitter oranges, and a tender green salad, and small pancakes of caviar topped with cream. Then tall bombe ices like pale coloured cones were served, and baskets of fruit so perfect it seemed a pity to eat it.

There was, of course, champagne, most of the bottles iced, because the Americans liked it that way.

Soon after they were seated, Arthur moved a candlestick so that he could see Emma across the table.

"Now I can see you," he grinned, adding approvingly, "You are looking charming." Indeed, he thought Emma was looking particularly well tonight, for her eyes were sparkling as with some inward fire, and her cheeks were pink as with some inward fever.

Emma had not seen Arthur since the morning. "Thanks for your flowers," she said. "They are lovely. I am so glad to have them."

"They suit you, Emma." There was a waxen purity in the fragile blooms that seemed to Arthur when he chose the flowers as being particularly suited to Emma.

Tim turned his head to look at Emma critically. He was feeling a little out of it in this gay company, rather confused at the profusion of luxury about him. It annoyed him to see Emma wearing Arthur's flowers. He thought vexedly, 'Why didn't I think of that?' He had been so excited by the event of the day he had not thought of giving Emma flowers. So he said sourly — because he must vent his ill-humour on someone, and why not on this mousy little thing? — "You should never wear black."

"Don't you like black?" Emma asked quickly.

"No, it is too funereal. You are too young. Besides, it doesn't suit your style."

It could have been Geoff speaking, his tongue bitter because of his frustration and complexes — a Geoff who seemed to enjoy making complications of simple things.

For a moment Emma was silent, overwhelmed by a rush of bittersweet memories. Then she remembered that this kind of thing, even in Geoff, must be checked, as it would reach a point when she could not stop it.

She said coldly, without glancing in Tim's direction, and looking into the heart of a red rose: "I had not thought to ask your opinion about what I should wear, for what could it matter to you what I have on? I know my taste is good because some of the best dressmakers in the world, whose opinions count, have been kind enough to tell me so."

"Conceited, aren't you?"

Emma made no reply, and Tim went on: "It does matter to me. Don't ask me why, because I can't tell you. I only know that you'd look prettier in white or even some colour."

Emma did not smile. She said, "If you speak so plainly to your friends about your likes and dislikes of their clothes, you won't be popular."

Tim paused. Emma was snubbing him. He did not mind much. But it surprised him to find that he had thought her mouse-like, for underneath that quiet manner she could obviously be quite sharp. It had the desired effect however, for he recovered his temper, saying good-humouredly, "So to be a success, it is essential for me to flatter my friends."

"It is half the battle."

"And the other half?"

Emma opened her mouth to speak, and turning her head chanced to meet Tim's inquiring, brooding grey eyes. "That can wait," she said abruptly. "I'll tell you some other time."

Later, during dinner, Tim asked Emma what she did to earn her living. He was evidently puzzled by her position in Olive's entourage. She seemed to have the freedom of an honoured guest, yet there must be a reason why she was with Mrs. de Witt.

Emma looked puzzled. "I am Mrs. de Witt's secretary," she said.

Tim laughed. "I call that play, not work. I mean —"

"You think Mrs. de Witt pays me for doing nothing?"

"Hardly that, but I don't understand what —"

"You obviously know nothing about me."

"I don't."

"Why this sudden interest in my private life?" Emma inquired icily.

"I am interested."

There was fear in Emma's heart, and happiness, too. The fear was there because that was how Geoff would have spoken to her, and she did not want a repetition of that part of her life. It was ended. Yet the happiness was there because Tim had shown his interest in her. It was strange how mixed up emotions could be.

She did not say much more to Tim. Resolutely Emma spoke to her partner on her other side. Sometimes she talked across the table to Arthur. Yet she was acutely conscious of the loose-limbed man with the reckless grey eyes on her other side.

Towards the end of dinner, Tim touched her arm.

Emma started. The touch sent a flame through Emma's veins. She turned her eyes inquiringly to him.

"Yes?"

"I've scarcely had a word alone with you this evening," he complained.

"That is surely your fault. As a matter of fact, I know you won't understand, but I am on duty. Even if you wished it, I could not have given you all my attention."

Tim looked blank. "I don't understand this set-up. What do you mean by duty? Do tell me. I really should like to know."

"Well, it is a part of my job to see that everything goes smoothly between the guests. If a guest is not pleased, or well taken care of, or the food or wines are not right in quality or quantity, or a waiter is lax, I report that to Mrs. de Witt. What is wrong is noted to be complained about and corrected next time. That is why Mrs. de Witt's dinners are so perfect; nothing is left to chance, and every detail is noted and arranged."

"I see. You are, in a sense, your hostess's ambassador?"

"Hardly that. Mrs. de Witt would have made an excellent one for her country. As a matter of fact, the Press welcome her as the uncrowned queen of Biarritz."

"That kind of duty must keep you busy — you don't get much time to eat."

Emma laughed. "I have more than I want."

"Don't you ever get any time off?"

"Lots. Why?"

"Because I should love to see you sometime — alone."

Emma looked down demurely. "You know where I am staying," she said.

"Yes — but can I phone you? I should never have the courage to face that grand, bewigged, silk-stockinged major-domo who stands holding a wand near the reception-desk of the Palais. He looks like an effigy from Madame Tussaud's."

"Everybody in the hotel thinks he is lovely. When did you see him?"

"I called in this evening with Arthur de Witt. Well — may I give you a ring?"

"Yes," Emma heard herself saying.

"Is there any special time I must get you?"

"Yes, about lunchtime. Usually I have my meal at my desk in the *salon*; I am on the spot for the phone."

"All right. I'll give you a ring tomorrow at one."

At midnight Olive's party left the Château Basque, and returned to the Palais, where a *fête des chrysanthèmes* was in full swing. The orchestra was embowered with chrysanthemums;

the candelabras of the *salon*, which was used for dancing, were wreathed in flowers. The waiters wore flowers in the lapels of their jackets, and each guest was presented with favours of the flowers whose long stalks were covered in silver paper. The younger members paired off at once and began to dance.

Arthur came up to Emma. "We've both done our duty for tonight," he said. "Now for a little relaxation."

She went willingly, glad of the exercise. They danced for half an hour — tangos and waltzes mostly, not speaking much, though Arthur pressed his cheek to Emma's, a position which he seemed to like, and which she did not appear to mind.

Once, moved by the sentimentality of the music, Arthur moved his cheek, and kissed her gently several times.

Emma drew back. "Don't!"

"Why ever not?"

"I do not like it."

"Being kissed by anyone or just me?"

"Anyone."

"Okay, just once again and I won't bother you any more tonight," Arthur begged, suiting the action to his words.

They sat on cushions around the edge of the dancefloor and watched a cabaret show of noted Spanish dancers, who had come across the border to entertain them. Tim's eyes met Emma's across the room, and he smiled. It was a sweet, frank smile and made him look almost boyish.

Emma was suddenly happy, but why she could not say.

The stars were paling, and dawn was coming in when Arthur walked back with Tim to the Carlton. They went arm in arm, like old friends.

"I often stroll about at this time of day, before I go to bed. A breath of fresh air often sends me straight off to sleep." Arthur sniffed deeply. "Smell the ozone?"

Tim yawned. "I'm usually thinking of waking up at this hour," he pointed out.

"Do you good to get a change."

"All the good in the world," agreed Tim.

"Like it tonight?"

"Loved it. To be frank, I've never been to a party like that one. But don't get me wrong if I tell you I'm worried at the expense. It must have cost Mrs. de Witt a packet of money to give such a party."

Arthur laughed. "I can see you have been encouraged to save, not spend."

"Yes. My father thinks spending for pleasure is a crime."

"And so you don't know the value of money."

"I think I know its value better than you," retorted Tim.

Arthur chuckled. He let go of Tim's arm and turned to face the breeze, walking backwards.

"That's the answer I thought you'd make. I was brought up in a different school, that for a man to know the value of money he must not only understand how to save, but how to spend. Fun, the jam that makes life worth living, the incentive for existing, is a necessity, and necessities have to be bought. Without the jam, a nation would soon become dull and stupid."

"What if one hasn't the money to waste on jam?"

Arthur shook his head. "There you go, talking about wasting money on jam. If my Aunt Olive saved all her money and sat on it instead of spreading it around, many people would go short, while quite a number would be out of work. She has cultivated a zest for life, and she is willing to share it with less fortunate people. So what?"

Tim laughed. "If you look at it that way —"

"It is the only way."

"You sound almost plausible. Anyway, I'm too tired to argue, especially after such a wonderful evening."

"Fine! Now don't you bother about preserving a perspective in this town. Remember you are on holiday. Let yourself go. When you return to work, you'll feel a new man."

"I suppose you're right," said Tim dubiously.

"Of course I'm right."

Privately Tim wondered how such a rich young man could be so guileless about money — or was he? Arthur was a successful businessman. He could not be such a fool as he pretended to be.

Emma was singing next morning, when Louis, the *valet de chambre*, who was gay and romantic, brought her *café au lait* into her room. He was a friend of Suzette's, and reported to her, with accompanying expressive gestures, that the sad-eyed Mselle, the protegee of Madame, was singing like a soubrette from Paris.

"It is lof," Louis told Suzette dramatically, blowing a kiss from his fingers with an airy gesture. "Me — I know the signs — *toujours l'amour!*"

Louis' news made such an impression on Suzette that sometime during the morning she went out to the garage to look for Alphonse. He was in the courtyard, his head inside the open bonnet of the Rolls-Bentley. It was the latest model from England, and Alphonse, who had taken a refresher course at the Rolls company and brought the car over, was still finding out its secrets.

Without preamble, because Olive, though engaged with the dressmaker, might want her at any minute, Suzette said, "Have you noticed that Mselle Ferrer is happy again, M. Alphonse?"

Alphonse's head emerged from the bonnet of the car. He closed it quickly.

"So! That is a strange thing for you to come and tell me. How do you know?"

"I thought you would like to know."

"Of course," was the simple answer.

"Louis says that she was singing and dancing when he took in her *petit déjeuner*."

Alphonse smiled. He could not visualize Emma behaving like that.

He said: "Possibly the good Louis exaggerates. But even if it is but half true, then Mees Ferrer must be happy. *Bien!*" Alphonse was delighted to hear that Emma's spirits had returned, but he sighed too, for with Emma's return to normality, there would now be no need to cheer her up. There would be no further excuse for him to suggest a play or cinema or any pleasure to distract her — and so give himself the pleasure of being with her.

Suzette watched him with her little dark eyes. She knew all about Alphonse's heart. She well knew that it had long ago been given to Emma. She was even a little jealous, spiteful and catty. It gave her a certain delight to tease him.

She ventured, "Perhaps it is because M'sieur Arthur is here once more?"

"Pstt!" It was an exclamation. Alphonse often used it either to call a waiter's attention, or with annoyance to shut someone up. It was used in the latter sense now. Alphonse spoke sharply, as though he had been shot. He glanced at Suzette.

Her face told him nothing, and Alphonse replied tersely, "Perhaps."

"Of a certainty," agreed Suzette.

Alphonse was torn between joy and misery, joy because Emma had recovered her spirits, and misery because Arthur was the instrument in making Emma happy. He himself had been the only man-friend near Emma for months, and he had not succeeded in making her want to sing or dance, yet Arthur had done the trick in a couple of days.

So sure was Alphonse that time and not people would cure Emma, he had not thought that Arthur's coming would influence her so soon. It certainly did not occur to him that a new face had come on Emma's horizon.

Just before one o'clock, after Alphonse had taken Madame de Witt to Casanova for lunch, he had a longing to find out for himself what change Suzette and Louis had noticed in Emma. He looked into the *salon*.

Emma was busy typing, her dark head on her pretty neck bent over her work. She glanced up at Alphonse and paused, wondering if he wanted one of his suggested tours typed quickly to make it easier reading for Olive de Witt.

But Alphonse's hands were empty. He came in and closed the door, saying: "You must be dying with hunger. I will sit here and take any telephone messages. You go and get some *déjeuner*."

Alphonse knew by the quality of Emma's smile, and her quick look of interest in what he said, that Suzette's report was true. There was obviously some new influence at work within Emma, something that gave a brightness to her eye and a flush to her cheeks. She was almost gay.

"I am not hungry, and I don't feel like dying," she replied lightly. "You are very kind to suggest it, but I am in no hurry.

You go and get your lunch, and come in afterwards. There will be time enough for me then."

"I should not dream of going first."

"Oh, do, please," begged Emma with one eye on the clock. Her nerves were tensed. She had a black thought, wondering if Tim remembered today what he had said under the influence of a good dinner and lots of champagne last night. While if he did remember, would he call her punctually? Even as Emma spoke, and the doubts which made her feel dithery about Tim flashed through her brain, the telephone-bell shrilled.

Emma's hand shot out automatically to pick up the receiver. Quick as she was, Alphonse was before her. (There was nothing odd in Alphonse doing this, for he often came in at mealtimes to take Emma's place so that she could lunch or dine at a proper time.)

"Allo! Allo!" he cried. "Yes. Mees Ferrer. Can I do anything for you?"

Alphonse's voice changed subtly. It had been impersonal; now it was clipped and sharp. He frowned.

"Oh! She is here. You want to speak with her. Who is it, please?"

Alphonse held the receiver out silently to Emma, and his face was no longer easy and kind, but set, and the brown eyes that met Emma's mutely questioning blue ones were hard, bright and suspicious.

"A personal call, it would seem," he remarked coolly.

Emma took the receiver.

"Hello!" Her voice was soft, sweet and intimate. She gestured to Alphonse to leave the *salon*. This was an entirely new suggestion.

After a long pause, Alphonse turned sharply on his heel and marched with almost military precision out of the room, opened half the large door, then closed it after him with a bang.

'Oh dear, now I've hurt his feelings,' thought Emma. 'But what can I do?' At any other time she would have laughed at this show of jealousy and displeasure, because it struck her as comic.

She had no time to dwell on Alphonse's behaviour, for Tim was speaking. He sounded amused.

"Oh, hello! At last! I was beginning to think I wasn't going to be allowed to talk to you. Was that Frenchie speaking? He sounded angry — in a pistols for two and coffee for one voice with a P.S. to it — 'I shall win'." They both laughed, and Tim went on: "I suppose he doesn't think I should ring you up at the hotel. I hope he doesn't report you to the boss for using the office telephone."

Emma retorted laughingly: "Of course not. Alphonse isn't like that. He wouldn't dream of telling tales even if there were any to tell, which there aren't."

"Then I haven't done wrong?"

"I should have hated it if you hadn't given me a call."

"Then you aren't angry? I thought you might be."

"No. I like it."

"Well — now for my say. Will you come out somewhere with me this afternoon?"

Emma hesitated. A look of longing came into her blue eyes. She longed to go out and play. She glanced at a pile of work to be done waiting in her tray, and wished it would disappear; then she would feel free to relax. But no miracle happened.

Tim went on: "Perhaps we could go over to St. Jean de Luz and bathe there."

That settled it. St. Jean de Luz was a whole afternoon's pleasure. "Must you go so far away?" she asked.

"I thought of St. Jean de Luz because I want to talk to you alone without any of your acquaintances butting in and spoiling our fun."

Emma shook her head regretfully. Tim did not see the action, but he could hear her voice as she said: "I'm afraid I can't go. It would take too long."

"Does that mean you can never have a few hours to yourself?"

"Not if it interferes with my work." She knew that Tim thought she did no work, or none that counted. The only good point about refusing was that it made Tim understand she was not a kind of female spiv who lived on others and did the least work she could for her wages.

"Then it will have to be somewhere in Biarritz." There was keen disappointment in Tim's voice.

"I should love to go, but not this afternoon."

"Then tomorrow?" Her refusal seemed to make him more urgent.

"Thank you, I will try for tomorrow."

"Can't you make it a date?"

"No, because even at the last moment I may be wanted here. I have always to make a reservation."

"But surely you don't have to break your own engagements to suit someone's whims?" Tim said. So many refusals made him impatient, as frustration of any kind usually did.

"Not for anyone's whim or wish, but because I should think it wiser."

"Well..." Words failed him. "You are a conceited girl, thinking yourself indispensable."

Emma laughed and answered serenely, "Am I?"

"Don't you want to come with me?" There was doubt in Tim's tone, for the idea had just struck him that Emma sounded half-hearted. Perhaps she did not like him well enough to want to spend an afternoon with him. It was an unusual thought, but then Emma Ferrer was an unusual person leading, according to Tim's standards, a remarkably strange life.

Her next words dispelled his suspicions, for she said impressively, so that he could not mistake her desires:

"Oh, I do — I said so, but you really must understand that I would not be in Biarritz at all if I were not working here. I could not afford it."

"Frankly, I don't understand. One hour I find you dressed grandly at a dinner at the Château Basque drinking soup out of gold cups and eating caviar, and the next you have your pretty freckled nose at the grindstone, and won't see me because you are here to do a job of work and not play. It doesn't make sense. Even you, with your values mixed so that you can't distinguish them clearly, must know that."

Emma laughed heartily. "Since we are both being frank, at the risk of making you terribly displeased with me, I must tell you I love it all. That's how it is with me. Everything, work or play, is lovely — or as Arthur would say, dandy."

"You don't displease me. You just exasperate me," cried Tim.

Then Emma told him, "But I have an afternoon off the next day."

"Oh, that's ages off. I can't wait that long. The fun would all be lost in the waiting," said Tim impatiently. "We are bound to meet often, of course, but I am anxious to meet you alone. How can I be expected to make any headway in our friendship in the midst of a crowd of people? I'm not like Arthur. He never minds what he says in public. It comes naturally to him, just as it comes naturally to me to be tongue-tied."

Emma wondered what Tim meant by 'making headway' with her.

She said reasonably, "We could go up the Rhune."

"What's that?"

"The purple mountain at the back of the town."

"What is there to see?"

"Scenery and eagles. It's one of *the* tours of the district. We could go up by funicular, and have tea in a café when we come down. You can book some coach seats."

"Would you like that?" Tim sighed. "It sounds too simple a pleasure for you after last night."

"I think it would be lovely."

"All right. That's a date for the day after tomorrow. Now — about tomorrow…"

"I hope to make it. Where shall we meet?"

"In front of the Casino?"

"That will be a good spot. About 2.30?"

It was Emma who brought the talk to an end. Tim would have gone on talking for a long time.

When she had rung off, Emma went over to the window which was wide open and looked out on to the beautiful sea, seeing but not observing, her eyes dreaming because her mind was full of Tim Crake. A soft smile played about her mobile lips.

A feeling that always welled up in her heart whenever she thought of Geoff was now by some queer stroke of fate transferred to Tim. It had happened without her knowing, almost overnight, and because of that chance likeness and a similarity of character and temperament with her late fiancé.

It alarmed her a little because while she forgave Geoff his faults and loved him in spite of them, she saw Geoff's faults mirrored clearly in Tim and could not forgive them because she did not love Tim. But that did not prevent this feeling rising in her heart. It was certainly not love.

Emma thought: 'There's nothing in it. I could not begin all over again.'

She did not hear Alphonse come into the room. But presently, instinctively, she felt that she was not alone and turned around, her eyes full of dreams, and seeing it was Alphonse asked:

"You've had lunch?" Her eyes strayed to the clock, and she saw that it was late.

Emma moved quickly, prepared to leave the room, but Alphonse's reply, and the tone of his voice, stopped her.

"I have *not* had my *déjeuner*."

Emma's eyes widened. "Don't you want any?"

"No."

"Why ever not?"

"I have waited outside until you finished your long talk with your new boyfriend." He spoke angrily, and now that she looked at his face Emma saw that Alphonse was deeply moved. With some compunction Emma recalled that she had sent him summarily from the room. Perhaps he did not like waiting outside, an object of interest to passing *femmes de chambre* and *valets*. But how was she to know that Alphonse would be foolish enough to wait?

She cried, "Alphonse, what on earth has come over you?"

"Nothing, but I am very angry."

"What about?"

"You — your behaviour — the way you treat me. Fancy going behind my back and making dates with a new friend."

"How do you know I have?" Emma flared up.

"Why else should M'sieur Crake ring you up?"

"Well, why shouldn't I? Or must I ask your permission first? Really, things have come to something if I have to ask you whether I may go here or there."

Alphonse breathed heavily. "All these months you have made use of me. I have tried my best to interest and please you. It has been of no use. Now you have taken up with a stranger. I am thrown aside. Naturally, I ask myself why?"

It was clear that Alphonse was hurt, and he was disappointed in her.

Emma said at once: "There is no need for you to be so upset. It is true that Mr. Crake rang me up asking me to go out with him."

"Does M'sieur Crake not think you have enough pleasure and entertainment with Madame? *Must* he provide more?"

"It isn't that, but — he wants to see me alone."

"Alone! That is most odd. Why should a stranger wish to see you alone? What has he to say that he cannot say in public?" Alphonse sounded distant. Emma dubbed him 'difficult'.

Emma shrugged. Alphonse was deliberately spoiling this new friendship. "How should I know?"

"You are intelligent. You can guess, I suppose."

Emma's mouth tightened. "Yes, I can guess."

"And you have said 'no'; or is it 'yes'?"

"I said 'yes'."

"Because you wanted to listen to M'sieur Crake's secrets?"

Emma raised her eyebrows stubbornly.

"Partly."

"And the other part?"

"I won't say another word. Yes, I will though. I like Mr. Crake. He attracts me. I want to see more of him. I am glad that he rang me up because…"

Emma paused, overcome by an odd emotion. She was sorry to quarrel with Alphonse about Tim. She faced him squarely.

"Well, if you must know," she burst out passionately, "he reminds me of Geoff."

With his swift Gallic mind, Alphonse understood at once. He came close to her and took her hands in his.

"Emma, *chérie!*" No man could have said the word more lovingly. "Oh, but I am so sorry. Imbecile that I am, I did not understand."

She raised tear-filled eyes to Alphonse. "Have you seen a likeness?" she breathed, hoping that he had.

Alphonse shook his head. "No, I cannot say I have. This new gentleman is nothing like M'sieur White — not one bit."

Emma frowned and hung her head. "Perhaps I imagined it," she said quietly at last, and thought, 'Subconsciously I must have wanted to find things in Tim that were like Geoff.'

CHAPTER 4

That evening, Olive de Witt asked Emma to telephone her hostess and cancel a dinner invitation to Chez Ramuntcho.

"Don't you feel well?" Emma asked with quick concern. She recalled that there had been a cold wind blowing in from the sea at Chambre d'Amour plage this morning, and wondered if Olive had caught a chill.

"I am quite all right, thank you," replied Olive, with just that reserve in her tone which forbade closer questioning about her health, and which Emma had learned to recognize and respect. "But I had to battle with the wind when leaving the plage this morning, and I am rather tired. I shall stay quietly at home this evening, and catch up with some personal business and my reading."

Emma looked anxiously at Olive's face. She knew that the 'personal business' meant that Olive would rest. The reading would be a pretence.

She said, "They are giving a firework display on the plage."

"Then I will sit in my window and watch them. They are sure to be good," said Olive. "If Armand de la Tremblay has no engagement, perhaps he will call in and read to me. If you have half an hour to spare, Emma, perhaps you will run along to the English bookseller and choose me some books." Olive glanced at the clock on her bed-table. "That is, if the shop is still open."

Emma said she had plenty of time. It was stretching a point, but Emma intended getting Olive those books even if the shop were closed, and she had to make the shopkeeper open it. She went off at once. The shop was open. Emma chose several books she thought Olive might like. It was not difficult, for Olive had a catholic taste in literature. The print had to be large and easy to read, and the theme light enough to catch Olive's interest if she were in pain, and exciting enough to make Olive forget her pain.

On returning to the Palais, Emma would have found Suzette and told her that Madame had cancelled her engagement, and Suzette would have gone to Olive and perhaps massaged the pain away with her clever cushioned fingers. But this was Suzette's evening off. She had gone with an easy mind, saying she would not be in until late. Olive had suggested that Suzette should not look in on her but go straight to bed.

Emma therefore went into Olive's bedroom and put away the black evening dress which glittered with sequin and diamanté trimming, and the accessories, which Suzette had laid out on the brocaded bed in readiness for her mistress to wear out to dinner.

Then Emma prepared the bed for the night, laying out Olive's peach-coloured silk nightdress and little coatee, the long wrap to match, if Olive wished to sit in her large chair when undressed but not feeling like sleep. Lastly she put out the cool nylon built-up shoes which were so chic and so comfortable to wear.

Emma rearranged some flowers in a vase and put it on Olive's bedside table by the pile of books and the softly shaded lamp.

The windows were open to the grey-green sea, and sounds from the plage outside came thinly over the air. Emma looked out for a moment. Far out to sea was a white yacht making for the old port of Bayonne. It had probably come up for a run from Santander, where sailing yachts were racing. For some minutes Emma watched its bows rising and dipping in the swell of the ocean. Most probably it belonged to one of the wealthy South American business men, some of whom had been attracting great crowds around them playing baccarat at the Casino. It was said that fifty thousand pounds were on the table at one time.

There was a worried frown on Emma's brow. She was excited about seeing Tim tomorrow, but there was a maggot of worry which spoiled the pleasure of anticipation. So long as Olive was able to go through her endless round of engagements, for she was greatly sought after to make a party 'go' with that success which an expensive party must have, then all seemed well. Yet Emma knew, as did all those who were in close contact with Olive, that the heavy list of these dates taxed her strength. Often Olive's body failed her, though her spirit was game enough to go on forever. She liked to see a full engagement pad. It became more crowded every day. It was at times like these that Olive's hip troubled her most. The pain became so bad that Olive was obliged to rest to recuperate. For Emma's part, she would have welcomed these periods of rest if they had not meant that Olive suffered. Emma could not bear to see Olive suffer. There was something so stoical and heroic about Olive at these times. She seemed to Emma almost inhuman, for she bore pain without a murmur of complaint, and was often brighter and more cheerful than when she had no pain at all. At these times, too, Suzette was snappy and ill-tempered, while Alphonse was desolated. The Comte de la Tremblay would be Emma's shadow. He kept whispering to Emma, asking her to take kind messages to Olive from him, and like all her friends, sending lovely flowers, so that the *salon* and bedroom took on the appearance of a graveyard, for the sight and scent of the exotic flowers were overpowering.

Emma's one hope was that the threatened attack would pass off, her one fear that it would not. Olive ate no dinner, though the manager of the hotel himself came to see why she would not eat. From his face, one gathered that the chef and kitchen staff of the hotel were miserable failures.

Later, Emma, Olive and the Comte sat at the open window in the *salon* and talked while they waited for complete darkness, when the fireworks would begin.

Olive had some knitting which she picked up and occasionally worked a row. Emma sat slightly in the shadows, half her mind listening in a kind of somnolent delight to the lovely voices of Olive and the Comte, the rich fluting contralto, and the mellifluous resonance of the Frenchman's, and the other half busy with Tim, wondering where he was and what he was doing and if he were thinking of her. She knew that Tim had been on the plage Chambre d'Amour in the morning, for Olive had mentioned it. He had been with Arthur on the Chiberta links in the afternoon, and the two men were dining together. Tim had said so on the phone. He was going to the Casino this evening. He had heard that fortunes were being won and lost at baccarat and Tim said he was tempted to try his luck. Emma had smiled to herself when she heard it, knowing that Tim would risk such small amounts it would be impossible for him to make a big fortune. Also, of course, Tim had to keep within his travel money in a foreign country. That was why he was so ready to cultivate Arthur's friendship, for the American had unlimited dollars at his disposal, and was willing to spend royally on his friends.

Emma woke up from her daydreams to see that the town spread to the left of her around the Miramar plage was a fairyland of lights which festooned the darkness. There was a big moon coming up. The sky, a beautiful Prussian blue, was thickly patterned with stars of all sizes, some of them just stardust. The sea looked a cold heaving waste.

It was chilly and Emma fetched a fur wrap for Olive, while the Comte tucked a rug about Olive's knees.

Suddenly, with a burst of many rockets that hissed and roared high into the sky and burst into a thousand different coloured lights, the display opened.

In the light of the fireworks they could see that the plage was crowded. Above the snapping and cracking and popping of the fireworks they could hear the cheering and the clapping. There were set pieces that took fiery shape and colour against the dark backcloth of the sea, some comics, pictures of the presidents of the various republics whose nationals were now visiting Biarritz, and the flags of nations, ending up, of course, with the tricolour of France.

When the fireworks were over, Emma closed the windows and switched on the lights. She saw that Olive's face was strained and drawn. She said:

"Would you like a drink now, or shall I mix you something hot when you are in bed?"

Olive looked at her with shadowed eyes. Then she smiled, "I will have something hot and soothing when I go to bed." Olive turned to the Comte, who had taken Emma's hint that he should go, and had risen, waiting to bid Olive goodnight. She said: "You must have a drink, Armand. Help yourself."

The Comte went over to a table where the drinks had been put out on a tray. There was a profusion of bottles to choose from. He mixed himself a drink and brought his glass back to where Olive was sitting. He did not especially want the drink, but it gave him an excuse to prolong his visit.

"Shall I read to you a little, Olive?" he asked, wishing he could do something, however trivial, to ease the burden of her pain.

"Not tonight, thank you, Armand. I shall go to bed." She broke off to say, with a laugh: "Now that is front-page news for the local reporter. 'Olive de Witt comes to Biarritz because the night life is the best in the world, and avoids it by retiring to bed at eleven o'clock.' But the air coming in across the Atlantic is strong and has made me tired." Olive turned to Emma, saying, "What will you have, Emma?"

"Nothing, thank you," said Emma. She went away for a little while and sat in her room mending a ladder in her stocking. But the secret worry pursued her. It was as though subconsciously, when Olive was unwell, Emma realized how much her own life depended upon Olive. That feeling of security, peace and contentment which had grown up in her heart since she became Olive's secretary was threatened. Emma felt that if anything untoward happened to Olive, her whole world would topple over.

When she returned to the *salon*, the Comte was alone.

"Where is Mrs. de Witt?" inquired Emma, looking about the room as though she expected to find Olive hiding behind one of the brocaded curtains.

"She has gone to bed," said the Comte, looking troubled. He had finished his drink but had not thought to put down his empty glass, and remained nursing it. "She is not at all well tonight, Emma."

So he had noticed Olive's looks too. Emma said: "I'm afraid not. It is a pity Suzette is out, for she knows so well what to do to ease Mrs. de Witt's pain. I do what I can, but I am not Suzette. I haven't her nice cushiony fingertips."

"I am sure you do very well," said the Comte kindly. Then he added: "Never hesitate to call me if I can be of any help — at any hour of the day or night. I can read. Mrs. de Witt has said that I can send her to sleep. You won't forget?" He put down his glass.

"No, I won't."

"You have my phone number. I am only around the corner and can quickly be here."

He was an ineffectual little man, but he meant well, and Emma knew that he was devoted to Olive. While, of course, he was blessed with the most delightful voice.

He came and stood before Emma. Clicking his heels, he bowed deeply.

Emma waited, thinking, 'I feel like royalty.' The little ceremony never failed to please her.

Then she held out her hand, hoping that he thought it as languid and lily-like as she imagined it was. The Comte took it, carried it to his lips, kissing it lightly. Or rather, he brushed his lips against the back of Emma's hand. Then he let it drop and stepped back a pace.

"Goodnight, Emma," he said. At the door he turned and smiled. "And now I must go to the Casino and take my nephew home. I have no doubt but that he has staked and lost all his daily allowance — as usual."

When he had gone, Emma prepared a warm food-drink for Olive. She took it to Olive's door.

She knocked and Olive called, "Come in."

Emma went in and closed the door after her.

Olive was in bed. She was sitting up reading, but put the book down when Emma went in, and in silence watched the girl put the cup of hot food beside her bed.

"Oh, you have managed to get into bed. I wish you had waited so that I could help you," said Emma.

"Then why did you leave me?"

"I thought you and the Comte might want to talk to each other."

"Tactful Emma!" Olive laughed. "Armand and I have long ago passed the stage when we want to be alone together. That is what makes our friendship so easy and comfortable. We can be natural and relaxed." Olive continued: "It did me good to make the effort. I mustn't get into the habit of relying on you and Suzette. Once I do that, I can give up all hope of returning to my old ways."

Emma nodded to show that she understood.

She did not sit down, but stood beside the bed watching Olive take a few sips of the hot drink, asking if it was as she liked it. They talked for a little about tomorrow's engagements and an orphan in whom Olive was interested, who was behaving so badly the authorities wished to place her in a special home. Olive had great faith in this child. "She must have another chance — and another — and yet another until we find the good that is hidden somewhere inside the child," she said. "I may even have the child with me for Christmas, and try to find the good myself."

Then suddenly, without warning, her passionate interest, which had been so vivid a moment ago, died away.

Emma said, "You are tired."

"I am — a little," confessed Olive.

"Then I must leave you to go to sleep. Have you got everything you need?"

"Everything. Thank you for your help. You do so well that I shall not miss Suzette when she goes out; then she will be jealous," smiled Olive.

"I wish I could feel it was practical help."

"Well, it is — more than you think."

Emma took a last look at the bedside-table to see that Olive had everything she might need for the night — books, a few flowers, a good but soft light, a glass and small syphon. Then Emma's eyes widened. She saw, half-hidden by the lamp-stand, a little phial of white tablets. Olive never took drugs except when in great pain, for she did not want to acquire the drug habit.

Emma knew then that Olive was still in pain, and she wanted to have the tablets handy. She made no comment because Olive had not mentioned them, or even that she was in pain. When Emma said 'goodnight', curiously enough she felt the older of the two. She patted Olive's arm reassuringly, and as she turned away laughingly blew a kiss to her. But outside the door, when there was no longer any need of pretence, the smile left Emma's face. She walked slowly across the *salon* and out into the corridor to the lift which would take her upstairs to her own bedroom.

It was then that Emma thought of Alphonse. She had not seen him since lunchtime, when he had been so kind and angry at the same time. Feeling lost and in need of advice, Emma went downstairs again, not in the lift which would land her almost in the arms of the magnificent major-domo with his long wand, whose appearance had such a terrifying effect on Tim, as it did on most people, but by a back staircase, where the carpet on the stairs was of second-best quality. She found her way eventually to the huge courtyard at the back of the hotel where the magnificent cars of the hotel visitors were parked in serried lines, and looked about her for the Rolls-Bentley, or Alphonse. The car, black, sleek and gleaming, looking a prince of cars among other elegant and foreign models, was there, in one of the best positions in the garage. Alphonse always managed to get the best place for his car.

But Emma could not see Alphonse's familiar figure. Why he should be there she did not think. Having telephoned earlier to the garage to say that Madame would not need the car, she had forgotten Alphonse. It was only later that Emma discovered he had put a wrong meaning to her ambiguous message. He had thought that someone going to the dinner was calling for Madame in his own car. It had not occurred to Alphonse that Olive was ill. Had he known, nothing would have kept him away from her.

Alphonse was not staying at the Palais. He had found quarters for himself in the town. This was his custom when Olive's party stayed at an hotel for any length of time. If they remained under a week, he usually had a room in the hotel. Lately Alphonse had changed his rooms, where there was no telephone.

Disappointed, Emma hurried back to the hotel, and sat working at her desk in the *salon* until one o'clock. She kept a wary eye on a slim pencil of light beneath Olive's door, and made up her mind not to go to bed until the light went out, showing that Olive had settled down to sleep.

At two o'clock the light disappeared. Emma crept over to Olive's door and listened. All was silent.

She went up to her bedroom, undressed and went to bed, but could not sleep. She was worried about Olive. It was not right that she should be left alone. Someone should be on the spot in case of need. Emma decided to go downstairs again. Slipping on dressing-gown and shoes, she went down to the *salon*.

It was in semi-darkness. The moon shone whitely through a side window, and cast sharp shadows in the room.

As Emma had feared, there was a light under Olive's door. Without hesitation she knocked gently on it. There was no answer. Emma opened the door and crept in.

Olive had not heard her. The bed was disordered. Olive was lying on her 'good' side, her body hunched with pain. She must have been restless for some while, but seemed now to have passed into a state of exhaustion.

"Oh, my dearest!" cried Emma in distress, and ran over to the bed. "Why didn't you send someone to call me?"

Olive raised a tortured face to the girl. Beads of perspiration glistened on her forehead. Her eyes were sunken and dull, and her lovely complexion grey as lead. She looked an old woman.

"Why should I disturb your sleep?" Olive demanded in a hoarse voice.

Moved by love and pity, Emma impulsively put her arms about Olive, much as she had done once before, when she had first discovered how sensitive Olive was about her infirmity, and how successfully she hid it from the world.

"Because I might be able to help you, my dear," Emma replied brokenly, tears raining down her face.

Olive drew away from her and said in a lighter, stronger voice, "Emma, you are crying!"

"No, I'm not." Emma freed a hand and brushed it fiercely across her eyes. "Have you taken some tablets?"

"Yes, two in a little syphon."

"You will feel better presently," Emma remarked hopefully.

Emma loosened an arm and patted up the flat pillows until they were soft and generous again. She laid Olive back amongst them. "That's better." She took a damask face towel and sprinkled it with toilette water, wiping Olive's forehead, behind her ears, and the palms of her hands. All the while she was talking softly, scolding Olive in a loving kind of way for not phoning the office to send for her.

"Tomorrow, Suzette and Alphonse, Mr. Arthur and crowds of your friends will put me on the carpet for not looking after you better," Emma said ruefully, trying to draw Olive's attention from her pain.

Olive replied: "Suzette may, but when Suzette's nerves are upset she is angry with everybody. But neither Arthur nor Alphonse would ever hear a word against you. Both look upon you as an angel — and so you are. What I should do without you, I don't know."

Olive seldom revealed the sentiments of her heart. Emma told her: "It's so lovely to hear you say that! It is like being wrapped in a mink coat on a cold day."

They both laughed. "You always use extravagant terms to express luxury, Emma."

"That's because I shall never get used to luxury. Sometimes I look up my favourite words in a dictionary, and get quite a kick out of seeing them in print, and saying them aloud to myself. Listen: 'orchids and ermine, gardenias and sables, caviar and mink, strawberries and cream.' Don't they sound lush?"

Olive was amused. "They are only outward expressions and soon pall."

"Oh no," persisted Emma, "not to me. They are signs of a full pocket, a life free from want, a secure existence. You don't want them especially because you have never been in a position to want them. I have. When I used to share a flat with Jennifer — you remember, my friend who had the twin girl babies not long ago — and we treated our boyfriends to a meal, we usually had to go without lunch or breakfast to make up. I was hungry. Then I used to close my eyes and imagine I was eating lovely meals. You can't think what banquets I consumed."

"You didn't grow fat on them," Olive pointed out. Then she said, "Tell me about the boyfriend."

"I have. It was Geoff White."

Olive thought: 'That man! He was never good enough for my Emma — a selfish, conceited, domineering pig of a fellow.' But she only said, "Was he your only friend?"

"Yes," was the simple answer. "The one desire of my life was to marry him."

Olive shook her head. "It is nonsense for a girl of your age and intelligence to talk about 'one desire'. Why not a second, or a third…?"

Emma smiled, but she did not reply.

Olive said, "Tell me something to make me laugh — quick!"

Emma searched her brain frantically for something funny to say, but all she could think of was, "Do you think Mr. Crake is like Geoff?"

Olive knitted her brows. "Is it a riddle?"

"Just a question."

"No — I don't think the men are a bit alike. Why? Is Mr. Crake a relative? Or is it that imagination of yours at work again, Emma? Wishful thinking will always be your problem."

Emma laughed. "Mr. Crake phoned at lunchtime asking me to go out with him."

"That is understandable. I should go."

"Alphonse doesn't want me to go."

"Nonsense. You don't have to ask Alphonse's permission. Besides, his views are coloured by jealousy. Don't take any notice of him." Then Olive added, "But do not go because you think Mr. Crake is like your Geoff — go to enjoy yourself, Emma."

At that moment Olive was suddenly overwhelmed with a new spasm of pain, and she dug her teeth into her lip to stop any sound from breaking out and frightening Emma.

With a courage and boldness born of desperation, Emma suggested: "I can't do what Suzette is experienced in doing, but let me massage your spine. I will try to be gentle."

Olive's consciousness was blurred by the strength of the pain, and for a moment she did not take in Emma's meaning.

After a while she said, "Do what you like."

Gently but compellingly, Emma rolled her over a little and put her hand on the back of Olive's neck.

It was extraordinary the effect Emma's touch had on Olive. It was as though the crescendo of pain that had Olive in its thrall was suddenly stemmed, and her tensed nerves relaxed. The pain did not stop suddenly. It was still there. But the feel of Emma's small fingers passing gently up and down and over her spine was like a soothing overlay on Olive's ratched nerves.

She groaned aloud, and Emma asked anxiously, "Am I hurting you?"

"It is exquisite — a relief and yet a pain. Go on. Don't stop."

The gentle movement was like a flow of healing water over Olive, and she became still and quiet.

Presently Emma sat on the edge of the bed; then she sank to her knees beside it. Emma's arm began to tire. She became hot and her face was flushed, but even to herself Emma would not admit weariness. Olive dozed, and Emma must have dozed too, for she woke to the realization that her hand was still. Emma began to move it, hoping that Olive had not noticed.

Olive's muscles relaxed. That part of her face which was visible was cool and healthy again. The greyness of suffering had disappeared. A metamorphosis took place so that Olive no longer looked old and careworn but young and beautiful again.

At four o'clock, stiff and clumsy, Emma got to her feet. She switched off Olive's light, and staggered rather than walked to the door. Groping for the handle she went out, closing the door after her.

At first Emma was too tired to notice that the light in the *salon* was on. Then she saw that Arthur, still in his dinner-jacket, was halted at the other side of the room. His hands were in his jacket pockets. He had evidently been walking about, but stopped when Emma entered the room.

He cried out in an amazed whisper: "You, Emma! I thought it was Suzette. I came in about an hour ago and saw the light on in Aunt Olive's room. I heard voices and guessed she was ill again. I was afraid to disturb her." He came over to her. "What are you doing here?"

"I came to see if Mrs. de Witt was all right," was the whispered reply.

"You look dead beat."

Emma stumbled, and Arthur put out a hand to steady her.

"Hold everything, old lady, or you are going to topple over." He did not let go of her arm, but asked, "How is Aunt Olive?"

For answer Emma put her finger to her lips. "Asleep. She's had a terrible night."

Arthur looked relieved.

"So have you by the look of you," he said. "Sit down here. I'll get you a drink." He led her to a chair.

"At this hour! I'd be sick."

"Then have some tea. I'll get the night porter to make some."

"I don't want anything, thank you, only bed and a little soda water."

Arthur went over to the tray of drinks which had been removed to a side-table by the floor waiter, and opened a syphon. He brought the glass over to Emma.

Her hands shook so badly that Arthur took the glass from her, knelt down by the side of the chair and held it to her lips.

"Where is Suzette?"

Emma sat back in the chair, and Arthur got up and put down the glass.

"It was her night out."

"But she must have come in long ago. Why didn't you call her?"

"I could not leave Mrs. de Witt."

"Aha! You're a great girl, Emma."

"If you say that sort of thing I shall cry. I'm not a bit great, but I am in the right mood for self-pity."

"Cry if you like. It'll probably do you good. I've got a broad shoulder and a big handkerchief. But for pity's sake don't soak my tuxedo. I hate the idea of any dame messing my clothes with tears. On second thoughts, Emma, because I love you, I'll let you soak my shoulder."

Then because Arthur was deeply attached to his aunt and grateful to anyone who was kind to her, he said to Emma: "Thank you for being so sweet to Aunt Olive. I don't know how we shall ever begin to repay you."

Emma looked stern. "I'd hate you to try. The boot of repayment is on my foot when I think of all the kindnesses Mrs. de Witt has showered on me."

Arthur was silent for a long time. His mischievous face was graver than Emma had ever seen it. There was a serious side to Arthur's nature, Emma knew, for Olive de Witt had told her so, but it was so seldom visible that Emma often forgot it was there.

Arthur stood looking down at Emma. He said, "I know many people like Aunt Olive for herself, because she is good, kind and generous to everyone; but there are a few who only like her for what she gives or can give to them or for what they hope she may give."

"I don't," whispered Emma fiercely. "If she hadn't a sou tomorrow I should like Mrs. de Witt just the same — more, because then I could at last prove to her how much I love her."

Arthur bent and took Emma's hands in his, pulling her to her feet, taking her in his arms and pressing her to him.

"You're a wonder kid, Emma."

He was growing sentimental, and Emma did not want this. She yawned tiredly, neither giving in to him nor repelling him.

"My eyes won't stay open, Arthur. I'm going to bed."

"I'll take you up."

"No, one of those night porters, or the man who goes around the corridors collecting and cleaning shoes, may see you. I'd soon get a bad label."

Arthur smiled, and for a moment Emma loved him for there was so much kindness in it, and somehow just now she felt in need of all the sympathy and kindness she could get. The night with Olive had shaken her, for usually it was Olive who was the brick wall between Emma and the world. She had grown to like the security that being under Olive's wing gave her. Tonight, having to take the lead had made Emma realize the temporary nature of the security. Her own position was too tenuous for her to contemplate it with equanimity.

Arthur said, "Being a Frenchman, he'd be too tactful to remark on it."

"To us — but I still have a wholesome dread of other people's opinions."

Arthur went to the door with her.

Late revellers were coming back from parties and night-clubs. They had a slightly bedraggled appearance as hurrying and giggling they tore along the quiet dimmed corridors to their rooms.

CHAPTER 5

Emma overslept. The *valet de chambre*, carrying in her *petit déjeuner*, was the signal for Emma to awake to a new day. She ate her brioche and butter quickly and drank the *café au lait* while it was still hot. After that she felt better, and able to cope with the trials that would shortly await her when she went down to Olive de Witt's suite.

As Emma had expected, Suzette met her in the doorway, her face dark with displeasure, her frizzed hair seeming to stick out like a fuzzy halo about her face, a sign which Emma had learned by experience betokened displeasure. Suzette was angry because she had not been called up in the night to help Madame. She did not voice her anger in English, but in rapid French which was more of a gabble than distinct words.

Emma tried to explain but gave up the effort. She could have said everything in English, but that language was not Suzette's strong point. Emma's French was excellent, but she was not a mistress of Suzette's *patois*. When she chose, too, Suzette pretended not to understand.

Having had her say, and having refused to listen to Emma's explanations, Suzette flounced into Madame's room and closed the door.

Alphonse also was in the *salon*. He had been forced to stand aside while Suzette spoke. He, too, was no match for Suzette when she considered she was in the right.

He stood patiently by the side window, holding a huge bunch of gardenias in a cellophane box which he had just brought in for Madame. His face was long, without a smile, and desolate. Emma had the wretched feeling that Alphonse would never smile again. He was more understanding than Suzette. He was not upset because Emma had failed to call him. He knew that she could not have done so. He blamed himself.

"This shall not happen again," he said severely. "Already I have been to the chief of the Post-Office to connect my landlady to the telephone within an hour. I have told him that if it is not done, I will go to the Institute of Hoteliers and report him. They know the worth of Madame to this town, the prosperity she creates in it. They will see to it that my order is carried out."

Alphonse gestured dramatically. "Anything might have happened." Then he scolded Emma for not telling the night reception clerk to send for him.

"But you couldn't have done any good, Alphonse."

"That is not for you to say. My point is that I should have been called. Now what do I find when I call for my orders for the day? Your desk is empty. The flowers are not arranged. You are asleep because you are tired. You are tired because you have been up in the night with Madame. Madame is ill today because you did not call Suzette, whose experience would have made Madame better."

"I did the best I could," protested Emma.

"But the best, it is not good enough. You look like a ghost — a ghost of an old lady of ninety. *Quel malheur!*"

Emma had no answer to this. There was nothing to say. Alphonse and Suzette had been with Madame for years. Her service was about five years.

"I'm sorry."

"So you should be. Now do not worry. Everything is in good hands. Go and rest. Go for a walk. It will freshen you up. You will feel better, and able to cope with the messages that will come in this afternoon."

Thus dismissed, Emma went out of the hotel and took a tram to Chiberta, where she walked among the pines on the sand-dunes, and picked a bunch of wild *oeillets*, which seemed to grow in profusion among the prickly grass growing on the sparse nutrition of the ground. Though Olive would have many bunches of expensive flowers arriving for her before the day was over, she liked the unpretentious wild ones too.

On her way back, Emma met Tim. He said he had been bathing in the rougher seas of the less-frequented Côte des Basques.

He hailed Emma, saying: "I went to Chambre d'Amour, but your people were not in their usual spot. What has happened to them?"

"Mrs. de Witt is resting in bed today."

"I thought it was something to do with her. The lifeguard on the beach was in a bad temper. I suppose he missed Mrs. de Witt's fat tip. She seems to be the hub of your special little universe. I am beginning to understand her importance in this town." Then Tim added: "Don't keep me waiting this afternoon, will you? Or those *gendarmes* in their comic-opera uniforms outside the Casino will run me in as a suspicious character."

He was in good humour at the thought of the afternoon's outing. It was with surprise and anger that he heard Emma say quickly:

"I'm awfully sorry, Mr. Crake, but I can't go with you today. I expect to be busy, and so I must stay at the Palais."

Tim glared at Emma for a moment in silence, not knowing quite what was at the back of this change of plan.

"But if Mrs. de Witt is in bed —" he began, his anger rising because he was thwarted.

"That's just it…" Emma interrupted, anxious to explain matters before Tim lost his temper and said things he might regret, which would spoil their friendship. "As you said, Mrs. de Witt is an important person in Biarritz. When the Press hears that she is ill, everyone will send her flowers and messages of sympathy."

Tim listened with tight lips. His disappointment was keen. Attached to the powerful Mrs. de Witt's entourage, Emma had acquired in his eyes a little of that magic halo which hovered with golden resplendence about her employer's smooth head. Also there was something in it all, for Tim thought of Emma as 'a nice little thing'. She was his countrywoman, too, and he did not have to bother about talking in French. She had more or less the same outlook as he had, and would make a good companion for him during his holidays. Indeed, she was more in his mind than was wise for his peace. She intrigued him immensely. There were times when he did not know what to make of her and was determined to find out. That was one of the reasons for his wanting to see Emma alone, away from the crowd she knew. So Tim had decided — and now this. It was too bad!

The news made him touchy to a degree. He was not to be talked or teased into a good humour.

He demanded shortly, "Who tells the Press?" There was so much of Geoff's arrogance in Tim's manner that Emma thought, 'I don't care what anyone says: Tim *is* like Geoff.'

She shrugged, not liking Tim's tone. Some of the remnants of her former meekness with Geoff must have been in her still, for Emma was not greatly put out by Tim's overbearing manner, though she would not have tolerated it in Arthur or Alphonse or any of her other friends. Not that any one of them would have dreamed of treating her so cavalierly.

She said equably: "The hotel management tell the Press. They tell them everything. One person tells another, too. If Mrs. de Witt does not show up at somebody's lunch or dinner, or at a fête or night-club, people remark on it and wonder where she is, and why she isn't there. They make inquiries, and of course I must be there to answer them."

"And they send her flowers, I suppose," added Tim disagreeably.

"Naturally."

"What a waste!"

"I thought that once, but I don't know. Flowers give lots of pleasure."

Tim glanced at the flowers Emma was carrying. He said suddenly: "You are expecting masses of expensive flowers to arrive, yet you waste time this morning picking those. They're half-dead already." And Tim looked scornfully at the little *oeillets*, their puce-coloured heads wilting in the sunshine. Then urged by a sense of frustration that he could make no impression on Emma, whose face was tranquil and calm, certainly not expressive of disappointment, he flicked the flowers with his thumb and forefinger saying: "Or are those your contribution to the festival of the flowers — or should I be poetic and call them the 'Blossoms of Biarritz'? I must say, for a gift they don't look up to much. Couldn't you have sported a few francs on some lilies?"

Emma smiled palely. "They will revive in water," she said. "Mrs. de Witt likes them."

Tim laughed. "She'll have to say so," he commented acidly.

Emma was stung to say: "I think you are perfectly horrid, Mr. Crake. You don't seem to see good in anyone. It is rather a silly outlook."

"Well, I am disappointed that you've boshed up my day. You don't care because life is one long holiday to you, while it is two weeks out of a year for me."

Emma knew that many people envied her delightful job. She thought herself lucky to have it. She said, "Don't you think I am a little disappointed too?"

Tim rumpled his hair. He stared moodily at Emma. "I don't know what to think," he confessed. "Sometime in your career with Mrs. de Witt you have certainly acquired discretion and subtlety. One does not realize how clever you are at once. Your simplicity of manner and dress are deceiving. They combine to hide your true personality."

"Thank you. I take that as a compliment. It shows I have progressed. At one time I could not possibly hide my feelings from people. I was so shy I would rather go hungry than walk into a restaurant. I would never have had the cheek to tell people what I thought of them."

"That is one for me, I suppose." Tim recovered his temper and said in a more persuasive tone, "I am sure that if Mrs. de Witt knew we had a date this afternoon she would be the first to tell you to keep it." Then as he saw Emma shake her head slightly, he continued: "It isn't as though you could do anything to help her. You're not a doctor or a nurse — only a secretary."

Tim meant nothing derogatory to Emma in saying this. He was only trying to prove how useless she was to a sick woman.

"I should not dream of telling Mrs. de Witt about our date, even if I had the chance, or suggesting I should enjoy myself while she is ill. In any case, I am far too worried about her to feel pleasure in leaving the hotel. My duty is to stay at my desk."

"You are horribly firm about duty," he complained. "When is Mrs. de Witt going to be well?"

"I do not know. She may be up and about tomorrow. I hope so."

"Then we'd better postpone our date until tomorrow," he said unsmilingly.

"We must." Then she said deprecatingly: "There is a fête at St. Jean de Luz. Half of Biarritz will be there. Do you think you will enjoy that?"

"Oh! That settles it. I want to talk to you, not to the dames of Biarritz." Tim had an idea. "Let's go up the Rhune."

Emma brightened. "Yes, let's," she agreed. "I've never done that trip, but I've often wanted to."

"Make it two o'clock then. You said it was your half-day."

Emma nodded. "I think I can make it," she said smilingly. "I'll try, anyway."

CHAPTER 6

Emma returned to the hotel in time for *déjeuner*. Before going into the restaurant, she put her flowers in a basin of hot water. She looked in Olive's *salon*, but no one was there. A tray was on a table. There was a half-eaten omelette on a plate and a peach skin and stone. Emma's spirits went up because Olive had eaten some lunch. She must be better. The thought made Emma feel hungry. She took her seat at a table in a secluded corner of the big restaurant, a spot shielded by glass screens, which was reserved for secretaries and companions of distinguished visitors. It was a unique position, a kind of vantage point for seeing without being seen, for those who were not eligible for the stewards' room. Normally, Emma sat at Olive's table in the big bay under an enormous chandelier whether guests were with her or not. If Olive wanted privacy, then Emma had a tray in the private *salon*. But if she were alone, Emma liked eating behind the screen. She met many foreigners this way and learned so much in talking to them about their countries. Emma's thirst for knowledge was insatiable. She had barely begun to eat her lobster cocktail when Suzette sent in a message to say that Madame had been asking for her and would she come at once.

Emma rose from the table immediately. She ran upstairs to her bedroom, quickly picked out some of the best of the *oeillets* and hurried down again to Olive's room.

To her surprise Olive was sitting in a chair in front of the open window. It was a shock after last night to see Olive looking her usual self, and Emma exclaimed at the sight of her.

"Why, you look better than ever. The rest has done you good."

Olive smiled. She looked so rested that the pale shadows under her eyes were hardly noticeable. There was a queer light in the eyes themselves which told its own tale to the observer of suffering.

"That's why I sent for you, Emma — just to tell me that. You can always be relied upon to provide that special tonic and make me feel better. Have you had your lunch?" Olive's tone was rich and light.

Emma nodded and her spirits soared. This was all so much better than she had expected.

"Then sit down and talk to me. What have you been doing all morning while I was asleep?"

Emma gave Olive the wild carnations. "I went to Chiberta and picked these for you," she said.

Olive took the flowers as though they were the choicest orchids, and Emma watched anxiously to see if she really liked the flowers or whether, as Tim had pointed out, Olive had to say she liked them.

"Put them on this table where I can look at them and pretend I roamed among the pine trees and picked them myself." She glanced at Emma and saw how bright she was.

"Wasn't it dull by yourself?"

"No, I went by tram, but I walked back through the pine woods. I met Mr. Crake. He had been bathing on the Côte des Basques. He asked after you."

"That was kind of him," said Olive warmly, as though it were an honour to be remembered by Tim. "We must see more of him. I know Arthur met him on the journey down in the train; but left to Arthur's mercies, Mr. Crake will spend most of his time in some bar, or gambling or flitting about from one night-club to another, showing no discrimination about its quality — spending all his foreign travel allowance, getting nowhere, and end by being disgruntled."

Later on Olive did a little business with Emma, but the effort wearied her, and Emma said:

"I can get on easily alone."

"Can you? Then I will leave it to you."

Arthur sent a glorious sheaf of roses to his aunt. They had arrived with an enormous bunch of flowers from the hotel manager. Alphonse sent in a few lilies, fragile, pure blooms, but unassuming in quantity, with a note begging Olive to *get well quickly!*

"So quickly," commented Olive, when she read the note, "that tomorrow I should like Alphonse to take me for a drive into the country. I have been here several weeks, but have seen little of the people in these parts. Emma, will you kindly ask Alphonse to think of an interesting drive tomorrow afternoon?"

Emma said she would. "But will you be well enough? You should rest —"

"Rest! What for? There is too much to do and see and learn for me to rest when there is no need," said Olive vigorously. "I am not an invalid, and I won't be treated as one." She pointed to a sheaf of invitations, and the thick pad of engagements written in Emma's neat hand which she had been studying before Emma came into the room. "There is the antidote for my illness. I must fill in every minute of my waking hours so that there will be no time to think of pain."

Emma picked up the list and studied it. Except for four hours of business daily, it was all pleasure. The list grew longer daily. There was a visit to Santander to watch the yacht racing in the lovely blue crystal sea from the Spanish club-house.

Emma knew Santander was a great resort for international yacht racing, mostly wealthy Argentines competing. They seemed to divide their interest between yacht racing and playing polo out at Beyris. There was a special bullfight at San Sebastian, where the chief attraction was to be the great Velasquez, a noted matador from Madrid. Olive did not care for bullfighting, but she had friends staying at the Hotel Santa Cristina and could visit them while Arthur went to the bullfight. They would all join up afterwards at the Bar Coris for cocktails before going home.

"It reads like a page out of the *Arabian Nights*," Emma said, but there was warm satisfaction in her voice.

"You love parties and people, Emma."

"I've never been to a dull party."

During the next three weeks, Olive de Witt had arranged for visits to friends either at their hotels or in villas at Chiberta, Bayonne, or on board yachts at Bayonne or Pasajes; a *super-dansant* party at the beautiful casino at La Roseraie at Ilbarritz; cocktails in the Bar Basque; a never-ending list of lunches and dinners at famous restaurants where cosmopolitan crowds collect day after day, throughout the season: the Château Basque, Chez Ramuntcho, Chez Henri, the Café Madrid and Restaurant Normandie; Casanova, which is entered under vine-covered arches preceded by powdered footmen holding aloft taper candles, and where one dances on a floor open to the star-spangled sky; L'avenue; La Petite Chatte.

Emma read out the list in breathless haste. She fluffed the pages and closed the book. Both she and Olive laughed, knowing that Suzette scolded at the waste of energy, and Alphonse openly wondered how long Madame could keep it up. But Emma always enjoyed immensely those to which she was invited.

The Palais led the way in gala dinners. One night, the restaurant was transformed into a Basque village, when double-yoked oxen paraded between the tables with bovine dignity: when a game of Pelota was staged, and the waiters were dressed as Basques in national costume. Another evening, the restaurant was turned into a battleship, complete with mock guns, and the waiters were dressed as sailors in winter duck uniforms. There were a *gala Argentine, gala Manhattan, gala des gardenias, Le bal des cent baisins; fête Louis XIV, fête des dames blanches.*

"It is one enjoyment after another," she cried again, recalling all the pleasures in store, "a hectic life far beyond my dreams of what I once thought was the perfect way of life."

"One thing I know, Emma, is that pleasure does not spoil you," said Olive.

That was true. All this gaiety about her, in the past, now and for the future, seemed to give Emma an added stimulus for work. It came easily to her.

As Olive once said, "You were certainly born with a flair for my special work."

Emma was the perfect liaison between Olive, her lawyers and her bank manager. She was excellent, too, at keeping in touch with all those charitable institutions and private help which made such large holes in Olive's fortune.

There was a knock at the door, and Emma said, "That is Alphonse."

"You know his knock?"

Emma smiled. "I should know it anywhere — so softly discreet." She rose to answer it, and said, "Is there anywhere particular you would like to go for your drive tomorrow?"

"I will leave that to Alphonse. It will be a surprise for me."

Emma went to the door, and as she expected Alphonse stood there.

"How is Madame?" he whispered.

Emma went outside and closed the door. She had been laughing at the 'carnival' list of Olive's engagements and her eyes were full of merriment. She had made the teasing remark about Alphonse's knock which had added in some way to her inward fun.

"Madame is much better, thank you. She is dressed and enjoying the air by the window."

Alphonse was delighted. "*Bien!*" he cried, his face lighting up. "But that is wonderful."

Emma went on, "Madame feels so much better that she wants you to arrange a little outing for her tomorrow afternoon."

"Impossible! I shall not do it. Absurd! It would be too tiring for her. This time I take a stand." Here Alphonse struck an attitude. It was meant to impress Emma. But she only laughed.

"Madame has made up her mind that it will do her good," she told him demurely, looking up at him under her lashes. It was something Emma had not done for over a year, and as soon as he stopped to recognize the teasing flash, Alphonse forgot his dignity and smiled.

Emma continued: "You can arrange it, Alphonse, so that she will not be tired."

"That goes without saying."

Alphonse knew that once Olive de Witt had made up her mind to go to a special place, it was up to him to see that she had an easy and comfortable journey.

He asked, "Is this your suggestion?"

"Alphonse!"

"Because if it is, I think I shall shake you. It is such a crazy idea. All night Madame was ill and in pain…"

Emma agreed. "That's right, and she is better today, resting quietly because Suzette has bullied her into keeping quiet. Tomorrow Madame wants to get out into the sunshine. What is so dreadful about that?"

"Nothing, providing Madame does keep quiet."

"Oh, she means to. There will be a quiet little lunch in the restaurant with Mr. Arthur, the Comte de la Tremblay and his nephew, and a few others —"

Alphonse groaned. "A *few*! To you or to me a few might mean three or four. To Madame, a few can mean anything up to twenty."

"Then Madame and Mr. Arthur and the Comte will go for a picnic — a gentle drive around the countryside and a picnic tea. I can give you some tea. I brought it with me from India last year."

"Are not you coming too?" Alphonse asked with surprise in his precise English.

"No. It is my day off."

Alphonse had forgotten it was Emma's half-day. Anyway, half-days did not count with him.

"Is that immovable?"

"It is in this case because I have a date."

"Oh?" Alphonse's voice was sharp. Emma had seemed in so much better spirits today, more like her old self. He had put it down to Madame's quick recovery. Now Alphonse was not so sure. He did not ask who Emma was going with. Perhaps he knew.

"Where are you going?" he inquired in an unfriendly tone, and Emma's expression grew wooden.

"You mustn't ask me."

"Is it a secret?"

"Oh, no. It is just that I don't think you have the right to inquire," was the bland retort.

Alphonse did not press the point. He looked at Emma for a long moment in silence, then he said: "I shall try to arrange a pleasant afternoon for Madame. I will give you the route in the morning."

Arthur came into the *salon* after dinner. Sitting comfortably in an armchair, his legs draped over the arms, he talked amicably to Mrs. de Witt for a long while. Often he glanced across the big room to Emma, whose head was bent over her work. The smoke from the American cigar he was enjoying acted as a kind of screen.

Arthur thought: 'Emma makes a picture in that blue dress with the rose brocade curtain as background. I bet she knows it, for Emma has a keen eye for effect.'

His aunt asked, "You are lunching here tomorrow, Arthur?"

"Yep. Emma put the date down on my pad."

"And you are joining in my picnic in the afternoon?"

"Yep, that, too, is down on my pad." Then he inquired suddenly, "Is Emma going, Aunt Olive?"

"I don't think so. It is her afternoon off."

"Does that matter?"

"Not to you, but it matters a great deal to someone whose time is not her own."

Arthur seemed disappointed. "Have you asked her?"

"No, but you can."

Arthur rose with alacrity. Carefully, with his little finger, he removed the ash from the tip of his cigar so that it fell into an ashtray. Then he sauntered across the room to Emma.

He came up to her quietly, and spoke softly, but she was too engrossed in her work, and did not hear him at once. Indeed, it was a drift of smoke from his cigar which made her aware of his nearness — that, and when he put his hand flat on the paper in front of her.

Emma glanced up with a smile. "I didn't see you."

Arthur grinned. "That's a blow to my self-esteem. I try to flatter myself that when I enter a room, everyone knows it." He laughed good-humouredly. Then he said, "Please, Emma, if I ask you nicely, will you join the picnic tomorrow?"

She looked up at him, and it came to her suddenly that a picnic with Arthur would hold more fun than one with Tim Crake, for with Arthur she could be herself, but with Tim Crake she would have to be careful not to annoy him. She could aggravate Arthur, but she must not tease Tim for he would not understand.

So there was genuine regret in her voice as she said, "I'm sorry, Arthur, but I have a date."

"That is rather a blow," he told her. "When I said I would go, naturally I counted on your being there. We could amuse each other."

"If I'd known —" Emma was beginning, but Arthur cut her short by calling across to his aunt, who had taken up some knitting and looked quiet and contented:

"I've asked her nicely, but Emma won't come, Aunt Olive. She's got a date."

"You weren't quick enough," replied his aunt. "A girl like Emma soon gets dated up."

Arthur made no reply. He was thinking: 'Something's going on here — something I shan't like. I understood from Aunt Olive's letter that Emma had passed the ice age and was in circulation again. That part is right. Emma is better. She is lovelier than ever. In a week or two we shall be on the friendliest footings: or shall we? I sure did not read in Aunt Olive's letter that I had a rival. I must get to the bottom of this, for how can I take up the old threads with Emma if another fellow's image comes between us?'

Arthur went through a list of Emma's boyfriends, the ones she had met since he joined his aunt's party, but none of them seemed to fit the bill.

Some more people came in and the party played Canasta for a couple of hours. It gave Arthur a vicarious pleasure to suggest to Aunt Olive that Emma should join in the game. He sat next to her. He was his usual gay self — but underneath Arthur was puzzled.

As she lay in bed that night under the snowy net folds of her mosquito curtain, and reviewed the happenings of the day, which was her usual habit before she slept, Emma was a little distressed because she had forgotten Geoff for a whole day. Not only had she not missed him, but, what was worse, the day had seemed complete without him. She thought soberly, 'Perhaps I am getting over Geoff, just as Olive said I would.'

She felt guilty of doing Geoff a wrong, and forced herself to think about him.

Curiously enough, Emma fell asleep on that thought, and spent the whole of the night in a deep restful slumber.

She awoke in the morning and thought of Tim and the glorious time they would have together in the afternoon.

Later, when Emma went into the *salon* and sat down at her desk to open the huge stack of morning mail, Alphonse joined her. He had recovered from his mood of yesterday and seemed anxious to please her. Having inquired after Madame's health, which was a ritual with Alphonse, he said happily:

"I have planned a lovely picnic."

Emma felt a tinge of regret that she was not taking part in it. Alphonse's picnics were always a success.

"Where?"

Alphonse looked straight at Emma. "To the Rhune…"

Emma stared wide-eyed and open-mouthed at him. How unfortunate! What could she do about it? They were sure to meet, and if they did then Emma knew that her picnic would be a failure. There would be no more talk *à deux* with Tim. He might even think she knew about Olive's drive and copied her purposefully.

"What is the matter?"

"Nothing. I hope you enjoy yourselves. The weather will be perfect. I sometimes think you must have some private communication with the weather prophet, for your picnics are always blessed with fine weather."

"You are talking to gain time," accused Alphonse. "What is wrong? You look as though you have swallowed a sprat complete with spine."

"I suppose it is quite settled that you are taking Madame to the Rhune?"

"Yes, and not only to the Rhune, but up it. We shall, of course, go in the funicular."

"Well, you'll have to think of something else."

"So!" Alphonse raised his eyebrows.

"You mustn't go there."

"Why not?" Alphonse's eyes were fixed innocently on Emma's face.

"Because…" Emma passed the tip of her tongue over dry lips. "I am going there."

"Are you?" It was Alphonse's turn to show surprise.

"That is why you must quickly choose some other place." Emma laughed a little. She was not quite at ease. She did not much like the way Alphonse was staring at her. She had a feeling that it was not going to be easy to make him change his plans as she had hoped.

Emma went on, gabbling in her nervousness, "What a blessing I found out in time, before you saw Madame."

"Do not worry, Emma," said Alphonse kindly. "The Rhune is massive — so big. We shall all go there — our two parties. We shall not meet, I promise you. If only you had been frank with me yesterday I could have arranged something else, but now it is too late. I am so sorry."

There was a pause. Emma was furious. What on earth was she to do now? She stamped her foot to show how angry she was at Alphonse's stupidity.

"You are absolutely hateful. I believe you like spoiling all my fun. You are not a bit sorry. If you were, you would help me."

Alphonse was shocked. It was notable that he did not lose his temper with Emma, only saying mildly:

"You are behaving like a child, Emma."

Emma could have wept with frustration. The trip with Tim to the Rhune was off. How was she to explain to him? He would never understand. Tim would think she knew that Olive de Witt was going when she suggested the Rhune, that she, Emma, did not want to go out with him alone.

In perplexity Emma stared at Alphonse. This was all his fault. He was not looking at her, but out of the window, a look of patient resignation on his face. It was only afterwards it occurred to Emma that Alphonse was acting a part.

Now she said defiantly: "I am not. You are being difficult. I shall speak to Madame…"

The words died on Emma's lips, and she wished they had not been uttered. For what could Olive do about it all? Why should she be bothered? It was not her business. Besides, Emma knew the futility, the disloyalty of telling tales about Alphonse to Olive. Yet the words were said — brave enough if one had the courage to carry them out.

But Alphonse forced the issue. He urged softly, "I should."

At that moment Olive came into the room, and Emma composed her face at once.

"Good morning, Emma," she said brightly, and to Alphonse, "*Bonjour*, Alphonse."

Emma replied with a swift smile. She noticed with pleasure that Olive was using only one stick.

"*Bonjour*, Madame," Alphonse bowed with deference from the waist. Then he brought a chair forward for Olive to sit down.

Olive did so, and glanced sharply from one to the other.

"Yes?" she asked, for she liked to come straight to the point. "What is it? Something wrong?"

Emma shook her head. She *could not* tell Olive that the pleasure of the day had gone for her; but she felt sick at heart.

It was Alphonse who spoke — softly, clearly. "I have planned to make an expedition to the Rhune this afternoon, Madame."

"Oh, that will be lovely," exclaimed Olive, clapping her hands with almost childish delight, for mountaineering of any kind fascinated her, perhaps because climbing was denied her. "I should never have thought of it, but now you mention a mountain, I think it will be the nicest picnic I could have."

"Unfortunately, Madame, Mees Ferrer has also arranged to go with her friend to the same place."

Olive paused. She did not want to forgo her own pleasure; but at the same time she was not the sort of woman to stand in the way of anyone else's enjoyment.

She looked penetratingly at Emma, whose face was slightly averted.

"Is it Mr. Crake, Emma?" she inquired softly.

"Yes, Mrs. de Witt."

"Well, then, we can join up and make one party of the excursion, for I, too, know Mr. Crake. Don't you think that is a good idea, Emma?"

There was no anxiety in Olive's tone. She was so sure that her idea was not only good but welcome to Emma, that she said to Alphonse:

"With your cleverness, and fate's help, that problem is easily solved. You are pleased, Emma?"

Thus appealed to directly, Emma had to agree. She swallowed her disappointment, and said with a good grace:

"I think it is a wonderful solution, Mrs. de Witt. May I ring up Mr. Crake and tell him?"

"Of course. He is young and might be annoyed to arrive and find himself in the midst of a crowd with the plans rearranged without consulting him. Don't forget to speak tactfully to him, Emma."

To Alphonse, Olive said, "We shall require another car."

"I have already booked a small coach, Madame."

"Good. You think of everything, Alphonse. That will give the party a chance to swell."

Emma left the *salon* and went downstairs to telephone. She would not speak to Tim with Olive and Alphonse listening.

When she had gone Olive's eyes met Alphonse's, and she said enigmatically, "I am not quite sure, Alphonse, at this moment, whether the crown of Solomon's wisdom has descended upon your head or mine."

"Even if I had a certain amount of wisdom, Madame, I have not the power of Solomon."

CHAPTER 7

Tim was still in his bedroom when Emma got through to him.

Directly he knew who was on the telephone, Tim said quickly: "Now don't say you are going to put me off again, because I shall refuse to listen. I have made up my mind that we are going up the Rhune this afternoon, and I won't change my plans. It is a perfect day and visibility is good. We should get a wonderful view from the top."

"It isn't quite that," Emma said placatingly. "We can still go up the Rhune, but we are doing it with Mrs. de Witt's party."

"Who says so?"

"I do."

"Oh!" There was a disagreeable pause. Then Tim said: "I am beginning to get sick of those words, 'Mrs. de Witt's party'. They are dinned into my ears by one or another all day; asleep they make a nightmare of my dreams. Why on earth did you have to tell her what you were going to do on your day off?"

"I didn't. I have only just heard that she was going up the Rhune today..."

"Who told you?"

"Alphonse."

"Frenchie! Then it's with a party," Tim mimicked. "Well, let them go. What has that to do with us?"

"Nothing really, only when Mrs. de Witt heard that we were going she suggested we should join her party and all go together."

"The cheek of it! Without consulting me!"

"I am doing that now."

"I hope you told her we didn't want to go?"

"I couldn't do that."

"Why not?"

"It would hurt Mrs. de Witt's feelings. She thinks we should love to go with her."

"What conceit! Because she likes chasing around *en masse*, it doesn't follow we do. You mustn't be so frightened of hurting people's feelings, Emma. You must assert yourself. Just say, *I want this or that* — be democratic."

Emma laughed. "Oh," she said, "would that be called democratic?"

"What else?" inquired Tim pugnaciously. He was temperamentally enthusiastic, but usually on the 'wrong side of the fence'!

"I should call it being rude."

"I say, is that one for me?"

"Silly! How suspicious you are."

"Well, I said you were subtle, didn't I? So I must be on my guard."

"Anyway, I can't take your advice. Mrs. de Witt would not understand. But you are sure to enjoy yourself, because Mrs. de Witt's picnics are always done so well."

"There you go again, kowtowing to her wealth, and what it can do for people."

"We do not talk about money," said Emma stiffly.

"You don't have to. It is easier perhaps to talk sentimentally about poverty which one has never known."

Emma had no answer to give Tim.

He blundered on. "Who exactly is Mrs. de Witt that people here run around saying her name with bated breath?"

"She is an American." It was a comprehensive word as Tim recognized, but Emma felt that it was impossible to explain that though wealth might have influenced the make-up of

Olive's personality, it was the woman herself that people were drawn to like a magnet, and liked so much.

"America is a large country," Tim pointed out.

"I know," Emma said so coldly that Tim realized he was trying her patience too far.

He said quickly: "As you were! That was a stupid question. A woman like Mrs. de Witt does not have to explain who she is. Her pocket does it for her."

"Now you are being vulgar. All this is, I hope, between you and me. For your own sake I should not air your opinions to your concierge or to anyone — he might be a friend of Mrs. de Witt's. I don't know what to say except that I wish you knew her better."

"Do you think I shall change my views?"

"I know you will eat mountains of humble pie." Emma's tone was warm.

Tim did not speak for a while, then he said in a chastened voice, "I am sorry."

"So am I about this afternoon, Tim."

"Tim! Is that how you think of me?" he asked swiftly in a changed tone.

"Yes."

"I dream about you as Emma. Surely that makes us friends." Then he added: "I give in. I apologize for my churlishness. I am rude, entirely without manners, and you have every reason to hate me; but, Emma, I hope you don't. We'll make another date for your next afternoon off. Perhaps we'll have better luck next time. Now where do we meet today?"

"We can pick you up at the Casino, about three-ish. It is on our way."

During the morning, Arthur came into the *salon* where Emma was busy typing at the little table beside her desk. He went over to her and sat on the edge of her desk, one foot on the floor, the other gently sawing the air. It was a favourite attitude of Arthur's. With that zest that was a speciality of Arthur's, he brought some chocolates with him. They were in a thin cardboard container which was smothered in coloured pictures of the stars now performing at the Bal Tabarin in Paris, and Emma examined it with amusement, recognizing some of the actresses whom she had seen either with Arthur or Alphonse, or some other escort.

She opened the flap, and raising a doyley looked at the chocolates.

"What temptation!" she cried.

"Count it as today's blessing."

"But what will it be tomorrow when I find I have put on weight?"

"Tomorrow is another day! You always were on the thin side. D'you remember what a sober little rag and bone you were when I first met you? You could do with a little fattening up."

"Though I have learned to dress the bones better?"

"Very much better." His eyes went over her figure. "Is that one of Conrad's dresses?" he asked.

Emma laughed and pretended to be shocked.

"For goodness' sake, don't tell Conrad that. He would have a fit. This dress is one I bought off the peg in Paris in June."

"It looks pretty good to me," said Arthur sturdily. Then he asked in a pleading sort of tone, "Who is the guy who has dated you for this afternoon, Emma?"

It was in her mind to tease Arthur, for that was the lightness of spirit between them, skimming over the surface of things,

116

each enjoying the other's company this lovely sunshiny morning. Then Emma chanced to look at Arthur, and met his eyes, and at once Emma sobered, for there was an appeal in Arthur's brown eyes such as an adoring dog might have for his master, and she knew it would be cruel to tease him. Emma had no doubt that even if Arthur were hurt, he would suffer it in the same stoic way that Olive accepted her pain. Aunt and nephew had that in common between them.

So she said simply, "It is Tim Crake."

There was a long silence.

"Crake!" Arthur was astounded. "But you've hardly spoken to him."

"We have talked quite a lot to each other at parties, on the beach, and the phone."

"Crake didn't mention it to me, yet we played a round of golf together at Chiberta yesterday. I also saw him last night. We had drinks together." Then Arthur said steadily, "You know, Emma, I didn't bring that guy along to push me over to get in with you."

Emma did not answer at once. Then she said, "We had arranged to go up the Rhune today, but when Mrs. de Witt heard of it she kindly asked us to join her party."

Arthur's face, which had grown despondent, lightened, and he cried boisterously: "Good old Aunt Olive! So we are all going together after all."

"Yes, in a coach."

"That'll suit me, especially if it's the way *you* want it."

Emma smiled. "Well, it is. I love picnics, especially Mrs. de Witt's."

When they met Tim in the afternoon, Arthur, who had been seated beside Emma in the coach, gave up his seat to Tim. He

117

sat behind the two, from which vantage point he could watch them, lean forward with his arms on the back of their seat, and talk.

"You didn't tell me you and Emma had a date this afternoon," Arthur said at once.

Tim looked a little confused, but he quickly recovered.

"I did not think to say so," he replied, "but there is no secret about it." He wondered whether Emma had been indiscreet enough to discuss him with Arthur. "But there are so few English in Biarritz, and I'm not a good linguist. It is natural for Emma and I to cotton on to each other. It is human to like one's kind in a foreign land."

"That's so," agreed Arthur. Then he said to Emma, "Where are your sunglasses?"

"In my bag."

"Well, put them on, for the glare is blinding and will give you a headache."

The coach drove past the shuttered villas, magnificent in their whiteness, towards the undulating curves and peaks of purple and mauve mountains which faded away into the distance until misted mauve mountain toned in with misted blue sky.

Alphonse, driving the Rolls-Bentley, was on the road somewhere ahead of them. In their party in the coach besides Emma, Arthur and Tim were young de la Tremblay, a couple of Americans, a German, some Argentines, two Spaniards and a French woman — a cosmopolitan crowd gathered into the net of Olive de Witt's hospitality.

The afternoon stood out as a landmark in Emma's life. After all the colour, sparkle and feverish rhythm of the holiday spirit in Biarritz, where bathing from at least five beaches, and sunbathing were as much a cult as the fêtes and galas, casino and night-clubs; where life was swift and gay, and one excitement seemed to feed on another, the change to quiet, simple pastoral scenes had a soothing effect on the nerves.

The coach passed through Bidart with its pretty white villas set amid pines, then through typical green Basque country towards the dark purple line of the Pyrenees, with the massive Rhune guarding the tip of the range. Here the hard-working peasants with their large doe-like eyes and clear skins, delicately shaped noses and small mouths appeared to have borrowed something from the serenity of the landscape.

The coach was held up by a slow-moving yoke of fawn-coloured oxen drawing a load of hay, their sleek flanks smooth as velvet, and with sheepskins between their horns.

It took little imagination to see that the great stretches of verdant pastures on either side of the streams that watered this fertile land were laughing in the sunshine.

Every inch of the rich brown earth was cultivated so that the country looked like a gaily patterned tapestry woven in rich colours that were a joy to the eye. It was as though some loving Power had put a kindly benediction on the land.

A clump of pine trees stood out almost black against the flawless light blue sky.

Olive was waiting for them at the funicular-railway station. She was seated and waving a fan languidly, not so much because she was hot as to keep the flies from bothering her.

The shrilling sound of the cicadas among the tough coarse grass bordering the little station was loud and continuous, or it seemed noisy in the quietness about them.

Alphonse and Suzette saw the party off in the single coach. With the chauffeur of the coach, they were remaining below.

"Are you sure you can manage, Madame?" asked Alphonse, just before the train started on its upward journey.

"Quite. Please have tea ready when we come down," said Olive.

Tim unexpectedly offered to look after Olive, and she accepted his offer gratefully.

The train travelled slowly in the dazzling sunshine. The party were in tourist spirit. They did not talk much but looked out of the observation windows of the coach. In a kind of enchantment they observed the beautiful valleys bordering the Basque country.

Away to the north there was a big forest fire, for clouds of smoke over a great area rolled and billowed blackly against the cerulean sky.

There was a thin softness in the air at the top of the Rhune, and a light capricious wind. Olive was glad of Tim's arm on one side. She chose Arthur also to help her for he was young and virile, and for all his lackadaisical manner, had great strength.

Near to the summit the train had disturbed a golden eagle. It sailed effortlessly above and around them, a bird of prey of great power and beauty, looking like a small monoplane.

Arthur had brought a cine-camera, which he used tirelessly.

"These pictures will amuse my family some winter's night, in the future, when we are shut up in the cosy warmth of my hunting-lodge in the Adirondacks," he told those around him confidently, with the calm assurance of stating an accepted fact.

"You are certain of being a family man," someone suggested jokingly, because it was hard to visualize Arthur as a man with family responsibilities, and those within hearing smiled derisively too.

"Oh, yes: I know my destiny," Arthur replied easily, not at all put out by this general disbelief. "My wife will be there with me, and our children." Under his breath, and with barely a flicker of an eyelid in Emma's direction, Arthur added piously, "I hope."

As though for the first time in their friendship Emma caught a serious undercurrent in his tone, she turned her head to look into Arthur's guileless eyes, and wondered at the sweet smile that suddenly illumined his face. It was something personal for her — between them. It was disturbing to think she had known Arthur for several years and been with him under all kinds of conditions, and not to have noticed this facet in his character. She glanced quickly away.

At that moment Emma felt happier than she had done for a long while. A curious thing happened too, for she had already thought the scenery about them perfect, but everything suddenly took on a richer colour. There was meaning and beauty in life which for so long had seemed arid and empty. The change in outlook was astonishing.

Drawn as by a magnet, Emma looked again at Arthur, to see if he, too, had changed. But one of the Argentines had drawn his attention to something far away, and he was no longer smiling in that special intimate way.

The party sat about for a long while in the sunshine, picking out places which they knew in the surrounding country, for the visibility was perfect.

It was Olive who closed her fan with a decided click which attracted everyone's attention, and suggested they should make a start to go back. She had noticed that the lighthouse lantern down on the plage at Biarritz was lit. As the beam swung round, she had thought at first it was a pale distant flash of summer lightning, for the sea had darkened, and the white lace-like foam which edged the sable sands showed up vividly against the dark sea.

The sunshine had faded around them. A storm threatened, obliterating the colour and beauty around them, and the mauve shadows of the Pyrenees turned black. Slowly they prepared to go to the train.

"It will die away when the tide goes down," prophesied the Comte de la Tremblay. "These summer storms are always promising to come, but before they develop the tide turns, and they drop to nothingness."

Everyone was duly impressed, for the Comte did not often offer his opinion, yet when he did it was worth listening to.

Olive laughed lightly. "That sounds like an allegory," she said.

Turning quickly to speak to Arthur, Olive saw that he was looking at Emma. There was such love and longing in his eyes that Olive was sorry for him. She was afraid lest Emma would never love him and he would be disappointed in life. She wanted to help him.

Her eyes fell on Tim, who might well cause some trouble with Arthur, if only because Emma was foolish enough to imagine she saw a likeness between Tim Crake and her late fiancé.

Immediately Olive drew Tim's attention from Emma, so that Arthur might have the undisputed pleasure of her companionship.

Emma was daydreaming — even when walking over the grass towards the little train.

Olive had taken the Comte de la Tremblay's arm, and leaned on her stick for support.

Arthur turned towards Emma, saying: "A dollar, Emma? Or are they worth more?" And he thought, 'It might be truer even to offer the exchange in another country's currency.'

She replied vaguely, for her thoughts were hazy but light. She was absolutely content, her nerves never more serene.

"I wasn't even thinking. Isn't it nice not to have to think? I seem to have brought 'doing nothing' this afternoon to a fine art." She smiled. "I hope Alphonse has made a decent cup of tea. I have taken such pains to teach him. A poor cup of tea can spoil a picnic."

Then Emma stopped suddenly, aware that she was speaking because Arthur had asked her something and she must reply — but what he had said she did not know.

Arthur appeared to notice nothing wrong, and said kindly and fondly, "Little sybarite!" And to Tim who was free for a moment from Olive's attentions, and was listening to what they were saying, ready and willing to join in their talk, he said:

"Emma adores the easy way. She makes a lovely cup of tea herself, but she has taught Alphonse so well that he can make it for her. All she has to do is to sit back and be waited upon."

Emma and Arthur laughed together as at a joke. Tim could see nothing to cause them such merriment.

He had been feeling out of it this afternoon. He had been a fool to offer to help Olive de Witt. Tim could not think why he had done so. Perhaps, subconsciously, he had not really meant her to take him at his word. That was the penalty of being too polite. People took advantage of it. She had taken possession of him nicely, smiling in that sweet way she had, thanking him graciously for any small service; using him, Tim thought with annoyance, much the same way as she did that courier-chauffeur fellow, or whatever the label was Frenchie had tacked on to himself. Indeed, Alphonse's position was an enigma to Tim. He could not understand it. The fellow dressed well. He behaved like a courtier at Court. Mrs. de Witt was the gracious queen, and seemed to like the position.

Tim felt disgruntled, and said sourly, "It is marvellous how attractive anything under the name of luxury can be."

"But you wouldn't call tea a luxury to me," objected Emma. "Everyone else prefers coffee."

"You make it seem a luxury."

"It is in France."

Arthur said: "Crake doesn't know it, but he's paying you a compliment... Well, we shall all look forward to the tea presently, and woe betide Alphonse if he doesn't produce a good cup."

Emma was aware that Arthur was protecting her tactfully from Tim's barbed tongue, reassuring her, anxious that she should not feel hurt. She recalled the tenuous and delicate happiness she had felt a short while ago; and now a warm glow came over her as Arthur's protective kindness did a little more healing to her spirit and soul, giving proof that there was something more solid and lasting in that feeling than she had at first thought.

Arthur's consideration surprised Emma. Often she had seen him kind, considerate and loving to his aunt. Though he had always treated her, Emma, kindly, he had also let her go her own way without let or hindrance. He was young and impressionable, and a little spoiled by girls, as all rich, pleasant and personable men must be, and he had, at times, been sentimental when she had laughed at him. There had been a period when Arthur had fancied himself in love with her, and had even asked her to marry him, not once, but many times, but that was when he had known that she was in love with Geoff. She had never taken Arthur seriously, for Mrs. de Witt, his aunt, was her employer and might not like her secretary to marry her nephew. There had been no fear of Emma losing her job over Arthur. One did not take Arthur seriously, for he was a blithe young man, tanking happily through life, working and playing with zest because that was his way, how he was born. Today Emma felt that perhaps underneath there was something worthwhile in Arthur, something she had not bothered to probe for or to understand, taking him at his own surface value which spelled 'playboy' to so many people.

CHAPTER 8

As it happened Alphonse made a wonderful cup of tea, but Emma was the only one who drank it. Olive, following the French custom, had coffee, but she liked it black because it gave her energy. Tim and Arthur had iced coffee, and all of them ate *foie gras* sandwiches and *petits fours*. Afterwards they smoked cigarettes and gossiped, but Arthur, following a wartime habit, lit a small American cigar. Having lit his cigar, with a deft twist of his tongue Arthur rolled it into a corner of his mouth. He clenched his strong white teeth on it so that it stuck out at an angle. He did not talk much but listened to the gossip, his body and mind relaxed. Tim, too, seemed to enjoy the interlude. Directly she got out of the train Alphonse took charge of Olive, helping her to walk forward to meet the driver of the train with whom she chatted for some moments. So Tim took a seat on a fallen tree beside Emma, leaning forward, resting his forearms on his knees, his hands clasped. The crickets chirruped merrily and tirelessly.

They were quiet for a little while, and Tim said:

"I'm so glad I know you, Emma."

"Are you?"

"Why do you say it in that tone?"

"Because you seem to use me as a flogging post to get relief from some frustration."

"You don't like that."

"Would you?"

"Well — no…" Tim admitted. Then he said: "Thank you for holding the mirror up to me. I promise to behave in future."

"Don't worry about that." Her tone was indifferent. Emma had thought: 'I could walk away from him and never speak to him again. I might lose my temper with him and tell him some home truths.' She had done neither of these well-deserved things, and she knew why. It was because of Tim's likeness to Geoff. Tim was not important to her, but she was able to find excuses for him. Nevertheless, he wearied her today.

"It's a relief to talk to you after an hour with Mrs. de Witt. Her ego is too pronounced for my taste. Now with you it is different. You are so restful that I can relax. You are not like those other women, gossiping about their sex."

Emma's mobile lips twisted. "Oh, I'm no different from anyone else," she disclaimed lazily.

"Yes, you are, though there must be others like you, but where they hide themselves I do not know. They are not at the parties or restaurants or night-clubs. Perhaps they are secretaries like you, and kept behind a kind of *purdah*."

Emma roused herself to say, "You certainly are an adept at giving a back-handed compliment."

"You know what I mean," Tim told her comfortably.

"Yes, I do," and Emma thought, 'But it does not forgive your clumsiness.' She wished that Tim was more tactful. If only he learned to hide his feelings he would be more popular.

They lingered over tea, for there was a tranquillity around them which they all noticed and were anxious not to break.

Even when people moved to go back, Emma and Tim did not stir. A few moments before it seemed as though they had found plenty of trivial things to say to each other, light subjects that did not call for much thought or exertion, or break the peace that was about them.

After a little while Alphonse came and stood before them. He looked kindly at Emma and he said, "The coach is waiting."

Emma jumped up and apologized for keeping everyone waiting. She felt excited and happy, though what about she could not say, unless it was that she had been a little bored with Tim, and Alphonse had arrived at the right moment to relieve her. She hurried after Alphonse's slim figure, for he had returned at once towards his car which was standing ahead of the coach.

Tim was behind Emma. She heard his shoes cutting through the long coarse grass, and called out over her shoulder:

"It has been a lovely day after all, hasn't it?"

"Far more enjoyable than I expected," he agreed, "but we haven't had our own special outing yet."

"You must give me a ring when you have a few spare hours, and we'll fix something up."

"I like that. It isn't *my* time that is so full up. It's you who are so busy."

Emma laughed. There was a mocking note in it which made Tim determined that he would make a date with her soon.

"We'll strike lucky someday," she told him.

The journey back to Biarritz was uneventful. Both Alphonse and the driver of the coach were in a hurry.

Emma and Tim sat together as before, but Arthur no longer sat behind them, forced to be content with a view of Emma's profile, and a few stray words which she threw at him now and again. He was with some gay Spaniards. There was no chance of quiet talk for anyone, because the party had somehow 'got together' and were like one big family rather than many separate units.

"Why this breakneck speed?" inquired Tim, when the coach driver stamped on everything to avoid hitting a stray dog.

"Because Mrs. de Witt is dining at Ciboure at ten o'clock, and she must rest first."

Tim groaned. It was useless finding fault with Olive, for she was the hub of Emma's little universe. He exclaimed: "What an hour! I have my dinner at half-past seven in London."

"And I bet you are ready for another meal before you go to bed?"

"I wouldn't refuse a snack. I'm hungry now. I should die of starvation if I had to wait until ten o'clock."

"The friend at Ciboure is a Cuban: most Cubans and Spaniards dine about ten."

"What are you going to do this evening, while Mrs. de Witt is out?"

"I shall work. You have no idea the amount of work Mrs. de Witt's charities involve. It isn't her part, for that is simple enough. Mrs. de Witt's methods are simple and straightforward. It is the complications and muddles the Charity staffs make about the smallest thing."

"Then it would be useless asking you to dine with me? We need not dress, and could eat as early as you liked."

"I'm afraid so; but I like dining late, Tim. I'm used to it anyway, now. There have been times when we have dined at midnight, and left the dinner-table at three o'clock in the morning."

Tim looked shocked and disbelieving.

"Even hotel staffs have to sleep at times," he said.

"It wasn't in an hotel, but in a *casa* which Mrs. de Witt had taken furnished at Tenerife."

"What terrible people! What's wrong with eating meals at the proper times?"

"Oh, just that it was too hot, or we weren't ready to eat, or friends couldn't turn up until later, or — oh, several reasons, and all of them good when one was anxious to make an exciting event of an ordinary dinner."

"That is the jungle rule for people on *shikari*, who eat when they are hungry, and sleep when they are tired."

"I don't know. We have never been on *shikari*. It would be too rough a life for Mrs. de Witt. Whether you like it or not, Tim, it is an experience, turning day into night."

"You are incorrigible, Emma." Then he said pointedly, "But it is your day off."

"You mean my afternoon. Oh, I don't work to rule. That would be dull. Besides, I can only just manage to keep abreast of the business if I deal with it the day it comes in."

"I believe you are quite at home with these people and this kind of life, Emma."

"I like it, and wouldn't change it for anything."

"Don't you ever want to settle down?"

"Of course, but that's something in the future. I am content in the present."

On her return to the hotel in Biarritz, Olive went straight up to her room to rest before dressing for the evening. Suzette had closed the windows and drawn the blinds and curtains. The room was cool and bathed in a dark grey light.

When Olive was lying down, she asked Suzette to leave her. Then Arthur came, and sat down on the edge of the bed and waited for his aunt to speak.

"Are you doing anything special tonight, Arthur?" asked Olive out of the shadows. Arthur replied, "I am, but it is not so special that I can't chuck the lot if you have something you want me to do."

"It is what you wish, Arthur."

"What is it? I know: you have some old dowager you want me to take out and be sweet to. I'll do it, of course, but I'd rather it were a nice young thing."

Olive smiled to herself. "I have no intention of urging you to do anything you do not wish. I am going to Ciboure to dine with a close friend who has just lost her husband to whom she was devoted."

"Yes?" Arthur wondered if Olive wanted him to go with her. The prospect was not alluring.

"Can't you guess?"

"No: should I?"

"If you are smart."

Arthur pondered, then he grinned. "It would be too much luck for it to be Emma."

"It is Emma. You are getting slow, Arthur."

"I know. It is old age."

"Emma will be in alone."

Emma had spent countless evenings alone, and no one had worried much.

"Why not take her down to dinner in the restaurant at the Palais? Now don't rush to build on my suggestion by making a wild evening of it. Make it quiet. Let Emma see that you aren't living on your nerves and need excitement to feed them upon."

Arthur grinned. Olive could see his white teeth in the gloom.

"Thanks, Aunt Olive, for the tip. Of course I'll do it. Shall I go and ask her now?"

"Emma will be down presently," said Olive. "Of course, I don't know if she is free to go with you. She knows nothing of my suggestion. You mustn't feel disappointed if Emma has made other arrangements. She may be going out with Mr. Crake — or Alphonse. After he has run me out to Ciboure,

Alphonse has four hours to himself. He is clever in not only interesting himself but at amusing others, especially Emma. He had always liked her from the first, when he made Emma his protegee."

"Emma isn't going out with Crake. I heard him ask her in the coach, and she refused. As for Alphonse!" Arthur paused, then said reflectively, "If I get friendly with Emma again I shall be in his bad books, for Alphonse has a specially soft spot in his heart for Emma."

"Would you mind?"

"I'd rather lose Emma to Alphonse, whom we know, than to a strange guy. But I'd hate him to be my rival. I should not care to compete with Alphonse's polish, his French understanding of women, how to amuse them, and more important, how to make love to them, and his English accent which they seem to find irresistible. In other words, I'd be up against his experience. I have knocked about a bit, but I am gauche beside Alphonse. While, of course, there is always the late Geoff White's influence. How deeply Emma has hidden him in her heart I do not know. She still feels it, or would never have taken up with Crake the way she has; not, I feel sure, because she likes him, but because he has the fortune to resemble White."

Olive considered this. It was easier to get a better perspective of Emma's admirers at this distance and in the darkness. Not often did Arthur unburden his mind so clearly.

She thought, 'That's the way it is.'

She said: "Alphonse's one idea just now is to make Emma forget Mr. White. He will certainly not help to further Mr. Crake's suit, though I have reason to know that Mr. Crake admires Emma; but then, who doesn't? She is so enchanting in every way; no man could help but fall in love with her."

Arthur moved restlessly about the room, picking up an object and then putting it down again, his mind uneasy. "That is the trouble," he said in a low voice. "Emma is so cosy." Then he said: "Perhaps I have stayed away too long, but I did it for the best. There is always someone else ready to take my place."

Olive guessed at his anxiety, and she said cheerfully: "Do not worry too much about the past or the future. What has gone is finished; the future usually shapes itself on the present. Why not forget possible mistakes and enjoy yourself *now*?"

"You are right," Arthur said. His mercurial spirits were easily raised. The idea of having Emma to himself for a whole evening, with his aunt's blessing thrown in to make the pleasure perfect, gave Arthur happiness. He told himself he was crazy to be so happy considering what he longed for so much from Emma, and how little he had progressed in the whole period of their friendship towards satisfying his longings.

Emma came into the *salon* prepared for work. She was carrying an attaché-case and a leather portfolio. It had been a hot day, and directly they arrived back Emma had gone to her room and changed into a cool grey dress which was suitable for dining behind the screen in the restaurant.

She had begun sorting out her papers when Arthur came into the room from his aunt's bedroom.

"Hello," said Emma, looking up in surprise. "What are you doing here? I thought at this time you'd be having your first drinks in some bar."

He looked at her reproachfully. "You seem to have gotten a very poor opinion of me. You look upon me as a kind of barrel. I am not always drinking. There are other things in life."

Emma laughed as at a joke, and took no notice of his reproachful look.

He came over to her and asked, "What are you doing this evening?"

She glanced significantly at the pile of papers on her desk. "I am going to settle down to some hard work, catch up on some sticky letters I have to think out how to answer, which I have shelved because I am a coward, and write a long personal letter to London."

"There's no need to make a martyr of yourself because Aunt Olive goes out. I'll help you with the business letters if you will dine with me downstairs first," said Arthur. There was an unusual wistfulness in his voice that Emma noticed. It caused her to waver. She recovered, however, and said decisively: "No, thank you, I can't; you mustn't tempt me. I am not dressed. And honestly, I don't feel like exerting myself to be pleasant to people tonight."

"Are you tired?"

"No, not tired. It must be a mood."

"There's no need for you to exert yourself or work hard to be pleasant. There will be only the two of us."

"Your idea is that we shall dine alone?" Emma asked in some surprise, for Arthur, like his aunt, was a gregarious person, and liked to do everything in numbers.

"Yes, I was dining alone in any case."

"That *is* unusual."

"Yes, but somehow today has been unusual for me."

"How is that?"

"Oh, I'll tell you someday perhaps. It would take too long now. You don't mind dining alone with me?"

"Of course not. But I'd still have to change."

"Well, you've got a couple of hours to do it in. You look pretty good to me as you are — sweet and cool — but you wouldn't be happy in a restaurant filled with foreigners, all wearing models from Paris houses."

That was true. To be badly or wrongly dressed so as to be conspicuous in a crowd would be a sin to Emma. It was enough still to make Emma flush with mortification. She said suddenly: "I'll have dinner with you, Arthur. What time will you be ready?"

He could be relied upon to go out of his way to please her, to choose a meal she liked, to give her all his attention, to discuss people amiably and not spitefully, and to put her in a good temper with herself if only because he found so much in life to laugh at and could share the most trivial jokes with her.

"About nine-thirty."

Arthur strove not to be too elated, and to hide all his emotion. If the chance came for him to talk deeper, of more intimate matters, he meant to take it. There seemed no sense in making Emma aware of his intentions beforehand. She would shy away from them. Even now, though he loved Emma so hopelessly, Arthur could not bring himself to plead for favours she did not wish to give.

"That will do nicely. It will give me some time to get some work done."

She was evidently not making an event of the dinner-date, but taking it in her stride.

"Afterwards, we can come up here and I'll write those letters for you."

Emma laughed. "That's a promise," she reminded Arthur, but had no thought he would keep it.

"Cross my heart." Arthur went through the pantomimic ritual of crossing his heart.

CHAPTER 9

Soon after nine-thirty, Arthur, in a dinner-jacket, was waiting for Emma in the *salon*. He had been reading the letters which required answering, and which she had left out for him to study — if he still wished to keep his promise.

Directly she came into the *salon*, Arthur put down a letter without comment and gave all his attention to Emma.

She had put on her best white dress. The strapless bodice glittered with diamanté, and the full skirt was sewn with patterns of sequins. She wore a small spray of orchids which Arthur had sent up to her room earlier.

"You look enchanting," he told Emma, his eyes brightening and smiling as they rested on her lovely slim figure in the fairy-like dress. "Thank you for wearing my flowers."

"I love them. Thank *you*, Arthur."

He laughed shakily because for the first time in his life he felt shy with a girl, and all the facile compliments he was used to making when he met a pretty girl seemed suddenly inadequate and foolish.

To cover his own confusion, he said, "They say it is only one step from a thank-you party to a petting party."

He could have bitten out his tongue for being so silly, for Emma might misconstrue his meaning.

She said at once: "I'm unpettable tonight. I love my flowers and I'd hate them to be crushed."

"What does it matter? There are plenty more."

"Not for me. Don't be callous. I always treasure my dead flowers. They are pressed in a thick book which I carry around with me. Alphonse often remarks on my weighty baggage. If he knew what was in it, I believe he would force the lock of my case, take my book out and throw it away."

She laughed as at a joke, but Arthur did not laugh. He said instead, seriously, "You think a lot of Alphonse's opinion, don't you, Emma?"

"Sometimes — when he agrees with me," she replied lightly.

"You've kept his flowers, I bet."

"Yes, and yours too. I've got the first ones you gave me — the first any man had ever sent to me." She smiled at the recollection. "They *made* my dress then. I remember I felt as well dressed as anyone in the hotel. How young I was!"

"And fresh, Emma."

"But not very gay, I am afraid. I was far too terrified of saying or doing the wrong thing, of picking up the wrong fork or spoon, to be gay."

"Well, you've progressed some — and then some — since." Then he said, "Will you have a drink before we go down, Emma?"

"Nothing, thank you. But it is early yet, and I can wait for you…"

"No, I've had enough. I spent over an hour in the bar." Then as he saw her mischievous look: "Oh, not drinking all the time. I assure you I've only had a couple of small drinks since I left you ages ago."

"Then shall we go down?"

They were alone in the gilded lift except for a Cuban and his wife. The woman glanced coldly at Emma, but the man stared so hard at Emma that Arthur frowned with annoyance.

"I had half a mind to give the fellow a sock in the jaw," Arthur said when they left the lift.

"That would have created a scene and spoiled our evening," she told him calmly. "A cat may look at anyone — even a queen. He might even get stroked and petted. I am only Emma Ferrer. I like admiration even from a stranger. Such admiration makes me feel happy. I know then that I look nice and my clothes are right. The measure of the envy I create amongst women is also the measure of my personal success."

Arthur fell into step at her side, and they went towards the restaurant.

"Will you never realize your value, Emma?"

"What is it?"

"That even in shabby clothes you would still be the most beautiful woman in the room."

She flushed with pleasure. "It's very nice of you to say that, Arthur, but you did not always think like that. I remember —"

"Forget it. I mean it now; and everyone knows it."

They went into the crowded restaurant, Emma walking in with complete self-possession. Vandolini, plump and prosperous, complete with his enormous gold cable watch-chain and diamond fob, the perfect *maître d'hôtel*, met them in the doorway. He knew Olive well. It was understood among the staff that Mrs. de Witt was one of their best patronesses. Where she was, money flowed. Vandolini knew who Emma was. He had often done business with Mrs. de Witt through her charming and capable secretary. He had not, so far, seen Emma enter his restaurant with Mr. de Witt alone; or he had not observed her manner in doing so. Now his great liquid black eyes gleamed approvingly at Emma. She had the manner. Vandolini could not describe it, but he knew it when he met it. He personally led the couple to Olive's great round table, where two waiters and their attendant commis were ready to serve them, and where the flower decorations were the most magnificent in the room.

The two young people would sit alone at the table, the cynosure of all eyes, for Mrs. de Witt would allow no chance client to sit at the table which was reserved solely for her and her guests.

When they reached the table, waiters slid chairs into position under their knees. As they sat down, waiters unfolded napkins and helped to arrange them on their laps. Emma was presented with a fan.

Arthur said laughingly to Emma: "That was in the nature of a royal procession. The waiters know who you are, but many of the people here don't. They think you must be a princess. You look like one out of a fairy-tale book."

They were handed large menus, but neither read them for a moment. They were engrossed with what they were saying.

"And you?" Emma asked curiously.

"No one here asks who I am. I *look* an American, and all they wonder is, not if I *am* a millionaire, but how many millions I have." Then with rare cynicism Arthur said: "It isn't 'who' with me. It is 'how much'. I guess it's like that over here nowadays with any hundred per cent American."

"*I* don't think like that." Emma opened her fan and waved it languidly.

"No, but you are used to me, and know how simple I am underneath." Arthur had a sudden brainwave. "Unless —" he said rather shyly, "they think I am your husband."

"That would be funny," Emma smiled.

"I don't see anything funny in it at all," Arthur said stiffly. Then they both laughed, but whether because each knew something about the other that was amusing, or because the fact that people thought they were married made them nervous with each other, was not clear.

Arthur consulted Emma about the dinner. He read out some of the dishes on the gold-printed menu.

"Are you hungry?"

"Yes: are you?"

"Famishing. So let it be a real dinner, and not just titbits which never satisfy hunger, and spoil the palate."

They began with cantaloupe melon which was sweet and spiced and refreshing. This was followed by one of the 'royal' dishes of France — carp, which Arthur said gave him a nostalgia for his aunt's villa at Versailles.

"I'd like to go back there this fall, Emma."

"So would I."

"Well, as we think alike, I will ask Aunt Olive to think about it."

"Alphonse is arranging to go to New York."

"That appeals to me too; but not if you prefer Versailles."

Emma shook her head. "My wishes mustn't count," she said firmly.

"They do with me."

Emma did not pursue the subject.

They drank champagne, of course.

"There is no choice of wines for you, Emma," Arthur declared, examining the wine list.

"None. I make no excuse for my love."

"This is an occasion, so it must be a vintage year champagne, the best that the hotel cellars can give."

Emma would not have hers iced. "I can't bear to spoil it," she cried.

"You'll find it mawkish."

"You ice yours and lose the bouquet."

"No, I don't. It is still champagne. Okay, I'll try to like it your way."

Vandolini made a point of passing their table many times to pay homage to the slender figure in white who sat there with Mr. de Witt. He was never too busy to inquire if they had everything they wanted, if this dish or that was entirely to their liking.

They ate a delicate chicken dish for which the Palais was renowned. It was served with sauce made by an artist.

Arthur said to Emma, "Now tell me what you think of the champagne."

He held up his glass to her, his emotions a little turbulent.

Emma raised her glass and touched it with Arthur's. Their eyes met and held over the shallow goblets filled with the delicate amber liquid, pinpointed with tiny bubbles. They toasted each other, then drank a little.

"They say that champagne comes from laboratories, not the vineyards around Bordeaux," she said, putting down her glass, her slender fingers lingering on the stem. "This is marvellous. It has come straight from Heaven — fine and dry and slightly stinging."

An attentive waiter refilled Emma's glass. She watched the white froth on the top of the wine disperse, though the wine remained 'alive' with aerated bubbles in it.

"I am so glad you like it," Arthur said.

The wine mellowed Arthur. He was not used to drinking much at meals. That was done beforehand in a bar or lounge. If Arthur drank anything at all during meals, it was iced soda water.

He said now: "You seem very knowledgeable about champagne, Emma. Who taught you so much?"

"Alphonse."

Arthur had not expected that reply.

"Oh! I knew it was a man. I might have known it was a Frenchman."

Emma smiled.

"You must have dined out with him often."

"Quite a lot. Why?" Emma sounded slightly on the defensive.

"Nothing." Arthur thought, 'Old Alphonse knows a thing or two.' Then he laughed to himself, for Alphonse was not so much older than he was. "I bet Alphonse found you an apt pupil."

"I had to be apt. There was no choice. Alphonse takes food and drink seriously; and he is an impatient master."

The meal ended with little dishes of *Fraises du bois Chantilly*, served with white wine instead of sugar.

Arthur's eyes seldom left Emma's face. Once, they wandered a little to the exquisite curve of her throat and rested for a while on the hollow at the base of her throat. He gave her all his attention. If there were people in the restaurant he knew, and who recognized him, Arthur was not aware of it. He was engrossed with Emma.

Somewhere, unobtrusively, an orchestra was playing seductive music, and Arthur found himself growing sentimental. Emma reminded him of thistledown. Yet for all her softness in looks and manners which appealed to his senses, Arthur knew that Emma had a core of determination and directness of outlook that was surprising in one so youthful.

He said softly, "There's no one quite like our Emma."

He realized that if he were to get on an intimate footing of friendship with Emma, now was the time. As soon as dinner was over and Emma returned to the *salon* upstairs, she would resume her position as an efficient secretary to his aunt.

Tomorrow, if he tried to trade on anything said between them tonight, Emma would have no compunction in snubbing him.

He sat gazing at her fatuously, partly because Emma had never seemed so lovely or desirable as now, but partly, too, because he, who seldom drank wine with his dinner, had drunk too much champagne. Arthur was not drunk, he was not even confused, but his mind was soft, receptive and misty. He would have liked to go on like this forever, never exerting himself to do any business, but just being near Emma, looking into her lovely eyes and listening to her light silvery voice that reminded him of a happy brook, with the water gurgling gently over stones.

Emma noted the look in Arthur's eyes. She knew that his words were the outcome of that streak of sentiment in Arthur which was not his prerogative, but something which all Americans had, no matter how tough and hard-boiled they appeared to be.

She hesitated before speaking because it was so easy to say the wrong thing. She had loved every moment of this dinner. Not only was the food and drink superb, but being in that luxurious restaurant had created in her a feeling of well-being and contentment which wove a spell about her it was hard to break.

She had to make a move to go, and to do it in a way that would not hurt Arthur's feelings. So she smiled sweetly at him and said, "It must be nearly midnight."

"You are bored?" he said quickly.

"No, I've loved my evening."

"Then what does the time matter? You are not Cinderella whose lovely clothes disappear at midnight."

Emma laughed. "Not quite. But I have been a long time over dinner, and I really must do some work before I go to bed."

"Oh yes, those business letters. I had forgotten them. I'll tell them to bring some coffee, and we'll go up and see to them."

With a wave of his hand, Arthur called the waiter and ordered coffee, and some *fin champagne liqueurs*.

"I don't know much about wines, but I do know that one should never drink champagne without taking a liqueur brandy after it," he told Emma. "Is that news to you?"

"No, Alphonse —" Emma opened her fan with a click and waved it gently to and fro.

"Ah, Alphonse!" Though still not admitting to confusion, through the haze that bothered his mind, slightly misting the clarity of thought, Arthur realized that he was terribly jealous of Alphonse, who had not been obliged to go away and leave Emma in peace when her fiancé died. Alphonse had been behind her throughout her trouble. He had shared her sorrow and so must have some place in her heart. That was understood. It was rather late to worry about that now, but Arthur did worry. It was not fair. It seemed as though Alphonse had taken a mean advantage over him. Aunt Olive had told him, Arthur, to go back to New York and to come back later, when Emma had picked up again a few threads of her old life. He had obeyed Aunt Olive, not because he believed she was advising the best, but because he dared not take the risk of losing Emma forever.

After the waiter had served them with coffee — strong, black and sweetened with several large oblong cubes of sugar, Arthur said sourly, "I do wish Alphonse would change his name."

He watched the wine waiter, with some intentness, pour a little brandy into big balloon glasses. When his own was put in front of him, Arthur put both hands about the glass to warm the brandy, and lifting it gently, swayed the drink about at the

144

bottom of the glass. Then he raised it to his face, and moved his head from side to side, savouring the bouquet of the wine. Suddenly Arthur felt better.

Emma watched him. "Why: what's wrong with Alphonse's name?"

"I'm sick of hearing it."

"I think it is a very nice name: soft and musical. Anyway, I doubt if he'd change it to please you. Would you change yours for someone's whim?"

"No."

"Well, then; it's none of your business."

Emma drank her coffee slowly, and in between she sipped the brandy which was old and fruity, and like velvet to her tongue.

"You like Alphonse, don't you?"

"Yes, very much."

"Why?"

"I don't know. Because I can rely upon him. He is to be trusted. I like to feel that he is at the back of Mrs. de Witt."

"Aunt Olive can take care of herself."

"I dare say. Up to a point. But there are times when a man like Alphonse, with his knowledge and experience and steadiness of purpose, is especially useful."

"Is that why you like him?"

"Partly."

"As a friend, or more than a friend?"

"Just a friend," Emma said quietly.

The answer appeased Arthur. He forgot Alphonse and talked himself into a good humour. Emma finished her coffee and put down the cup. She was bemused no longer, but refreshed and invigorated.

"What time is it?"

Arthur glanced at his watch.

"Just upon midnight."

"Then I must go up. Are you coming?"

"Sure. Didn't I say I would?"

"I didn't know whether you really meant it."

"I usually keep my word."

Arthur called for '*l'addition*', and when it came he glanced at it and signed his name. Taking out his wallet, he put a generous tip on the bill.

They rose from the table, and said thank you and goodnight to the bowing waiters, and went out of the restaurant, which was still full of people, and along a broad-carpeted corridor to the gilded lift which took them up to the *salon*.

"Thank you for a lovely dinner, Arthur," said Emma at the door of the *salon*. "It is a long time since I enjoyed a dinner so much."

"Thank you for coming," he said formally. "I feel the same as you."

They went in and Arthur switched on all the lights. Someone had closed the windows and drawn the curtains. The atmosphere was heavy with the cloying scent of many flowers.

Arthur exclaimed, "Isn't it stuffy?" He drew the curtains back and opened the windows, and by the time he returned to Emma he saw that she was already at her desk, and looking over some papers with that air of detachment which usually came over her when she was doing business.

It seemed to him as though her charming social manner had gone. Her face looked tired and a little set. The fairy dress and the gay flowers on her corsage struck a wrong note.

She handed some letters to Arthur. "I shall be awfully obliged if you will give me a hint how to answer them — something not too firm, and yet firm enough; you know."

146

He nodded and took the letters.

"It won't take more than a few minutes to dictate the answers. If you don't like them you need not use them; or perhaps you can fit things to your requirements. People don't expect the precision from a woman they would from a man; or should I say that people will forgive a woman a mistake when they will never pass it in a man?"

"They are sure to be good."

"What makes you think so?"

"Mrs. de Witt says you are a sound businessman."

Arthur laughed. "I've had a sound business training if that's anything to go by. But I wouldn't lay too much store on Aunt Olive's opinion. She has a charitable outlook on most things."

Arthur was silent for a while. He found it difficult to concentrate on the letters because half of his mind was wondering what time his aunt was expected home. She would have to go through the *salon* to get to her bedroom, and if she came too soon everything might be spoiled for him. The other part of his mind was misted with an almost unbearable longing for Emma. He wanted more than anything else to take Emma in his arms and tell her he loved her. It was a kind of obsession with him. He did not care whether she liked his love-making or not. It was his own overpowering emotion that counted, and must be satisfied. He had to do something about it, and hang the consequences.

Arthur was sorry for himself, too, because he was too cowardly to do what his longing urged him to do. He was afraid of Emma. She was so coldly efficient, so aloof, so standoffish, and that silly dress made it all seem worse, as though it was a fancy dress and not a real dress, with a flesh-and-blood woman inside it.

Arthur dithered and hesitated. The hands holding the letters shook so that he could not see to read clearly.

He assured himself that he was afraid of nothing and nobody.

Then Arthur gave in. He felt deflated and depressed. Somehow he had misplayed the evening. He felt sagged, defeated and beaten. All the pleasure of the evening drained out of him.

Emma sat quite still on a horrid little hard chair which she used for typing. She was looking up at Arthur with interest, her lovely eyes shadowed by the soft lights, her pencil poised in slim fingers, ready to take down Arthur's answer.

Arthur felt her looking at him, probably wondering why he was so slow, perhaps noticing his shaking hands.

He pulled himself together. "Take a note," he warned harshly, surprised at his own horrid voice, marvelling greatly at the strange behaviour of the man, Arthur de Witt. He began to speak rapidly, and after that first startled pause, as though she wondered what he was going to say, Emma's pencil seemed to fly over the pad.

When it was done, Emma read aloud what she had written at Arthur's dictation.

'I suppose she is going to tell me I've been dictating a lot of rubbish,' Arthur thought gloomily, and waited for her to speak.

Instead, to his astonishment, Emma smiled broadly with pleasure.

"It is brilliant, Arthur. I didn't know you had it in you to think such inspired stuff. I shan't alter a word, but send it exactly as you dictated. That'll make them sit up. I could never have written anything so pithy and perfect. You are wonderful. Thank you so much." It was obvious that he had gone up by leaps and bounds in Emma's estimation.

He was taken aback for a moment, delighted with her unexpected praise. Then swiftly he thought, 'Perhaps though I have failed so far, I can cash in on this.'

He said, "And the reward?"

The words brought Emma up with a jerk. She was putting away her pad. She would type this stuff first thing in the morning and send it off. Arthur's strange words said in an even stranger voice made Emma pause. Her eyes grew round.

"Was there to be a reward?"

"Payment, then," Arthur cried savagely.

Emma looked at him and flushed, for there was no mistaking the look in his eyes.

"Oh!" she gasped, and then again, "Oh!"

She did not want to kiss Arthur or to be kissed by him or any man. But there was a queer feeling within her, an emotion which was rising rapidly in answer to his, the power and strength of which she could not control.

She whispered a little wildly, "Some other time, Arthur."

"When?" He was masterful, unlike his usual self.

"Tomorrow." She rose and glanced at the door as though seeking a means of escape.

"Tomorrow is already today. Anyhow, I'm not interested. I am no Spaniard to be interested in *mañana*. It must be now, Emma."

Arthur came close to Emma, and put his arms about her, drawing her to him, slowly at first, and then with a bold swiftness that brought her close to him and took her breath away.

"Oh, Emma!" His voice was endearing.

He held her close in arms that were like steel bands, and bent his head to hers.

Emma was carried away by his passion. She had been lonely for so long, loveless and unkissed. Now there arose in her soul something that insisted on being satisfied. As in a dream, she felt Arthur's warm kisses on her cheeks, on her closed eyes, the dimple in her chin, and last of all her mouth.

It seemed a natural happening, the culminating point in an enjoyable evening, every single minute playing its important part towards a perfect ending. It was only later, when savouring Arthur's hot, fierce kisses in retrospect that it seemed to Emma that she had never known what love was before. She had been in love with love. This was different, warmer and fuller. It was like being born again.

Arthur could not believe that all that was happening to him was true. He was aware that he held Emma, slight and warm, in his arms at last, her body leaning against his own. He knew, too, that she answered his kisses, shyly at first because Arthur's kisses were new to her, and she was still unsure of the strength of her own emotions which his love-making was awakening.

It gave Arthur a kind of ecstasy to feel Emma's soft lips under his own. He felt crazy with joy. He loved her. It was like being in paradise where only love counted and nothing else seemed to matter. His kisses were punctuated with soft protestations of his love for her. It was like being wrapped in cotton wool. What a seductive darling she was!

If it could only go on like this forever!

At last Emma broke away from Arthur. She seemed to wake out of her trance.

"Please, let me go," she whispered. "Mrs. de Witt will be in presently. I should not like her to catch us."

Arthur wanted to laugh at Emma, not in any nasty way, but tenderly, telling her she was a funny little thing to be afraid of Aunt Olive. But he did not want to offend Emma. It was a delicate moment, and could so easily be spoiled by rough handling.

He loosened his hold reluctantly.

"Where's the harm?" he asked in a thick voice charged with emotion. He stood away from her, grinning fatuously, his spirits airy, not master of himself.

"Mrs. de Witt won't like this sort of thing."

Arthur raised both hands and swept them over his head, not because he cared how he looked, but because his mind was still in ecstatic confusion.

"Oh, she won't mind; but I'll ask her if you like."

Emma had taken her powder compact from her bag, and quickly, quietly, she was repairing the damage which Arthur's kisses had done to her make-up.

She saw that the beautiful orchids on her corsage were damaged and broken; the white petals, tinged with green, were hanging limp.

She unpinned them, saying, "Oh, my poor flowers!"

"Don't worry; there are plenty more where these came from."

Emma put them on her desk.

"Are you going to press them?" inquired Arthur disparagingly. "I should throw them in the waste-paper basket. They aren't worth keeping in any form."

Emma touched the broken blossoms tenderly.

"These more than others," she said, and put them out of sight in her desk.

She was closing it when a piece of paper that had got caught in the hinge fell to the floor. It must have been put on the desk flap earlier, and she had not seen it.

Emma picked it up and read it curiously. It was probably some memo of Alphonse's. The writing was difficult to

151

understand. It was not Alphonse's but Suzette's. Her writing was as though spiders had fallen into the ink and then crawled over the paper.

"What is this?" she asked wonderingly.

"What?" Arthur came over to stand by Emma as she read the paper.

"Isn't Suzette's handwriting awful?"

"It isn't writing at all," laughed Arthur. Then he sensed a certain quietness about Emma, and asked, "What has she got to say?"

Emma replied in a little voice, "Only that Mr. Crake rang up about ten o'clock."

It was as though Emma were receding from him. Her voice was distant and her manner aloof.

"What did the fellow want?" Arthur demanded harshly. He was suspicious of Crake. He was beginning to dislike him.

Indeed, Arthur found himself readily disliking any man who took even a fraction of Emma's time.

"How should I know?" Emma felt guilty suddenly. She remembered that she had refused to dine with Tim — yet within a couple of hours she had accepted Arthur's invitation. She had completely forgotten Tim. What could she say to excuse herself? In itself that was nothing dreadful, for she would explain to Tim and hope he would understand.

That was not all, however.

What struck her forcibly was that she had also forgotten Geoff. She had allowed another man to make love to her, and what was worse she had enjoyed it. She had been false to Geoff's memory.

CHAPTER 10

Alarmed by Emma's sudden quietness, Arthur caught her arm. He smiled engagingly.

"It doesn't matter," he told her. "You don't have to worry about a chance friend like Crake anymore. He won't ever count with you again. If he rings you up tomorrow, just tell him about us. If he's got any decency, he'll hold off. If he has no decency, then I will deal with him. After all, it is our lives from now on, and he will have no part in them."

So spoke Arthur. He did not want to talk about Crake, he wanted to speak about the future — his and Emma's. There was so much to arrange — so many people would have to be told — the Press must be informed of their engagement. First thing tomorrow he must take Emma to a jeweller and buy her a ring worthy of her. He was bubbling over with high spirits. Emotion was nearly driving him crazy. He wanted to go on loving and kissing Emma. He could never make enough of her. He longed to pet her.

And now this fly in the ointment. It was too bad.

Slowly Emma put away her compact and closed her bag, a white beaded fold-over which Olive had given to her last Christmas. She looked suddenly pale and tired. Listlessly she picked up the fan that had been given to her at dinner, opened it, then closed it again with a snap. She was quiet because she was thinking hard.

Arthur felt a pang of fear. The gaiety and gentleness of her love, the passion in her kisses, the feel of her soft arms around his neck, might never have been. Emma stood half-turned away from him, remote and silent, just as though he were not in the room.

For a brief moment it occurred to Arthur that perhaps Emma had had too much champagne. It affected people in different ways. Some people's spirits rose after drinking champagne, and then when the first effects wore off they were depressed. Then he recalled that they had left the restaurant an hour ago, and whatever effects Emma may have suffered from drinking champagne would have worn off long ago.

Besides, Emma was the sort to know when she had had enough to drink.

"Emma!" Arthur's voice cracked sharply on a note of fear.

"Yes." How tired she sounded.

"What's gone wrong?"

"Nothing."

"Oh, yes there is; you can't fool me that way. One minute you were in my arms, soft and loving and enchantingly sweet; but now, since you've read that message, you are changed. Have I offended you in some way?"

"It isn't you," she replied quietly enough, though her breast heaved stormily through some inward and disturbing thought.

"Then it must be Crake. He's got some hold over you."

She shook her head.

"You are afraid of him?"

"Not *afraid*, Arthur."

"Then what is it? Come, I must know what is at the bottom of this. It is only fair to tell me. Or must I ask Crake?"

Suddenly emotion welled up into a kind of balloon inside Emma, and when she could stand the feeling no longer, it seemed to burst.

"Tim wouldn't know," she said with a catch of her breath — which was the prelude to a violent outburst of sobbing. She hid her face in her hands.

Arthur was aghast. What a climax to the beauty of their love-scene!

"Oh, for pity's sake, Emma," cried Arthur in sudden exasperation and frustration, "don't make so much noise. Someone will hear you and think I am ill-treating you."

"I can't help it," she sobbed, and put out one hand gropingly.

Arthur took out his handkerchief and put it into her hand.

"But *what* is it?"

"Haven't you noticed? Tim is like Geoff."

"Well, suppose he is," Arthur said in a puzzled tone. "What of it? Go on, I don't understand."

"I don't expect you can. But Tim reminds me of Geoff. Tim asked me out this evening and I said no; then you asked me, and I forgot his invitation and went with you. But in forgetting Tim I forgot Geoff. It was cruel of me. It shan't happen again. I promised I'd be true to Geoff's memory always, and I will."

She spoke thickly, her voice full of tears.

Arthur stared in amazement. "See, let's get this straight. Do you mean you won't allow yourself to forget Geoff?"

"Yes."

"You must be crazy. You don't seriously believe in ghosts or reincarnation or something?"

"Yes, I do, when I look at Tim. The likeness is uncanny. He has many of Geoff's mannerisms."

"I'm not in a joking mood, Emma."

"Neither am I." They looked at each other in complete misunderstanding and antagonism.

Emma began to laugh and cry together. No one would believe her or take her seriously. She said with a catch of her breath, "I know I sound funny to you, but I can't help it."

Arthur was perplexed. He could cope with most things, but not this. He could put up a show against a rival, but not with a dead man.

"So what?" he demanded, conscious of his weakness. "Supposing Crake is like your Geoff? I don't see it, but if you say it's there, it is. I'll take your word for it. But what of it? Geoff White is not here. We are concerned with the living, not the dead."

"I know, but at least I can try to be true to him."

Arthur's mouth tightened. He no longer looked easy-going. He was annoyed and frustrated. According to his lights, Emma was behaving like a fool, spoiling all their fun in fear of annoying a spirit.

He asked angrily: "Is it your intention to stay in mourning for Geoff forever? Are you never going to allow another guy to kiss you and pet you because you are afraid of offending a dead man? Because, if so, you're going to have a pretty miserable time for a few years. After that it won't matter, because the bloom will have worn off your youth, and who cares for yesterday's dead flowers?"

Emma frowned. "Now you are getting personal. What you say is not quite right; but I do seem to be forgetting Geoff quickly."

"Quite right, too. You are too young to wear black; besides, it doesn't suit you. Any decent fellow would want you to be happy. I do not think your late fiancé would like you to go through life lonely and wretched — unless, of course, you happen to be one of those odd people who are only happy

156

when miserable, in which case you will enjoy wearing a martyr's crown."

"I knew you wouldn't understand." Emma laughed and cried together, her emotions gradually getting out of control.

Arthur cried urgently, "Hold it, Emma!"

He remembered dimly reading how one should deal with hysteria. For a moment he hesitated, then with some determination, Arthur stepped swiftly close to Emma and lightly slapped first one cheek, and then the other.

He was undecided on whether to sink to his knees and beg Emma's forgiveness, or to run away and hide his shame for having struck a woman.

Emma gasped with amazement and put both hands to her flushed cheeks.

At that moment, Olive came into the *salon*.

She was wearing a black crinoline dress of chiffon trimmed lavishly with diamanté. There were diamonds in her hair, around her neck and in her ears. About her shoulders was a lovely white ermine wrap. In one gloved hand she clutched a huge painted fan and a small bag. The other rested on the crook of her stick. She was followed closely by Suzette and Alphonse.

Arthur exclaimed at sight of his aunt and her attendants. Emma was still hiding her cheeks. The hysterical fit had died. Olive's entrance stopped it completely.

"What on earth are you two doing?" asked Olive in some dismay and disappointment.

It was obvious that Arthur was surprised.

Emma did not answer. 'I must look a sight,' she thought, and wished that she had known Olive would come in just then, and given her time to hide the traces of her tears. She wished, too, that Alphonse was not there watching her, no doubt nearly collapsing with inward laughter at the sight of her.

Olive repeated her question, and Arthur was forced to reply.

He said, "We were only having a difference of opinion, Aunt Olive. Emma was being silly."

Arthur was quiet now and a little tired, his earlier exuberance gone, his high spirits sunk to below zero. It had been borne in upon him within the last few minutes that what had happened between Emma and himself was only an interlude in their friendship, and not, as he had at first thought and hoped for, the prelude to something more emotional which would spell happiness for both of them.

Olive looked from one to the other. She said clearly and decisively, "I have never seen Emma silly." Then she said directly to Emma: "You have been working, Emma. I will not allow it at this time of night. People will call me a slave-driver, and that is what I am not. You look dreadfully tired and I don't wonder. Do go to bed at once." She spoke to Arthur more severely because Olive had had experience of men. She guessed that Arthur had made love to Emma tactlessly and without proper preparation, and she was angry because carelessness on that score might well write *finis* to Arthur's hopes for future happiness. She said: "I left you to take care of Emma, but it seems you have been wasting her time. Goodnight."

She slipped off her lovely fur wrap and let Suzette take it away. Then she said in a kindlier tone to Emma: "Do go to bed, child, you look washed up. Goodnight, Emma."

Emma whispered, "Goodnight, Mrs. de Witt."

Olive left them and went into her bedroom, Suzette following her.

Arthur glanced at Emma. She was not looking at him, but at the floor. Her hands had tired of holding her cheeks, which were a deep pink.

He said: "Goodnight, Emma. See you tomorrow morning."

She nodded to show that she had heard. There was nothing to say.

Arthur shrugged, turned on his heel, and went out of the room, whistling under his breath. The spirit of bravado was not assumed on Emma's account, but for Alphonse's benefit, because Alphonse was staring solemnly at him. Arthur banged the door shut.

Emma, too, looked in Alphonse's direction. His expression was inscrutable, and for some reason Emma felt mortified. It was always her luck that Alphonse should see her when she was not looking her best.

As the door closed Emma stirred. She slipped a few more papers into her desk, picked up her bag, fan, and a big leather portfolio, and turned to leave the room.

As she did so, she felt rather than saw Alphonse stoop down and pick something up from the carpet. The movement was slight and did not disturb her curiosity.

As Emma walked across the soft carpet, Alphonse's mellifluous voice reached her. It was cool and precise, and she knew by the tone that for some reason Alphonse was angry with her. She did not know why he should be unless it was that the tears had made havoc of her make-up, and Alphonse believed that people should school themselves to have a good appearance in public. Anyway, he hated anything messy.

"Is this yours?"

Emma glanced back, but did not for the moment recognize what Alphonse was holding out to her.

"What is it?"

She tried to make her voice sound ordinary.

"A petal of a flower — to be exact, an orchid." There was cool distaste in his tone.

"Oh!"

"Is it yours?"

Emma nodded miserably. "Yes."

"Do you want it?"

"No, throw it away."

"Where?"

"In the waste-paper basket."

Solemnly Alphonse marched over to the big waste-paper basket standing beside her desk, and threw away the flower petal.

"If I should find any more, do I fling them away, too?" he asked, his voice a little warmer.

"I suppose so."

"You do not sound definite."

"I am. Throw away the lot."

"So, but where can they be?" He glanced vaguely about him.

"In my desk," Emma told him recklessly.

Deliberately Alphonse opened Emma's desk. Inside, under some papers, was the crushed spray of orchids. He took them out and closed the desk.

"Did you hide them from me?" Alphonse paused to ask suddenly.

"Good gracious, no. I never thought of you. I just didn't want Mrs. de Witt to see them."

"Why not?"

Emma did not reply.

"Because they were so crushed and she would guess why?" Alphonse sounded angry again.

How persistent he was! How inquisitive!

"If you like," Emma shrugged.

Then Alphonse said cuttingly: "Dollars are wasted on you, Emma... I have always said you have no money sense."

"So what?" she cried furiously, borrowing Arthur's expressive slang. "They are orchids."

Alphonse looked at her and then at the spray of broken blooms in his hand.

"Same thing," he said quietly.

He dropped them in the waste-paper basket. Then he dusted his hands.

"Any regrets?" he asked.

"None."

"*Bien!*"

Emma would have liked to tell Alphonse that she was the most miserable girl in the whole world, but in his present mood he was unapproachable.

It occurred to her that Alphonse was jealous of Arthur. That was nothing new, but an old tale. Yet Alphonse sat back when Arthur was there. Certainly he made no active attempt to rival him. That quip about dollars being wasted on her was the outward expression of some bitter inward thought.

At any other time Emma, in a better mood, might have taunted Alphonse with jealousy, but something in his manner froze her tonight.

Emma waited a moment in case Alphonse said anything which might tempt her to linger, but he said nothing, only seemed to be waiting for her to go. It was a tame ending to an exciting dinner. Emma went quietly out of the room and to bed. She heard subdued voices in the service room at the end of her corridor. Some of the floor staff were probably gossiping while at work on visitors' clothes. A *femme de chambre* looked out to see who was passing.

Emma smiled at the woman who wished her goodnight, and passed on to her room. She took off her lovely white dress, threw it over a chair, and put on a dressing-gown.

Emma switched off her light and drew back the curtains, and opening the window looked out to sea. There was no colour in the vast seascape, but she could see a white frill of foam on the edge of the dark sands, and hear the waves booming and splashing against the rocks near the lighthouse where the revolving beam of light in the tower lit up at regular intervals the lonely waste of tossing sea and the lonelier sands.

The vault of dark sky was alive with glittering stars.

A night wind lifted Emma's short curls and swept about her head, cooling her forehead and hot cheeks where Arthur had slapped them.

Emma was still deeply moved by all that had happened in the *salon*, her emotions in an excited state. But her thoughts were clearer now. She was ashamed of having let herself go with Arthur. 'If it had been anyone else,' she thought, 'I could have understood it. I love Arthur, but I could never love him in the way he wants me to, or that I could wish to love the man I might marry.'

That was a new thought, concrete again for the first time since Geoff's tragedy, and Emma faced it squarely. One day she might love another man enough to marry him, but it would never be Arthur.

There was a light knock at the door, and Emma turned sharply to answer it, wondering who was there. Sometimes the *valet de chambre* for her floor came to her door at night to inquire if she wanted anything pressed by the morning, but never so late as this.

Emma turned on the light and opened the door.

It was Suzette. Her wiry black hair appeared to be more unmanageable than usual.

"Oh, it's you, Suzette. Come in." Then quickly Emma voiced the fear that was always foremost in her mind. "Is Madame all right?"

Suzette was in her room by then, and the door closed. The French girl assured Emma rapidly in her own language that Madame was in bed and she hoped asleep.

Then Suzette said in English, speaking slowly because she was not familiar with the language that Emma had tried to teach her over the years: "It is about a telephone message… Tonight it was M. Crake. 'E ring up eleven o'clock and ask fer Mees Ferrer. I tell 'im you are in restaurant, with M. Artur. I tell 'im you mus' not be disturb. Okay?"

"Yes, Suzette, that was quite right," said Emma slowly, assimilating the meaning of what Suzette had said to Tim. To herself Emma said grimly: 'It could not well be worse. How can I explain things satisfactorily to Tim?'

"Is that all, Suzette?"

"*Oui*, M'moiselle. I could not say zis to you in the *salon*. I 'ad to wait until Madame, she is in bed."

"I see. Eh *bien*, Suzette, *je vous remercie*."

Suzette did not go at once. She caught sight of Emma's dress where it had been thrown carelessly across the chair. Suzette rushed over to it, and picking it up shook out the creases, exclaiming in her quick way and with a wealth of gesture at the bad treatment of a dress which everyone said was *ravissemente*.

When Suzette had gone, Emma turned off the light once more, and returned to her vigil at the window. But her thoughts were no longer clear, they were jumbled. They were not warm. She was critical about her hysterical behaviour which struck her as rather absurd viewed in the cold light of reason. How silly and dramatic she must have seemed to Alphonse over those orchids.

Emma yawned. She had better undress and go to bed and get what sleep she could from the short night left to her.

She undressed in the dark, and presently crept under the foam of mosquito-netting around her bed, got in between the sheets and sighed as her cheek met the comfort of her pillow.

When Suzette took in Olive de Witt's *petit déjeuner* in the morning, she also took in a message that Arthur was in the *salon* and would like to speak to Madame if she could spare him a few moments.

Olive sat up in bed and received her tray of brioche, croissant and butter, and hot *café au lait*. She had been up earlier to pull back her curtains and open all windows, and to clean her teeth. The room was full of sunshine and fresh air.

Olive looked astonished at receiving such a message.

"At this hour!" she exclaimed. Then she cried: "I have no make-up on. I look pasty and grim." Then she called out: "Come in, Arthur. I look a sight and you won't know me, but it must be important news to get you out of bed at this hour."

He came in quickly, and Olive glanced keenly and appraisingly at him as though to read in his face whether his news was good or bad.

She smiled hopefully at Arthur, not because she could gather anything hopeful from his face that would cause her to smile, but because it was policy to expect the best even if the reality was the worst. Meanwhile Suzette brought powder, mirror and lipstick. She stuck a pretty lace cap on Olive's hair, and brought in vases of flowers from the *salon*, then made herself scarce.

Arthur was in his bath-gown, a striped affair which gave him a jaunty look even though his face was devoid of joy. He came and stood by his aunt's bed, his hands plunged deep into the bath-gown's capacious pockets, and stared owlishly at her.

"It really is me," Olive assured him, using the powder and lipstick with striking effect.

"I know."

Olive de Witt tried again. "Have you nothing to tell me, Arthur?" She put down the mirror.

"I don't know. Should I tell you something?" he said evasively.

"Yes, about last night." Olive gave him all her attention.

"Oh, that! Well, honestly, I don't know where I am."

"You are not engaged?" his aunt asked bluntly.

Arthur shrugged. "I am all at sea."

"Why not pull yourself together and confess?"

"I don't know where to begin."

"Well, did you enjoy your evening with Emma?"

Arthur's face flushed. "It was perfect, Aunt Olive — at least, it was until Emma spoiled it all."

"Ah! I thought something was wrong when I came into the *salon* unexpectedly last night. I heard noise and movement in the room when I was outside the door. When I entered the room, you were both in a state of suspended animation which made me think that something violent had been disturbed. There was a look of supreme guilt on your face. As for Emma —"

Olive paused and waited for her nephew to speak.

Arthur nodded. The picture was correct enough. He said: "Perhaps you can straighten all this out for me. It is beyond my powers to do so, though I have spent most of the rest of the night trying to think out a successful plan."

"Yes?"

"We had a wonderful dinner together. It was one of those rare delightful evenings when everything is fine. After coffee we came up to the *salon* where I helped her with a couple of difficult business letters, and she seemed pleased." Arthur flushed, and his voice became loud and rapid as he said defiantly: "I told Emma I loved her. I held her in my arms. We kissed each other — lots of times. Then suddenly she picked up a scrap of paper from the carpet, and everything was changed. Crake, of all people, came into the picture, and then Emma's late fiancé. I think I went crazy, because it seemed to me odd and wrong that the dead should have influence over Emma."

"Emma loved him."

"I'll say she did."

"Such love fades slowly. One reads about it. Songs are written about it. Artists paint it — but one seldom meets it. Emma did."

"Maybe," said Arthur flatly, unimpressed by Emma's power to love a dead man. "But in the end Emma got me seeing things, too. I felt frustrated, angry. She grew hysterical. I slapped her lightly to jolt her out of it."

Olive was shocked.

"What a mistake!" she cried. "Marriage is a gamble, but to Emma an engagement is a gamble too, because she lost the last one. It will make her more careful in the future."

Olive drank her *café au lait*. The brown brioche and the crisp horseshoe croissant and the golden pats of butter had no appeal for her this morning.

Arthur's future was at stake, his happiness.

She sat back among her pillows. Arthur removed the tray to a place of safety, and sat down on the side of the bed, took his hands from his pockets and twiddled his thumbs miserably.

He said: "It's no good talking about past mistakes. How shall I behave to Emma when I see her this morning? Shall I take it for granted that we are engaged? Do I apologize for slapping her face? What do you think her reactions will be to last night?" He groaned. "Every moment adds to my torture, as with each passing moment a new difficulty occurs to me."

Still Olive did not speak, and Arthur, seeing that his aunt was turning the matter over in her mind, did not speak either.

When Olive spoke on such an occasion, with the assurance of a woman who is accustomed to making plans without interference or criticism, it was something in the nature of an oracle, and people listened, ready to take note of what she said and to accept her advice.

Now Olive caught his hand in hers, and tempering her words which she knew must hurt one of his buoyant nature, with gentle pats, soft smiles, and little endearments, she said slowly:

"I do not know what *really* happened last night. I have heard only your side, and naturally, I know nothing of Emma's reactions, though I am free to guess them. But I do feel that, in some way, probably unavoidable on your part, you missed a chance of greatly improving your relationship with Emma. How far you could, or would, have succeeded with her, and with a little more foresight, I cannot say. But I am certain that if Emma loves you as dearly and devotedly as you love her, it would be impossible for the present position between you to remain stalemate. Love and not Emma would decide that. For Emma, to love is for her to wish to give — even herself. Your emotions were aroused and influenced hers. Then I imagine she grew frightened in case she was committing herself in some way, like being engaged, which she was not ready to be. That made her hysterical. All of which proves clearly enough, my dear Arthur, that she does *not* love you."

There was a pause when Olive had finished, then Arthur drew his hand from Olive's, and cried in keen disappointment, "Is that all you have to say to me, Aunt Olive?"

"It is only what I think, my dear."

"Then I won't accept what you would like to call a 'realist' view. I don't have to."

"No, of course not," she soothed at once. It was too much to expect a man in the depths of sentimentalism to take a realist aspect of love.

"It would be too absurd for me to give up hoping to win Emma because you think she is not in love with me."

"I sincerely hope I am wrong." Above all, even if Arthur were wretched about the result of this friendship, Emma must be happy. 'If she marries the man she loves, I have no doubt but that Emma will be happy,' Olive thought, 'for Emma is a born wife and mother with the right man.'

"You only 'hope', you don't 'think'."

"Don't you know that I should love to agree with you, Arthur, to give you the answer you wish for? It is my duty to see this matter clearly, in a material way, and not through rosy glasses as you are doing. I, too, love Emma like a daughter. In times of trouble we have been very close together. She has never failed me. She is one of the loveliest girls in mind and body that I have ever met, and I have met many nice girls. She has suffered one disappointment, and I long for her to be happy. It would give me the greatest happiness to know that the two people I love most in this world are in love with each other. But I know that love cannot be bought, or directed, or wished for. It just comes. It is there, something of the spirit, and you and I are powerless to insist, coerce or invite — or even buy it if we would. Thank heaven that true love is priceless."

"Then what can I do? I won't give Emma up; and I can't let matters rest."

Olive shook her head.

"All I can suggest is that you do your best to allay the fears you roused in Emma last night. When you meet, as you must do presently, be your usual self, and try to make her forget all that happened; be Emma's friend rather than try to play the lover. Emma is probably feeling humiliated by her display of passion last night. As you know, she seldom shows anyone her deepest feelings. Hers is a shy nature. She will hold you off and be cold to you. Don't rush into more trouble by reminding her of what she hopes you have forgotten."

"As if I could. You are asking me to do the impossible."

"If you don't, you will frighten Emma away forever."

"You want me to retreat."

"Only so that you may advance with a rush later on." And to herself Olive said, 'Perhaps,' but she had not the heart to say it to Arthur. It would have been unnecessarily cruel.

Arthur groaned aloud. He did not want to take his aunt's advice, yet he knew that if he did not do so, it might be as she said and he would lose Emma forever.

He rose from the bed, rather an unhappy figure.

"I guess I'd better get dressed," he said, and Olive thought how ill-suited to his nice face was a look of sadness. It made him seem positively ugly. "Emma may go to bed at dawn, but she manages to get up with the milk without effort. Whatever time I go into the *salon* in the morning, she is usually there and at work, looking as fresh as can be."

Arthur did not thank Olive for her advice. Most of it, he thought, was silly, and could not apply to his case. Anyway, he would have a long hot bath, and try to think over what Aunt Olive had just said, and perhaps extract a few crumbs of comfort for himself. God knew he was in need of some.

As Arthur turned to go, a thought struck him, and he said: "You don't think Emma has fallen for Crake, do you, if only because she sees a resemblance to White in him? Perhaps they have been left too much together. You know how it is: you invite your best friend to a cocktail party, and he runs off with your best girl."

Olive shook her head. "It is the best thing that could happen to Emma to be thrown with Mr. Crake. The more she sees of him, the less she will like him. I intend on inviting him to go with us to San Sebastian tomorrow."

"Must you? He will spoil our day."

"Possibly, but he will also spoil his own future."

Arthur looked at his aunt for some seconds in silence, then he said, as if to himself:

"So that's the way it is?"

"That is the way."

CHAPTER 11

Emma, dressed in a simple pink dress which gave colour to her pale cheeks, looked anxiously at Alphonse when he came into the *salon* that morning to get the list of Madame's engagements for the day.

As he entered the room Alphonse paused, bowed slightly, and bade her good morning in French. Usually, if he were in a good mood, Alphonse greeted Emma in her own tongue. She thought his English accent enchanting, for he found difficulty with his 'ths', 'is' and 'rs' and seldom used an 'h'.

He carried his notebook open in his hand, as though his visit was to get his orders quickly and hurry away. So there was to be no gossip, or that exchange of light wit which sometimes passed between them as easily as a game of pat-ball, requiring little effort, each relying on the other's answer to make the next swift sally.

Alphonse's manner was cool, impeccable and impersonal. He stood by Emma's desk, examining the thick engagement-pad, and made copious notes of places and times in his pocketbook. There was to be the usual short journey to Chambre d'Amour later in the morning, when Olive de Witt, dressed in a loose bathing-gown and wearing her enormous tasselled Mexican hat, would sit outside her gaily coloured tent on the sand talking to her friends. So many friends liked to bathe and sprawl in the sun beside her, and chat idly in the intervals of bathing and playing with rubber sea toys, and sunbathing.

There was a small lunch party at the Palais. It meant that Olive would not need Alphonse's services from the time she arrived back at the hotel to get ready for lunch until teatime, when she would have tea under the pines at the golf club-house at Chiberta, and meet more friends.

After the return from Chiberta there was a free interval for Alphonse until ten o'clock, when Madame was due at a dinner-party at La Chaumière.

"It is not a busy day," remarked Emma, "and no place is far away."

"No, just taxi-ing about," agreed Alphonse solemnly. "That is as well, for the car must be got ready for the long day trip to San Sebastian tomorrow."

Emma flicked over a leaf of the pad.

"We start for San Sebastian at eleven o'clock," she reminded him.

"So!"

Alphonse looked sideways at the leaf, and made a note of the time when the car would be wanted.

"How many are going?"

"Madame, Mr. Arthur, the Comte de la Tremblay and myself."

"There will be a spare seat?"

"Yes. There is also the little car —"

"I know. I thought of sending some Chilean friends in that. Pierre, of course, will drive it."

They both fell silent. Indeed, there seemed nothing to discuss. Alphonse slipped his notebook into his jacket pocket. He turned to go.

Emma knew by then that she had somehow managed to offend Alphonse deeply. He was treating her like an acquaintance. It was hateful of him and unfair. She did not know what she had done to make Alphonse so moody and unlike himself.

But she could not let him go like this. She had a brainwave.

Emma plucked up courage to say, "M. Alphonse?"

He paused at once and waited for her to speak.

"Yes, Mees Ferrer."

"You remember saying the other day, when I mentioned buying some new hats, that you knew the name of a marvellous milliner who at one time made hats for Royal ladies?"

Alphonse bowed to show that he had heard what Emma said and remembered.

"I wonder if you would let me have his name and address — at your convenience, of course."

Alphonse looked at Emma keenly. She flushed under his gaze, and was cross with herself for doing so.

"No, I shall not do that," he told her deliberately.

Emma's eyes widened. Alphonse had taught her many things. French and other languages, all about wines, how to drive a car, and done her many big favours. But he was sticky over this little one!

"D'you mean you have lost it?" she echoed.

"I nevaire lose addresses," Alphonse remarked angrily.

Emma looked away. This was a rebuff and humiliating. Usually she was enchanted by Alphonse's accent. It was unending entertainment — as were his smooth, polished manners, the way he greeted her, kissing her hand as though she were a princess.

"Then you have changed your mind about giving it to me?" she said in a small voice.

"Yes. I have no intentions to do anything to make you more beautiful than you are. For what do you take me?"

"It is only a *small* favour. I hoped it would save me some francs. As you know, I can't afford to go to expensive milliners; and I like to look smart, just like other girls," Emma pleaded.

"*Not* for your own pleasure. I do not make that mistake. You want to look chic for someone else's eyes to make a feast. Mr. Arthur's perhaps? Or is it Mr. Crake? *I* am to make you look so sweet for them? Oh no, I shall not help you to do that. It is too much you ask me." Alphonse warmed to his subject. "You treat me as inhuman."

"That isn't true," Emma replied hotly. "I don't suppose in your present horrid mood you would believe me, but whenever I buy clothes or hats, *you* come to my mind. I think: 'What would Alphonse think of this? Would he like that?' You see, you are French and understand clothes."

That sounded logical enough. Emma was not flattering him. Alphonse's face cleared of the clouds and he even smiled dimly.

He said slowly: "That is different. Then I shall tell you the name. *Tiens*, I have changed my mind. I shall take you to this man myself."

Emma's face was suddenly wreathed in smiles. "Oh, will you, Alphonse? I *am* glad. Shall we go this evening about five o'clock?"

Now Alphonse smiled, no longer palely, but with warmth. "That will suit me very well. I shall come here for you." He came over to the desk. "What a child you are, Emma, one moment so sad and the next so happy — and all for such a simple thing."

"Is it so simple? You have your moods too, Alphonse."

"There is some reason for mine, while you are so pleased about a new hat." Then he sighed deeply. "You must promise not to wear one of these hats for the pleasure of Mr. Crake."

Then Alphonse added feelingly: "I cannot help Mr. Arthur. I wish I could."

Emma gave the promise readily. "I don't suppose I shall see Mr. Crake again," she told Alphonse.

"What makes you say that, Emma?"

Her face wore a curious brooding look. Alphonse, of course, was jealous of Tim and Arthur. It was perhaps a good thing she would not see Tim again. Perhaps, one day, when he returned to England she would write to him. In a letter she might have the courage to explain that she had actually forgotten him and his invitation to dinner when Arthur invited her to dine. But it was difficult to tell a man such a shattering truth to his face.

Emma hated herself for forgetting Tim's date. It was unpardonable.

Her mind was see-sawing between Tim and Alphonse, when Arthur bustled into the room. He brought with him an air of well-being and virility which acted as a fillip to her jaded spirits, so that in spite of herself Emma laughed in anticipation of a bright half-hour, something which Arthur's ebullient presence seemed to promise.

Arthur brought with him a glorious bunch of flowers which he laid with a flourish on Emma's desk, nearly burying her in the blooms.

Alphonse watched him, smiling wryly.

Arthur looked at the grave, lovely face with the direct and disturbing gaze from the frank blue eyes, and said: "These are for you, Emma, with all my love, and a hope that you will forgive my impertinence to you last night. They could mean so many things — a bouquet from a knight to his lady love, or a peace offering from a rude Yank; or just a gift from an adoring boyfriend. Take it as you like."

Out of the corner of her eye, Emma saw Alphonse stiffen... She wanted to laugh with relief because Arthur seemed to have no thought of playing the lover. He was his old mercurial self. She might have guessed Arthur could not remain serious for long, even about love.

Emma had been dreading meeting him this morning, rather at a loss what to say supposing Arthur, after last night, considered they were engaged. It could be a ticklish problem. She had been worried about this important moment of meeting ever since she woke up this morning. Somehow the matter had worked itself out agreeably, as she should have guessed it might.

Emma felt so light-hearted suddenly she wanted to laugh at Alphonse, whose expressive face and bulging eyes told her that his swift Gallic mind had hit upon the truth. She managed to keep a straight face.

Taking the flowers with both hands, she buried her face in their blooming sweetness.

"Oh, thank you, Arthur, they are lovely," she cried. "I will put them in water at once." She rose to fetch the water, and Alphonse said politely:

"I will get the water," but he did not sound enthusiastic.

"Don't bother —" Emma was beginning, when Arthur cut her short, suggesting:

"Aw, let old Alphonse get it, Emma. You stay here and talk to me."

It was the old cry. Emma recognized it. Arthur, a little bored, if he had nothing else to do, must be amused.

Alphonse marched out of the room in stately fashion, each step a protest.

When he had gone, Arthur laughed unfeelingly.

"Old Alphonse hates leaving you alone with me, even for five minutes. He never knows what we're up to."

There was a time when Emma would have laughed with Arthur, not because of an ill-feeling towards Alphonse, but because Arthur had the effect on her of making her light of heart. But this morning, the careless epithet struck a discordant note. It was poor sport to take a rise out of someone who neither would nor could answer back.

She said sharply, forgetting to feel shy with Arthur about last night:

"Speak for yourself. If Alphonse has any sense at all, he knows I've too much sense to be 'up to anything'. As for being old ... I took the trouble to find out your ages one day. You are exactly eighteen months younger than Alphonse."

"So what?" Arthur asked crisply.

"You have no right to speak of Alphonse as old."

"You don't say!" Arthur looked amazed. Then he burst out laughing. "Am I to lay off calling Alphonse old? Since when has he been in the spotlights with you?" He flung back his head with renewed merriment, showing his strong white teeth.

Emma coloured. There was no smile on her lips as she replied tartly, "He isn't, but I hate the way you talk about him at times, sort of — anyhow."

"*I* do? Guess again, sister. I respect Alphonse far too much to make him a butt of my feeble jokes. It's a — well, a kind of endearment."

"I know, like you say 'old Dobbin' about your trusty horse," she told him crossly.

"Now there, I don't get you."

"I didn't think you would," was the flippant reply.

Arthur studied Emma closely. He could not make her out this morning. She was brittle, snappy and touchy. Could he ever understand anyone so complex? His mind harked back to their first meeting nearly four years ago at the Rochester in London. Emma was raw, and her dress hung about her immature figure like a rag. She was shy and her manner gauche. He was younger then and liked to escort girls who were sure of a certain sidewalk admiration. There was none for Emma then. He had felt a little ashamed of being seen with her. Yet even in those days, Arthur had glimpsed the Emma that was to emerge after a few years' world travel with a woman of Olive's experience. His aunt had offered Emma the chance of a lifetime when she engaged her as secretary-companion, and Emma had made good use of that chance. There were still traces of the old Emma under the beautiful polish. Sometimes she had the same retiring 'mousy' look which Arthur remembered so well. She had moreover an unspoilable outlook on everything, and an engaging frankness which could only be excused by her youthfulness. In spite of Emma's poise there was still a shyness about her, a diffidence which men of the world like Arthur found enchanting. He had always suspected that underneath Emma's quiet, even prim manner, there were depths of feeling and passion which no man, not even Geoff White, had plumbed. Last night Arthur's suspicions were confirmed. Now with a swift glance at the door, and anticipating that Alphonse would be back at any moment, Arthur said quietly:

"Where do we stand in with each other now, Emma?"

The ready flush rose to her cheeks. "Just as you were, Arthur," she said in a low tone.

"I won't take that as final!"

Emma did not reply for the reason she could think of nothing to say.

"You may change your mind. Women do, you know."

"I may," Emma said evasively.

Then Alphonse returned to the room with the vase of water, and further intimate talk was impossible.

No sooner had Emma arranged the flowers, talked gaily to the two men, only one of whom was responsive while the other remained glum, than Olive entered the *salon* from her bedroom. She wore a heavy silk gown that swept the floor all around her, with a heavy corded girdle at the waist, and tassels that trailed on the carpet behind her.

The quiet room quickly hummed with work. Everyone seemed to be busy doing something. Arthur got up and sauntered away. He was not wanted here.

"See you later," he called carelessly to his aunt, who was already sitting at the telephone, scanning the slim book of telephone numbers, and making a personal call.

Then Emma and Suzette, two *femmes de chambre*, a porter and a *valet de chambre* passed to and fro between the rooms. Madame had asked for a piece of furniture to be taken away as redundant to her comfort, and they were doing what she wanted, and enjoying themselves making a great deal of noise over it.

As Olive rose from the chair by the telephone, Emma smilingly took her place. The telephone was never idle.

Olive spoke to Alphonse, who had been waiting quietly in the midst of the uproar to have her attention.

She discussed in detail tomorrow's proposed trip to San Sebastian, and told Alphonse to reserve a table for lunch at the Hotel Maria Cristina. They spoke in French. Alphonse repeatedly referred to his notebook and jotted down memos. He had a precise mind, but did not believe in relying on his memory.

"You have arranged with Pierre to drive the small car?" said Olive.

(Pierre was the under-chauffeur.)

"Yes, Madame. That is already done. He will drive the Chileans."

"Will they like that?" Olive asked dubiously. "They mustn't be allowed to feel out of it."

"They prefer it that way," Alphonse replied. "They have been married but three weeks."

"Then, of course, you know best, Alphonse," smiled Olive. "I leave it to you." It was almost a stock phrase with her, so much did she rely on Alphonse's judgment.

He inquired at last, "Have you anyone in mind for the spare seat in the big car, Madame?"

"It is filled. I have just phoned through to Mr. Crake at the Carlton. He will be delighted to come with us."

Alphonse said "*Bien*" in a curt, business-like way. No one could guess that his inward thoughts were a turmoil of fury.

He glanced across at Emma, but obviously she had not heard the news. She was busy talking on the telephone about some powder that had been ordered from a *magasin*, and which had gone astray.

"*Bête!*" Alphonse kept saying angrily to himself, referring to Tim. "Why should he come? How shall they sit? I shall not permit him sitting next to Emma." Alphonse knew he must keep his head clear when surely something might be arranged to keep these two English people apart.

Meanwhile Olive's voice reached his ears. It was calm, clear and low. She was saying, "I leave the details for you to arrange, Alphonse."

He bowed and thanked her.

Then Olive mentioned their return to the villa at Versailles in ten days' time. They spoke of the route to Paris. As usual, Madame had friends she wished to visit en route.

"There have been some big forest fires on the route, Madame. You shall not care to see vast spaces of old charred trees. It is not a pretty sight."

"No, but I should like to keep to the direct route as much as possible, for once I leave here I shall be anxious to get back to work in Paris."

When Olive had finished with Alphonse she turned to Emma, who had replaced the telephone receiver and was beginning to open the day's mail.

"You will come with us to Chambre d'Amour this morning, Emma?"

Emma was afraid of meeting Tim. She would have liked to laze away an hour or more on the plage in the lovely sunshine, but she could not face Tim.

She excused herself, saying regretfully: "I'm afraid not, thank you, Mrs. de Witt. I have so much work to do. There won't be time to do much work tomorrow, as we start so early." Emma indicated two big trays of letters, all of which must be opened and read, and many of them answered.

Olive nodded. "It seems a larger mail than usual this morning." Then she said: "Will you put through a call to the villa and ask Honoré to see that everything is prepared for our return at the end of next week? You have reminded him of our return, I know, but it might be as well to follow up your letter with a personal call. I shall be sorry when our holiday is over, for I love the smell and sound of the sea. But I must go home to the villa for a couple of months. There is so much work for us to do before Christmas." She enumerated some of the important items on her fingers. "I must visit my dear pensioners. Then the young orphans must have their party. They do so love parties, and it is a year since we had our last big one."

Emma nodded from time to time to show that she had heard. There was no need for comment. It was not only these big charitable projects, which brought comfort and love to many, which Olive de Witt loved to do, and which took so much of her time — and money. There were all the threads of the many committees, of which Olive was a member, to be picked up, and in which she was so interested. They were the reason for her existence. Interest in them made Olive forget her pain at times.

She ended by saying: "Even if there is a lot to do, there is no need for you to work so hard. You stay in too much. I insist that as you won't come to Chambre d'Amour, you go for a walk before lunch. If you don't get fresh air now, you will wilt when winter comes." To make sure that Emma did go out, Olive arranged for the girl to do some small errand at one of the big *magasins* in the town.

Meanwhile Alphonse, his good-looking face grim and set, chanced to meet the Comte de la Tremblay outside the hotel.

They met and spoke, for they had known each other for many years.

Alphonse said, "It will be a hot day tomorrow, M. le Comte."

The Comte agreed. "But it will be misty crossing the frontier." Then he asked, "Who is to be in our party?"

Alphonse told him, and the Comte said:

"Mr. Crake! Have I met him?" He searched his memory for a face to tack onto a name among Olive de Witt's legion of friends.

"You have, but naturally you could not be expected to remember everyone."

That odd answer said with a peculiar inflection in Alphonse's voice, which was meant to be derogatory in some way to Tim, gave the Comte a certain clue. As one man to another, as one Frenchman to another, he said:

"Is not M. Crake a friend of Mees Emma?"

"A great friend, M. le Comte," said Alphonse frigidly.

The Comte laughed gaily. He enjoyed a little intrigue.

"Then both M. Arthur and this M. Crake will want to sit by Mees Emma. It will be amusing to see which, if either, will win."

"Very," said Alphonse shortly.

As he walked away, the Comte looked after Alphonse's elegant slim figure. Stroking his imperial, the Comte smiled crookedly.

"Yes," he said aloud. "I wonder who will win — the Yank, the Englishman, or — the Frenchman?"

CHAPTER 12

It was noon when Emma, wearing sunglasses and a shady hat, went to the town. She walked beside the plage Miramar, which was like a gay animated carpet of bright colours. Sailor lifeguards in white duck were in attendance, a reminder of those old days when this was the most exclusive plage in Biarritz, and it was indecent even for a lifeguard to show too much unclothed body. Then she went up the winding hill-staircase, between the tamarisk trees, to the place where the biggest cars were parked in gleaming lines, looking more like ships than cars. She did her shopping in the Avenue Edouard VII, and returned to the Casino. Her mind was restless today. She was thinking of last night when Arthur had made love to her, and she had felt weak, with her legs like jelly, and thinking ahead of the work to be done in Paris, worrying lest she had been away too long and lost some valuable threads; and even if Honoré had sent on all the letters, or kept back some of the important ones. He would not do such a thing wilfully, but in his zeal not to worry Madame unnecessarily he might hold back some that did not *look* important, yet were so.

However, it was a bright morning and gloomy thoughts had no permanent place in the sunshine. Emma shook her mind clear of troublesome thoughts and began to take an interest in what was going on around her.

On the other side of the white-painted Casino, behind some palm shrubs, Emma saw Tim. He was leaning idly against the railings, not looking seawards, or at the swarm of people on the plage, but at the elegant passing cars, each one surely a winner in any *concours d'élégance*. Tim was in white flannel trousers and a thin short-sleeved shirt, open at the neck. He was wearing a white linen Basque cap at a rakish angle on his dark hair. There were no sunglasses to hide the moodiness in his eyes.

They spotted each other simultaneously, and there was no time for Emma even to think of retiring, something she might have done had she known he was there.

She said anxiously, "Hello, Tim," and stopped in front of him.

"Oh, hello!" Tim greeted her coolly, saluting casually, barely straightening his figure.

Emma was aware at once that Tim felt he had been slighted and was hurt. Quick to seize her chance to apologize, Emma said swiftly, "I was rather hoping to meet you."

"Were you? What for?"

"I wanted to explain about last night."

"Is there anything to explain?" he asked, coldly indifferent.

"Yes — but perhaps I should have said try to explain."

"I shouldn't bother if I were you. As a matter of fact, I shouldn't have known anything about you, only I was at a loose end and thought you were alone, and suddenly wondered if we could go places together. The French maid who answered the phone mentioned that you were dining in the Palais restaurant with de Witt. I understood the situation at once."

Something in his tone — a subtle nuance which was obviously meant for her — made Emma ask curiously, "Oh, what was it?"

Tim shrugged. "The almighty dollar at work. It was, wasn't it?"

Emma looked straight at Tim. His eyes were screwed up against the sun, and she could not see them clearly.

She did not speak for a moment. Then she said reflectively, looking above the heads of the crowd to the ocean which, even on a calm day, heaved ominously as though inwardly troubled:

"That is news to me. Most people often tell me that I have no money sense. If I had I might have married Arthur de Witt several years ago, when he first asked me."

Tim's eyes no longer glinted. He stared at her with new interest and respect. He did not know whether to admire Emma's courage in refusing the gilded de Witt, who was in the millionaire class, so they said, or to brand her a fool for letting such a glittering chance slip through her fingers.

"Is that true?"

"I am not used to telling lies."

"Oh, you would call them fairy tales. It sounds so impossible."

"Yet it has happened." Then she relented, for there was that same brooding, unhappy, restless and dissatisfied look about Tim as there used to be in Geoff, when life was tough, before fortune smiled upon him. "Are you busy?" she asked, but she knew he was not.

"Not a bit."

"I must be back in half an hour, but we can walk and talk for a while."

"As you wish." Tim turned to walk beside her. "You know the way." He said, "Actually, I was thinking about you when you turned up."

"Oh!"

"Mrs. de Witt rang me up this morning to invite me to join her party to go to San Sebastian tomorrow morning." He tried to speak casually, but the invitation had clearly impressed him. That was news to Emma. She did not know whether to be pleased or not. As one progressed in Tim's friendship so one's responsibility seemed to increase. She thought: 'This will complicate matters with Alphonse. In his present jealous mood he may even accuse me of bringing this about. He does not like Tim.' She said, "Are you going?"

"I said I would, but really it is for you to say. If you would rather I did not go, I can always ring up Mrs. de Witt and make some excuse to stay away."

"I shouldn't do that. If Mrs. de Witt asked you it is because she wants you."

"But do you, Emma?"

"Of course. It should be an interesting day," she said politely. "Don't forget your passport. Arthur and the Chileans who are in the party will want to go to the bull-fight. But I expect Mrs. de Witt will take me to the yacht club to watch the racing."

"Then I shall go. I have never seen a bull-fight."

"You will be all right with Arthur. You won't like it. English people don't; but it is an experience. Arthur knows one of the toreadors, and will probably take you round to the back to see the bulls in their *torils*. You know they are cared for in the same way as we run horse-racing stables. I have heard that bull-breeding is a more flourishing business in Spain than horse-breeding in England. There is even a little chapel behind the arena where all those taking part in a bull-fight go to pray beforehand."

"That sounds odd."

"To us; but it is a dangerous profession."

While chatting they had strolled down to the Grande plage, under the archway outside the Casino, and along the Boulevards des Tamaris, where a band was playing with vigour.

It was Tim's suggestion that they should sit down for a few minutes.

"Or will it bore you?"

"No, I like it."

"I shouldn't have said this kind of thing interested you," he said, as they sat down facing the band.

"Why ever not?"

"It's too cheap," he told her.

Emma felt a surge of annoyance. "D'you mean that I can't enjoy the music because it only costs a few francs to do so? Why do you spoil everything by harping on money the way you do?"

Tim confessed: "I'm not like it in England, only since I have been here. It must be the influence of the de Witt fortune."

"That is unfair and unkind. The de Witts made their money, and have a right to spend it as they choose. Personally, and I know quite a lot about their private affairs, I think they spend it very well."

"I expected you to say that. There is a glamour about exceptional wealth that appeals to some people."

Emma looked pained. She recalled that Alphonse had hinted as much last night. Was she influenced so much by the de Witts that everything about her was coloured with their personalities, to the detriment of her own?

She said resentfully, aware that in some way Tim was hitting both at the de Witts and herself, "*You* don't seem to mind accepting anything they offer."

"Rather not. They fascinate me no end. For all her drab, old-fashioned clothes, Mrs. de Witt is a perfect showman, or should I say show-woman? With her French maid in attendance, and her ubiquitous courier-chauffeur, with his '*beau geste*' manner, she is as exotic as a goldfish."

"Carp!" corrected Emma sharply. "In France carp is far more valuable than goldfish."

"Have it your own way — carp."

Emma thrust out her jaw. Her face had changed while Tim was speaking. Her expression was cold and closed to him.

She said, her voice deadly calm, a fact which if he had known her better would no doubt have penetrated Tim's obtuse mind and pulled him up: "I like the de Witts for themselves. If she hadn't a *sou* I should still love Mrs. de Witt."

"That is prettily said, Emma. There isn't a chance that Mrs. de Witt will ever be without a dollar. You are very loyal though. Whenever I offer the slightest criticism of the de Witt family, good or bad, you simply jump to their defence."

"Why not? No one has ever been so kind to me as Mrs. de Witt, certainly not one of my own countrywomen. I have nothing to thank *them* for."

"Well, I think you can have too much of a good thing. I admit it has its advantages. I don't say you haven't learned a lot from Mrs. de Witt. You have travelled considerably, something you could not have afforded to do alone, but everything has been made too easy for you and you have grown soft. I doubt whether you could look after yourself now, even if you wished. As I see it, Mrs. de Witt is bad medicine for her typist. She gives you undreamed-of luxury, and in return she has sapped the best out of you — your independence and freedom — for no matter how much you think you are free, you are tied to her by the invisible silken cords of luxury. You can leave her tomorrow, but you wouldn't know what to do with yourself. You would certainly not find it easy to get another soft post. But take my advice, vamoose while you are still young. In a few years' time it will be too late. You won't want to leave her, but in the nature of things she will leave you, drunk with luxury, dissatisfied that it can't continue and you are feeling the cold — unless, of course, you change your mind and decide to marry Arthur de Witt. There are many kinds of love, from dollar-worship to hero-worship, and the common or garden sort of love-in-a-cottage."

"Have you finished?" Emma hissed.

"Just about." Tim stifled a yawn. "I wouldn't have said all that if I didn't like you quite a bit."

"Then I wish you hated me."

"Silly girl!"

"Shut up."

Tim asked presently, "When do you leave here?"

"At the end of next week. I shall be glad to go because I love Paris, and I am looking forward to starting work."

"Work! My dear girl, you happen to have fallen soft, and some words have lost their meaning for you."

"I'm no fool, though I know I have been lucky for years."

"Until your luck ran out suddenly," Tim reminded her brutally.

Emma flushed. Then she said a funny thing. It came on the spur of the moment, yet somehow she was not surprised when the words slid easily off her tongue as though they had been waiting to be said for a long time. She spoke impressively and slowly.

"Perhaps I was mistaken, and my luck did not run out after all. Maybe it has been in all the time, and I didn't know it. How blind one can be at times!"

She thought: 'Supposing I had married Geoff and found that after all I had made a mistake? It would have worked out somehow. I should have stuck it. But it might not have turned out well. I am beginning to think it wouldn't have done. He died before I had the chance to prove it one way or the other;

but if he was at heart like Tim, what a living death it would have been. What an escape I had.'

She caught herself up quickly, aware that she had been guilty of disloyalty to Geoff's memory. Then she thought again: 'Why not hold the mirror to the truth? Why should I pretend? It is my life.' Quite suddenly her mind felt light, as though it had shed a burden.

Tim's voice pierced her thoughts. He said:

"Exactly what is your important work in Paris?"

Emma forced herself to reply. After all, she had been well-schooled by Olive in tact.

"There is all the charity work in which Mrs. de Witt is involved. Deserving cases are brought to her notice by certain organizations. I have often to visit the homes of those needing help and report to her on the family, their life and needs. Sometimes it is a matter for the public assistance bodies, or hospital almoners or convalescent homes or approved schools. There is plenty of clerical work attached even to one case. The routine work goes on all the time: countless invitations, begging letters, bills, receipts, a basketful of mail that has to be opened, sorted, indexed and answered."

"Or thrown away?"

"Or thrown away. Such a waste of paper! But I like my job. Mrs. de Witt has the knack of making routine seem like a pleasant pastime."

"What do you do in the evenings?"

"If I am free, I play hard. I study foreign languages, drive the small car, go to restaurants and theatres and — I look upon my evenings as my *larger* day."

"With whom?"

"Oh, I have many friends: and then I go out quite a lot with M'sieur Alphonse —"

Tim burst out laughing. He laughed so much that all the people about them turned to stare, while the band conductor positively glared. The mad English indeed!

"D'you mean Johnny Frenchman? Is he sweet on you, too? But of course he is. He is jealous of me. Every time he sees me with you I wait tremblingly for a glove to be slashed across my cheeks. I feel it is going to be pistols for two, and coffee for M'sieur Alphonse, or do you prefer the foils? Just as in the good old days."

"What utter nonsense! M'sieur Alphonse is devoted to Mrs. de Witt." But Emma spoke with heightened colour. "He is kind to me as he would be to his dog or cat — or pet mouse."

"Ah! Then there must be some sinister idea at the back of his practical French brain, for no man would look at Mrs. de Witt while *you* are there. But why talk of *him*? You would never even look at him with the dollar Prince in the lists — poor Johnny Frenchman!"

Emma was outraged. For a moment she was too astounded to speak. Then she cried at last in a strangled kind of voice that put an end to Tim's smug satisfaction: "How dare you suggest such a thing between Madame de Witt and M'sieur Alphonse? I will not listen to such monstrous talk. No such question has or will arise between them ever. It proves how little you know either of them even to think such a thing. My mistress is adorable, and adored by all her staff from the highest to the lowest. M'sieur Alphonse is one of the best, kindest and most honourable of men. If necessary he would die for Madame, and think it an honour to do so. She is his first consideration. He has made her so. *You* may think it odd, but I don't, but he is entirely uninfluenced by Mrs. de Witt's wealth in the way you suggest. One does not think of dollars in connection with her. That would be vulgar. One does not notice that she is lame because one is entranced by the calm beauty of her face. And let me tell you this, Tim Crake: if you knew Mrs. de Witt as I do, and you understood a quarter of the personal suffering she goes through, or a fraction of the beauty of her mind, you might consider it a privilege to die for her."

There was a little silence after Emma's dramatic outburst. Then Tim said lightly: "That peroration was worthy of the President of France. You are quite lyrical, Emma. Honestly, I didn't know you had it in you. I should never have had the courage to speak so emotionally."

Emma rose restlessly and did not realize that she had risen in the middle of the Overture to *William Tell*, or that people around her were hissing at her bad manners.

"Don't let's talk about the de Witts anymore," she said firmly.

Tim got up too. He was conscious of the disturbance they were causing, and the reaction of the volatile audience. He hurried after Emma's retreating figure.

"We don't seem to be able to hit it off for long, do we? Either you say something which makes me think you are priggish, or I have a tilt at the de Witts, and you get annoyed."

"Oh, it's all right, but don't do it again. I don't like it. Yes, we are touchy."

It was that talk which seemed to open Emma's mind to the fact that she did not like this man. He was carping and critical of everyone and everything, especially those who had more money to spend than himself. It was a 'thing' with him, and showed clearly his poverty of spirit. He seemed to have the power of wringing all the pleasure out of life for her.

She thought with secret annoyance: 'I know exactly the kind of husband he will make for some unfortunate girl. He will say: "Here is five pounds to spend on a holiday, but take care you don't waste it on pleasure. It is all I have; and the gas bill came in this morning." And he will say to his children: "Here is a shilling to buy some sweets. Buy the cheapest, and don't forget to bring me back some change."' She thought, too, 'How could I have bothered about this rude, rough boor even for a moment: a man who pleads frankness as a cover to vulgar attacks on people?'

Without speaking Emma hurried along the plage towards the Palais, Tim dodging about among the crowd, but keeping fairly close to her. He protested in vain at her pace.

Emma passed Alphonse returning to his pension for *déjeuner*.

He raised his hand in smiling salute, and made as though to stop for a chat. He appeared more like the Alphonse she had known so well a year ago, before Geoff came on the scene again after their separation. Alphonse was young and sweet and tender then, debonair and charming.

Emma could only look at him imploringly, silently begging him to understand. She knew it would be but a matter of seconds before Alphonse's glance slid away from her face and recognized her companion.

She watched, fascinated, with a kind of depression, the smile freeze on Alphonse's face, and observed the sudden recovery of his hesitation, and the quickening of his footsteps. What would he think of her? He might forgive any escort other than Tim, whom he hated.

Then he was gone.

Emma felt forlorn and inclined to cry with disappointment and rage. It had been a horrible morning, and all because of that stupid Tim Crake.

"Alphonse won't meet me this afternoon now," she told herself.

Nevertheless, in spite of her fears, Emma put on a freshly pressed white dress and went down to the *salon* at five o'clock hoping that her fears were mistaken, and Alphonse would be waiting as arranged.

He was.

Emma smiled with relief. She did not say anything for fear that what she said might be the wrong thing. She just waited for Alphonse to speak.

He asked, "Did you know this morning that you were going to meet M'sieur Crake?"

He spoke without anger, even gently — but Emma knew.

"Of course not. I happened to meet him outside the Casino, on his way back from bathing."

"Was it your idea that Madame should invite him to go with us tomorrow?"

Emma shook her head. "Mr. Crake told me. I was surprised to hear it."

"And you are glad perhaps?"

"No, I am sorry, because I feel sure…"

Emma paused and Alphonse urged her to continue.

"What are you so sure about?"

Emma had been going to say she was sure that Tim would spoil their day. Then she remembered that Tim was not her guest but Olive de Witt's, and therefore it was not her business to speak her thoughts.

"No matter." She shrugged indifferently.

"I must know."

"No."

"*Bien*, then I shall not take you to buy hats."

"How mean of you! I'll buy them without your help," Emma cried with spirit.

"So, and a sight you shall look — a pork pie, a pannier of flowers, a what-you-call-it, topknot on your head. How I shall laugh!"

Emma did not care what she looked like, or if she caused Alphonse laughter.

"You will be sorry for this one day," she cried childishly.

"Perhaps: but not today; some day, when you have decided to grow up."

Emma's temper had the effect of calming Alphonse.

"I put on this dress especially to please you because you said you liked it."

Alphonse stood back, his head on one side, his eyes raking over her slim figure.

"So I do," he said admiringly. He was smiling now, pleased that Emma was roused. "It is a pretty dress, but nothing shall make me go out with you."

Emma looked at him through her lashes. "Shall I ask M'sieur Crake to go with me?"

"*Bon Dieu*! No," cried Alphonse with horror. "Nevaire! That one would not know a hat from a cabbage!"

"Then you take me?"

"Oh no, no, no. I shall not."

Emma turned away. She was weary of being the butt of these jealous quarrels between Arthur, Tim and Alphonse. Somehow, each one contrived to put the blame on her.

She said quietly: "I am terribly sorry, Alphonse. Nothing of this is my fault."

He did not answer, and she turned to him, saying passionately: "What has come between us lately, Alphonse? We used to be such friends. Now is it *Bonjour*, *Au revoir*, and *Bon soir*, *Dieu vous benisse*, but nothing in between. Are you too tired to play? Don't you want to be friends with me anymore?"

He was silent for a while, looking at her down-bent head. The laughter had died out of his eyes.

Then he said quietly and a little sadly in English, his tongue tripping over the words in an enchanting way that seemed to tear at Emma's heartstrings because Alphonse still loved her so much, and she could do nothing about it:

"I am not too tired for you at any time, Emma; but I am not content with friendship anymore. You remember we talked this out long ago, and the problem was too difficult for us to solve. But you appear to forget, Emma, that I am a human being with all the frailties that are a part of human nature; and sometimes, as now, I feel I cannot go on living so close and so far from you any longer. There is a limit to what a man can endure, and I feel I have reached it."

Emma's head went even lower. She remembered clearly what had passed between them a long while ago. Madame had first claim on their services. They were not free to love each other like other couples.

She said softly, but with quiet determination: "You are more necessary to Madame than I am. Would you like me to go?"

"Oh no; not that. I could not bear it." Alphonse drew in his breath with a hissing sound.

"Then how can I help?"

"That is just it. I do not know. Sometimes I tell myself we shall come to a corner of the road, and the way will be clear for you or for me." Then he added whimsically, "But it takes time to reach that corner, and often I grow impatient."

She was quiet for so long that Alphonse put his hand lightly on the top of her head and fondled it gently.

"Cheer up. The bad time is over. I shall not be weak again. Let me see you smile, Emma." He put his forefinger under her chin and raised her flushed face, and their eyes met for a few seconds before hers fell. "Such a little mouse at heart still!"

Later Alphonse said: "Will you dine with me tonight? There is a new café opened at St. Jean de Luz. With Madame's permission I will run you over in the little car."

"I should love to go, Alphonse." Emma cheered up at once. The evening was sure to be enjoyable.

"It must be early, eight o'clock, I think. That will give us nearly two hours before I take Madame to La Chaumière at ten."

On returning from Chiberta, Olive went to her semi-darkened room to rest before dressing for the evening. She sent for Emma.

"Are you busy, my dear?"

"Not at all. Did you want something?"

"Perhaps you would read to me a little." Then she said in a different tone, "No, don't read: let's talk."

Emma sat down obediently. She looked straight at Olive, marvelling afresh at her roseleaf complexion, and the calm look in her lovely eyes.

"About you, Emma."

"Yes?" Emma wondered what was coming next.

"You are getting to be a 'yes' woman, Emma. It won't do, for it means you will soon be stale. You must learn to assert yourself more, and do a few things that you want to do, not always what I want."

"Yes." Then Emma smiled, and apologized.

"There, isn't that what I was saying? You use the word 'yes' so often it is growing like a mushroom on your tongue. I have never wanted to bind you to me with cords — even silken cords. I believe in freedom. If you don't wish to do something that I ask you to do, I want you to promise to say so. It is as bad for me as for you to have everyone agreeing with me, so for goodness' sake don't be afraid to speak."

"I won't," Emma promised hurriedly, for it was not often that Olive de Witt was so forthright. She marvelled at what Olive had said. It was almost as though Olive was aware of what Tim had said that morning, and saw that though it was rude and uncalled for, there might be a germ of truth in what he said.

Yet Olive was wise and far-seeing, and so what Tim had tumbled upon so crudely must also have been plain to her. She had probably thought it over for some time before speaking. But the criticism, if such it was meant to be, frightened Emma, and she thought a little wildly: 'I knew it couldn't last. What shall I do if Olive de Witt feels she wants a change in those around her? Perhaps she is tired of me already, and this is the thin end of the wedge, and soon she will be telling me to go.' It was a frightening supposition.

Quickly Emma stifled the idea, but she was determined to try to please Olive more than ever. Emma was not thinking selfishly, but selflessly, for Olive was very dear to her.

'One day, soon, when we get back to Paris, I shall talk it over with Alphonse. He will tell me what he thinks about it,' she thought.

Olive had no idea of the panic she had aroused in Emma's mind. The pinprick about asserting herself was deliberate, for Olive wanted to disturb the inner serenity of the girl, to make her think like other girls of marriage — perhaps marriage with her dear Arthur. That was a wish that seemed to be growing fainter, but it was a hope that never left Olive. She knew that youth does not bloom forever, that one morning Emma would wake up and find her admirers cooling off, for who wants the flower of yesterday's blooming?

CHAPTER 13

Overnight Olive de Witt decided to start the journey an hour earlier, so that they could reach San Sebastian before the heat of the day was too intense for pleasure. It was not that the journey was long, but the wait at the Customs on both sides of the barriers might be wearying, especially on a big bull-fight day such as this one.

As usual, Olive was punctual. For a short while the party stood outside the hotel in the brilliant morning sunshine. Olive spoke to the manager who, smiling, fat and urbane, had come out from his office to wish them '*Bon voyage.*'

Suzette, carrying a precious small box of red Moroccan leather holding everything that might be wanted for comfort or sudden illness on a long day journey, from pins to aspirin, smelling salts and brandy, came out with her mistress. Having given the bag into Alphonse's keeping she stood behind the party, waiting to see them off. Having stowed away the bag, Alphonse stood quietly beside the big car. He had already saluted Olive. His eyes rested for the fraction of a second on Emma, whose small slim figure was nearly hidden behind Olive. She wore a thin white dress, the pleated skirt pressed to perfection. She was hot, and fanned herself with a diminutive painted fan which had been given to her last night at the new restaurant in St. Jean de Luz. On her neat head she wore a charming little straw bonnet in fancy straw with a wisp of veil clouding the edge of the brim, which followed the contour of her face. It made her look young and entrancingly lovely. When Emma had appeared in the *salon* a short while ago, wearing the bonnet, Olive had exclaimed with delight: "Emma! How heavenly! Where did you get it?"

Emma, her eyes dancing, had said, "M'sieur Alphonse sent it to my room this morning with his compliments and hoping I would wear it today."

Olive said, "He could not have found a hat to suit you better."

Suzette had screamed in her high-pitched voice, "*Ravissante*, mademoiselle." She gabbled in French to Olive, and Emma caught the word '*épris*', and blushed, wishing that Suzette was not so outspoken.

"I congratulate you," said Olive. "I wonder where Alphonse bought it? I must have the address."

"It says 'Henri' on the box, Mrs. de Witt."

"I have heard of him." Olive had a second look at the hat, and she thought, 'If I could look only half as nice as Emma I should be pleased.'

Later, Arthur had stared hard at the hat and whistled softly: "Attaboy, Emma! Where did you get that hat?"

"It is a product of Biarritz." But she did not say that Alphonse had given it to her.

"It is wonderful — a perfect peach!"

Then, when Emma went out of the hotel, she looked for Alphonse.

Their eyes met for a split second. In that space of time which was both short and endless, Emma caught a curious look in Alphonse's eyes, before he gave his attention to Olive, who was coming down the steps towards him.

It was a disturbing look, and Emma was shocked at her own swift reactions to it. She was thrilled, and for a few moments a spirit of ecstasy seemed to take possession of her body — a feeling of power and triumph and delight. Somehow she had never associated Alphonse with passion.

Of course, she *might* have imagined it. To make sure, Emma looked a second time.

Alphonse was not even looking in her direction.

Olive paused to speak to the Chileans who were to travel in the small car with Pierre, the second chauffeur. Meanwhile, Suzette had taken a bundle of wraps from one of the porters and handed them to Alphonse.

He counted each one meticulously. He glanced with disparagement at Emma's thin tussore dust coat and flung it back at Suzette and said something to her.

Suzette went over to Emma. "M'sieur Alphonse insists that you take a warm coat, mademoiselle."

"Nonsense, it is going to be a blazing day. I only want a dust coat."

Suzette shrugged and reported to Alphonse.

He spoke sharply and Suzette returned to Emma.

"M'sieur Alphonse wishes to speak to mademoiselle, if you please."

Emma went unwillingly.

"Where is your greatcoat, Emma?"

"Don't be silly, Alphonse. I am baking already. You know how hot it is in San Sebastian."

"Yes, I know. I am thinking of the return journey. Please to get your coat." Then seeing Emma's indecision, he said, "If you don't, I shall fetch it myself."

"You wouldn't dare."

"Are you going, or shall I?"

"Oh well, if it's like that —"

Emma went back to the hotel and fetched her coat. She took it out to Alphonse.

"Here it is."

"Thank you." Then in a whisper and a different tone of voice, "Now please pull your hat one inch forward and sideways, over your right eye."

Emma tweaked the bonnet.

Alphonse glanced at it swiftly. "So. I am very pleased with my choice. Do you like it, Emma?"

"Do I like it? Oh, Alphonse! It is perfect. Thank you so much."

There was friendly rivalry by the car as to who should sit next to Emma.

Olive de Witt and the middle-aged Comte de la Tremblay had the wide seat at the back. They were already seated. Then Emma, avoiding the discussion between the men, took the smaller seat in front of Olive. Arthur and Tim put forth their claims to each other as to who should sit beside Emma.

It was Alphonse who mildly suggested that Tim, to whom the route was new, should have the front seat beside him. Once clear of the town, and he was able to talk to his passenger, Alphonse said he would point out many objects of interest.

Tim held back. His reluctance had nothing to do with Emma. It was, of course, the best seat, his view would be uninterrupted, and he would not be expected to turn around and talk to the others. But he did not like Johnny Frenchman. Tim did not trust him. He had a feeling that Alphonse saw and secretly laughed at his shortcomings. He could not air his French before Alphonse, sure that the latter would pick holes in it, and criticize his accent, probably dub it as awful. Tim recalled, too, that Olive had remarked once at Chambre d'Amour that Alphonse had a remarkably pure accent.

Hesitation to face Alphonse made him argue forcibly to be with Emma.

It was Olive who decided. She leaned forward to say:

"Of course, Mr. Crake must sit next to Emma. Arthur, you must sit by Alphonse."

With an impassive face, Alphonse held the car door wide open for Tim.

Then, when his party was stowed safely away, Alphonse asked Olive to excuse him a moment while he spoke to Pierre.

The Chileans sat in the back seat of the little tourer with the cape hood. Pierre was standing beside his car waiting for the Rolls-Bentley to start, when he would follow. He was a local man with a Spanish mother and a French father. His mother's people lived in San Sebastian, and Pierre was looking forward to seeing them today. Alphonse had chosen him to be second chauffeur because he was a first-class mechanic. Apart from that, a disinclination to work, a fondness for pleasure and for the company of girls were against Pierre. Alphonse knew of Pierre's weakness for women. Not that it was wholly Pierre's fault, for girls seemed to conspire to spoil him. Pierre was a handsome virile young animal with great brown liquid eyes, a ready smile, and a soft, plausible tongue. Alphonse did not trust him. But there was a great game of Pelota at Cambo today, and the attraction of noted toreadors at the bull-fight in San Sebastian, just over the frontier; and cars and drivers were at a premium. Indeed, Alphonse was considered lucky to have obtained Pierre's services.

Alphonse spoke to Pierre, his tone impersonal, telling him to keep behind the big car throughout the journey. Pierre agreed readily, showing his strong white teeth.

He crushed out the cigarette he had been smoking surreptitiously, and a look of merriment came into his great brown eyes.

Alphonse opened the door and spoke to the Chileans in the back seat, asking if they were comfortable, pulling the dust cover over the señora's knees, and letting down the window a little.

Then he returned to the big car, in which the atmosphere was intimate, for the glass screen between Alphonse and his passengers was kept down at Olive's request.

"Are they all right, Alphonse?" asked Olive.

"Perfectly, Madame, but that Pierre, he is truly a handful." There was a certain disharmony from the start between Arthur and Tim. Its foundation, of course, was jealousy. Each wanted to be first with Emma. Arthur for once was not in the best of humours. He had lately been going regularly to the races at the Hippodrome de la Barre, where he had enjoyed an amazing run of luck. Yesterday he had gambled heavily on an outsider, tried his luck too far and was annoyed when it gave out. Tim expected to have first place with Emma, partly because he was convinced that she had suggested to Olive de Witt to invite him to go to San Sebastian, but also because they came from the same country, and so she must necessarily prefer his society to that of a man from any other country.

The journey was not a long one, but it was timed for them to arrive before the day was at its hottest, and allowed for the long wait at the frontier. Also, Olive knew from experience that this would be a day of heat, crowds, noise and excitement.

As usual, Olive spoke little. She liked watching the pastoral tranquillity of the countryside, noting the industry of the Basque peasants, the tidiness of their houses with the overhung roofs and the bunches of pink beans tied up under the eaves to ripen and dry in the sunshine ready for the winter, and the small areas filled with flax just ripe for cutting.

The whole route was overshadowed by the purple line of the Pyrenees.

There were long straight roads over which Alphonse drove at a great pace between massed regiments of dark tree-trunks, some of them broken, and all of them scarred by recent forest fires, their green top plumes burnt away, with the scorched earth about them.

Here Alphonse stopped the car to inquire of some tired-looking woodmen when the fire had occurred, if it was subdued, and whether it was safe to proceed.

The men assured him that the fire had been out for several days. They stood watching the passing cars, commenting on a way of life so different from their own.

They drove on through an atmosphere sinister and heavy with the acrid smell of charred wood. Such destruction was depressing, even though there remained near the roadside clumps of yellow flowers which had miraculously escaped the fire, and were spilled like so much gold upon the brown scarred earth.

Emma spoke to Tim, but only half her mind was on what she was saying, and the other half was remembering her dinner with Alphonse last night.

It had been an evening to remember because Alphonse was truly French, in that he knew how to choose a lovely meal.

They had sat at a table on the balcony overlooking the bay, rimmed to the water's edge almost with the striped bathing tents, their domed canopies topped with a golden ball. Emma had a fondness for the artistic little town with its dolly villas painted fantastically in delicate colours.

They had drunk champagne partly because Alphonse said it was a long while since he had given her a treat, but also because he knew that she liked it.

And what champagne! It was dry and aromatic and delicately chilled, so that it stung the palate, and caused the blood to tingle in her veins.

After a wonderful dinner, they sat for a long time over coffee and cigarettes. They watched the twilight darken and the stars appear, so that the dark blue sky seemed to be polka-dotted with gold, and the flowers in the tubs on the balcony drooped their white heads and closed in sleep.

Alphonse had come to sit beside her. He asked, "Do you like M'sieur Crake, Emma?"

She had been in teasing mood. The first headiness after drinking the champagne had left Emma, but she was still vivacious.

"Why do you want to know?" She had glanced sideways at him, knowing that jealousy prompted him to ask the question.

Alphonse had sidestepped her reply neatly.

"Because I should not wish you to get hurt."

She had not expected him to think so kindly about her. She quickly forgot the slight feeling of disappointment which his reply caused her and said: "I liked him at first because he reminded me of Geoff. Then I began to resent his hectoring manner, and his attitude towards people who had made more of a success out of life than he had. Mr. Crake seems to take a delight in being on the opposite side of the fence."

She had realized at once how easily she had been able to mention Geoff. Perhaps Alphonse did too, though he made no remark about it.

He said: "I am glad, because what you say is true. My only fear was that you might not recognize the fact."

She had said the right thing. She felt reassured, as though Alphonse had patted her shoulder approvingly. She was touched by Alphonse's interest in her well-being.

Occasionally, Alphonse glanced in one of the mirrors inside the car. He had carefully tilted it beforehand so that he could glimpse Emma's reflection during the journey. He thought she seemed a little bored, but perhaps the white dress did not suit her so well as a colour. It made her look frail and a little remote — too pure for everyday use. He longed to put a glass case over Emma, and a red cord about it, and a notice, 'Please do not touch', before it... Perhaps she was tired after last night. Alphonse congratulated himself on his good behaviour. It had been an effort not to take Emma in his arms and kiss her — but it was only one of a hundred such efforts over the years. He had been pretty close to breaking down at times, but he had never let himself go. Perhaps the early return had something to do with his fortitude. He was not able to keep Emma out late because he had to be back to take Madame out; and, too, Emma had seemed a little distrait, and he was afraid of boring her. She had been quiet and thoughtful, as though there were something on her mind. Yet, when he had twitted her, Emma had been soft and sweet, so that whatever was on her mind was because of nothing that he had said or done. Of course, it may have been his fancy. Alphonse knew himself to be hyper-sensitive where Emma was concerned. Or it may have been that she was a little disappointed about the hat... That, too, had been taken care of.

In between his glimpses and thoughts of Emma, Alphonse listened courteously to anything Arthur might say to him. He said nothing to attract Arthur's attention to himself, because he wanted Arthur, who was irrepressible, to talk to Emma and M'sieur Crake, something that Arthur was finding it easy to do.

Below them, in the curving valley, was the Bidassoa, a grey little stream which seemed to play in the glittering sunshine.

Alphonse was glad to see it because now they would leave behind them the hard earth and broken trees that had been so tortured and stripped with the fire.

Presently, sweeping around the curve of the hillside, Alphonse saw a long queue of cars, and slowed down to join the tail.

"Is it an accident?" asked Tim, and Alphonse answered him briefly.

He had not been so ubiquitous this morning. He had been friendlier to Emma. To her surprise he had not made a single bitter remark, or flung at her a wisecrack about other people's riches. His tongue was not barbed but honeyed, and twice he had remarked on her pretty hat. The truth was that Emma fascinated him this morning. She seemed younger and softer than usual, or perhaps it was the hat.

He leaned towards her so that Alphonse should not hear what he said, while it would be difficult for Arthur to join in the talk without being rude.

"You are usually so grown-up and sophisticated you make me afraid of you," he told her.

Emma laughed in some amusement. This was not Geoff's criticism. His cry was that she was far too young for his taste.

"What's so funny?" asked Tim, on the defensive at once.

"Nothing really, only the cry used to be that I was always so young."

Geoff had attracted and repelled her at the same time, yet she had truly loved him. This man repelled and attracted her, solely because of that strange similarity with Geoff — but it worked out to the same thing in the end.

Then Tim said, "Don't forget before you go to give me your Paris address."

"I will, but please ring up before you bother to call."

"So that you can arrange another date?" he asked quickly.

"No, just to make sure we are there."

"Don't you expect to be?"

"I expect nothing. I don't know. When work is finished in Paris we may go off somewhere, and still land up in New York or Canada for Christmas. Last autumn we were tiger-shooting in India. Our host was a Maharajah."

Tim sighed. "There you go again —"

"Well, Mrs. de Witt has a zest for life — and why not?"

"I'll say she has," said Tim, "helped by you and him," and Tim pointed surreptitiously at Alphonse's back; "she is as restless as a flea."

Emma looked down at her hands, which were folded demurely in her lap.

"I wouldn't know how restless a flea is," she whispered primly, her eyes dancing with fun.

"No," Tim whispered back fiercely, "you wouldn't — no lady should." He began to laugh helplessly, until Olive leaned forward to ask what the joke was and if she might share it.

"That is the joke, Mrs. de Witt. There isn't one."

The car crawled through the rough cobblestoned main street of Béhobie, behind and in front of many cars of tourists, all going to the bull-fight.

Here, outside the mud cottages that flanked the street, seemed to be collected all the beggars of the town.

They were stopped at the bridge by French customs officers who gave them a cursory glance, stood back and beckoned them to proceed.

"That's soon over," said Tim with relief.

"Don't talk too soon. You haven't seen nothin' yet. You wait," said Arthur.

They crossed the bridge beneath which, lying like an emerald in the river, was the Île des Faisans, the no man's land between France and Spain.

On the far side of the bridge at Irun they were stopped by the officers of Spain — two young beaux, flamboyantly dressed in red and blue uniforms. They strutted up and down importantly, looking into the cars as they passed, looking not for contraband or dangerous criminals, but for youthful lovely faces.

They signalled for several cars to await their pleasure and concentrated on Olive de Witt's car. It was the largest there. They recognized American millionaires. They were infatuated by the glamour of wealth. They also saw Emma, English, lovely, and chic in the becoming French hat. They spoke gaily to Olive about Emma — not rudely, or because they meant to be impertinent, but because Emma was beautiful and they must stare at her. They asked no questions. All traffic was held up while they looked in at the open windows of the car and talked about the bull-fight and the cinema, and a fiesta that was taking place that night.

They spoke gaily to Olive because they liked her on sight, but their eyes were fixed on Emma.

Men in cars in front and behind hooted impatiently, but the Spaniards were deaf to the sounds. Arthur talked to them. He said he knew one of the matadors, and instantly Arthur was a hero, a man of importance.

Tim sat bolt upright. He had nothing to say, even if he could have said it in Spanish. He disapproved of these Spaniards. It was obvious to everyone that if he had known who to report

212

them to he would have done so. At last one of the Spaniards asked if the *Inglésa* was real or preserved in ice?

At length they were allowed to go on, and had to face jeers and catcalls from drivers who had been held up because of them.

Alphonse heard it all impassively. He drove through Irun.

Tim fumed, saying, "I can't think why your chauffeur didn't drive through the mob."

Olive laughed. "M'sieur Alphonse is very clever," she said amiably. "He knows that we have to go back tonight and will probably pass the same guard."

"Weren't you annoyed, Mrs. de Witt?"

"No, I was amused."

"They insulted Emma."

"Oh no, it was all very harmless. The attentions were meant as compliments."

"Emma would make a damned good smugglers' moll," announced Arthur. "She would get through every time. Trained to put it over, I have no doubt but that she could smuggle in the most bare-faced manner — right under their noses."

Tim pretended not to hear. He looked out of his window at the Spanish *casas* and the numerous *fondas* — and nothing was so clean-looking as in the Basque country.

Alphonse slowed down again at the old city of Fuenterrabia, with its climbing terraces, ornate churches, high old Spanish houses, closely shuttered against the heat of the sun, and its old grey lichened walls and gates of the city.

Here, in a wide street, Alphonse stopped the car.

"We shall wait here for half an hour," he said, turning half-round to face Olive. "There is a new parador on the top of the hill, which was once the home of a grandee of Spain. It has been turned into an hotel. The cooking, they say, is marvellous, but the service poor. Perhaps, Madame, you might like to lunch there."

Olive looked up at the height — at the old, grey and hoary building and shook her head.

"That must keep, Alphonse," she decided. "It is too hot for much exertion. Another time, perhaps."

"There is quite a good café across the road," said Alphonse. "You must stretch your legs while I refuel."

He got out and helped Olive across the road, and found her a table in the shade of trellised vines, and went to look for the proprietor. In the meantime the Chileans, driven by Pierre, had drawn up. Arthur brought them into the restaurant and Olive made a fuss of them.

Presently they were served by a Spaniard in a black felt sombrero, with sideboards on his cheeks, and wearing breeches that had once been white, but which were now grey and streaked with pipeclay. He offered them sharp red wine out of blackened goatskins, but they refused, asking for iced *apéritifs* which they knew.

It was hot now; the sun was high. The Comte and Arthur waved fans and mopped their brows with big handkerchiefs. Olive and Emma waved their fans gently, opening and shutting them with an expert click which betokened a familiarity with the fan.

Tim, sitting close to Emma, used a newspaper vigorously, disturbing the warm air and making himself hotter than ever. He went out of the café to watch a string of mules, harnessed with cord, dragging a rickety cart which was laden with sacks.

When he came back to the comparative coolness of the café, Arthur was sitting by Emma.

"Hi, de Witt, that's my place."

214

"It is mine now," was the comfortable but triumphant reply.

"That's not fair."

"Everything is fair in love and war."

The Comte de la Tremblay said to Olive, "It is war right enough."

Olive said plaintively: "*Must* you both squabble in this heat? Arthur, Mr. Crake *was* there first."

For all her gentle utterance Arthur knew that his aunt must be obeyed. He rose at once laughingly, but Emma knew by his flippant manner and the exaggerated bow to the seat he had just vacated that Arthur was angry.

Tim settled himself. "Right is right," he remarked to Emma.

She nodded. "Always insist on your rights," she advised. "It is better to satisfy your ego than to be popular."

"Is that aimed at me?"

"Not especially."

"Wasp!"

"Egoist!"

Emma knew that Olive heard what she said. It was rude, of course, but Emma comforted herself by thinking, 'I have acquired a lovely polish in the last few years, but underneath I am still the old Emma, uncouth, badly dressed, and — yes, I remember —' faintly the memory came back and she smiled — 'sticking out my tongue at a bus conductor because one wet night he refused to let me board his bus, saying it was full.'

Presently she rose and went to sit just behind and between Olive and the Comte. The latter, glasses to his eyes, was peering through the vines at the terraces of houses.

"They remind me faintly of the hanging gardens of Babylon," he was saying.

Olive was shocked. "They are one of the seven Wonders of the World," she said. "There is nothing wonderful in these. They are ugly. Do you see any resemblance, Emma?"

Tim, gazing over at Emma, heard her reply. He thought: 'Nothing is new to her. She has been everywhere. Who would have thought that a little English nobody from nowhere could have fallen so soft?'

Yet Emma fascinated him increasingly. He could not keep his eyes from her. If they did leave Emma for a moment, Tim found them back again the next. He began to wonder how he could make himself attractive to her. It would have to be something striking because Emma was so spoiled and blasé.

He thought with some discomfort, 'Is this love?' He began to count the days feverishly until the end of his holidays, and to wonder what his chances would be with Emma.

Arthur went out to the kerb in the sun and focussed his camera on the party.

"Hold it," he called out, "and for pity's sake don't squint." And to Emma, "I must get in that hat." He clicked the camera while they all sat and posed to show themselves off at their best. Special snapshots were taken of the Chileans, for Olive would not let them feel outside the party. Then Arthur came over to Emma. He picked up a small table and brought it over to her and sat upon it bang in front of her.

"Listen, Emma," he said eagerly, "when I am with my wife and children one fall, in my log cabin in the Adirondacks, and we are looking through the family album of old-time photographs, I shall say —"

It was Olive who rushed to the rescue. She realized that Arthur dreamed so much of Emma that the dreams were a reality to him. He was about to name his wife. She could well imagine the consternation of Emma and Mr. Crake…

She said quietly: "That is a pipe-dream of tomorrow, Arthur. We are in Spain now."

"Okay, Aunt Olive," Arthur replied swiftly. "It is all *mañana* here, so what?"

Emma understood. She knew that Arthur was trying to take a rise out of Tim, perhaps trying to ride him out.

The Comte put down his glasses. "You are as sentimental as all Americans, Arthur."

It was Tim who, irritated with Arthur, could not help saying, "Emma won't be there."

"No?" Arthur queried blandly. "Well, how do you know about that?"

Emma powdered her face and used her lipstick. "Have you quite finished, Arthur? I can't sit here much longer with this dentifrice smile on my face. It is getting stiff."

Arthur fiddled with the camera. He ran outside again.

"Hold it, Emma — atta girl, that's fine." And to the Chilean, "Hold it, Señora Huneues."

Alphonse called for them. He went inside the café and paid for the drinks, glanced at the two watches on his wrist, and put the little red Moroccan case beside Olive's chair. Then he went outside to talk to Pierre who, now that he was in Spain, was behaving more like a Spaniard than a Frenchman.

"Say it," whispered Emma fiercely to Tim. She had risen from her seat and re-joined him. She had seen the expressions flitting across his face as he watched Alphonse doing these little services for Olive.

"What?"

"What you're thinking."

"I'm not thinking about anybody," Tim said mildly. He did not feel like squabbling with Emma.

"Shall I say it?"

"If you like."

"You don't approve of M'sieur Alphonse. No, don't deny it. I can read it in your face. As if he cares!"

"Fortune-teller!"

"I don't have to be a fortune-teller to know that."

"Americanism! You are becoming hybrid, Emma." What barbs there were to his tongue!

"It must be because I like it. I shan't change."

She left him suddenly, going over to Olive and helping her up. The Comte de la Tremblay took the Moroccan bag which Olive had opened, using some toilette water on her face. Olive also took out her purse in case she might want it. Alphonse had put *pesetas* and *centimos* in it, but there were dollar bills too.

They went past the bowing proprietor and crossed the road to where Alphonse stood beside the great car studying a roadmap, and watched, at a distance, by a crowd of small boys with large lustrous and longing black eyes.

Olive opened her purse. "I can't resist them — tomorrow's chauffeurs," she said. "They look so pathetic."

Alphonse closed his map with a bang. He shooed the boys away unceremoniously, speaking to them in their own patois. Then he sprang forward to stop Olive.

"No, Madame. I beg of you. The pathos is a pretence. They are really monkeys. Do not give them money. They will never leave us — or others after us."

"It is only a little jam, Alphonse, a few *centimos* for today's bread," she begged, but slowly she put the purse back.

"No. It will make them dissatisfied for tomorrow, when it shall be only bread."

He took the Moroccan case with the purse inside it from Olive and handed it to Emma with a disarming smile. "Pardon, Madame."

Olive went over to the little car and stood in the sun and talked to the Chilean couple, who were shy and much in love with each other.

They were soon on their way. The road was congested with traffic. There was much speeding and cutting in. For a while there was a burst of conversation among those in the car.

Between Arthur and Tim a kind of tension arose. Both talked a great deal to Emma, each trying to monopolize her.

Once Tim said crossly, "*I* was speaking to Emma, when you chipped in."

Arthur cracked back: "In America, we believe in cutting in at a dance. It gives the other fellow a chance."

"This is not a dance," snapped Tim.

"You're telling me! Same principle applies though."

They drove through Pasajes, a long narrow town with a busy dirty port, and a bottle-necked exit to the Bay of Biscay between rocky cliffs which Arthur said made him feel 'kinda homesick' because it was like a canyon in Arizona — if only because of the shape of things in the brilliant sunshine.

Tim was suddenly full of despair. He cried aloud, "I believe before the day is out that someone in this car is going to be reminded of the lost continent of Atlantis." He was incensed because everyone laughed heartily at him.

Olive said, "Now we really have come to something that reminds me of the suburbs of Pennsylvania — the inevitable street-car lines."

That was more feasible, and no one commented upon it or laughed for street cars, or trams or buses, are all very much alike.

They travelled over rough roads, along sidewalks bordered by snow-white *casa*s in large tropical gardens with palm and eucalyptus trees and pampas grass, purple bougainvillaea and scarlet poinsettia bushes — and, of course, masses of roses. In the suburbs of San Sebastian were dark, open-fronted shops filled with golden pumpkins, citrus fruits, amber melons and long strings of white garlic, and mounds of green almonds.

Emma stole a glance at Alphonse. She approved of the clean line of his head where the hair was cut short above his collar.

She was accustomed by now to Alphonse's kind attentions. They were a part of the man, inseparable from his nature. He would be the same to a peasant as with a princess. It was natural for him to treat all women and old men and children kindly.

Yet today she was freshly astonished with his kindness and consideration and gentleness towards Olive. It seemed to show up against Tim's egotism and selfishness, and his timorous approach to living, and making friends with people by first proving himself to be a friend.

Tim's first thought was, 'What do I get out of this?' just as Alphonse's first idea was: 'How can I please? What can I do to help, to make life easier for her?'

Emma thought, too, how strange it was that she never felt isolated and alone when Alphonse was near. All through her trouble he had stood staunchly behind her; and, looking back, Emma wondered if all her grief and misery had been given to a false loss. She saw now that Geoff's nature was poor and weak and stunted — bitter because no plums of life seemed to come his way, and venting his frustration on her. It was as though something inside her had awakened, and while it showed her Alphonse's solid worth and moral strength, it also showed her Geoff's poverty of spirit. She had often been unhappy with Geoff, but Alphonse's friendship had given her happiness.

They had reached the centre of the beautiful white city. Here the big shops had plate-glass windows, and were full of goods and chic clothes, lace mantillas, and wonderful fringed shawls embroidered with flowers, and, of course, the ubiquitous fan in all shapes and sizes.

Alphonse was driving the car, not merely getting it along, and concentrating on the road. But somehow Emma knew that he missed nothing of what was going on around him. She knew that first of all he would be aware of Olive, what she was saying in her melodious velvet voice, and above all how she was feeling, if tired or in pain. Then, when Olive was labelled to his satisfaction in his mind, swiftly and efficiently as he did everything, Alphonse might notice her, and the way Arthur and Tim were bickering, scarcely able to hide their growing dislike for each other, and all because of her.

Then Olive touched Emma's arm, and she turned swiftly with a smile to see the calm, beautiful face close behind her, and at once the embarrassment that the two men were causing her by their childish behaviour died away.

"Have you a notebook and pencil, Emma?"

"Yes — in my bag." Emma opened her bag and fished for what she wanted.

"Could you make a memo that next week, on our way back to Paris, I must stop off at Bordeaux, and raid the Châpon Fin cellars for some of their famous wines?"

The Comte said that he, too, would like to order some, and he told them that when he was young and his mother had a villa at Arcachon, he and his brother used to visit the Bordeaux market to buy peaches as big as turnips for a few *sous*.

CHAPTER 14

Within moments of Emma making the note, the car drew up before the Maria Cristina hotel; its white facade, with every *persiana* closed against the sun and heat, was dazzling in the hard glitter of noonday.

Though Olive had used her fan continuously she looked weary.

Alphonse and Arthur, with two hotel commissionaires in attendance, helped Olive out of the car. The under-manager hurried out to meet the party, for Alphonse, with that sense of showmanship which Tim so loudly deplored and hated him for, but which obtained the maximum of comfort for his employer everywhere, had made reservations for a large room for Olive, where she could have a short siesta before lunch.

While Olive was being greeted just inside the hotel by the manager, Alphonse took the opportunity of saying quietly to Emma: 'Please, see that Madame she rests. You must rest too, for it will be a long day before we are back at Biarritz. I have known San Sebastian to be hot, but nevaire like this. If you want me, I shall be in the courtyard for a while. I must look after young Pierre. He has met already some charming relations, and he wishes to go off with them. It cannot be permitted except for two hours in the afternoon."

As Olive was being escorted to the lift, Arthur said: "My throat is dry with heat and dust. After a wash I shall go to the bar for a long, cool drink. But I shan't desert you, Aunt Olive. I shall stick around until lunchtime, either in the bar or the lounge. So if you should want me, you will know where to find me. Coming, Crake?"

Tim nodded. He, too, was thirsty. There was no prospect of seeing Emma again until lunch; besides, he wanted a little time to think things out, for his brain felt hot and bothered. Perhaps it was the heat, but he thought not. It was something to do with Emma, who, despite the heat, seemed to manage to *look* cool even if she did not feel so.

He said: "Surely they aren't going to have a bull-fight in this heat? I understand it is held in an open arena. The beasts will go mad if they do."

"The bull-fight does not begin until four o'clock, when the worst heat is over," said the Comte de la Tremblay.

"I can't wait for it," cried Tim. He hated hot weather at any time, but today it seemed unbearable.

The Comte went with the two men as a matter of course. He took Señor Huneues' arm. "You will join us, señor," he said.

Olive smiled her thanks to the Comte. She spoke in Spanish to Señora Huneues, inviting her to go upstairs. She went into the lift with Olive, and Emma brought up the rear.

While Olive and the young señora rested and talked in semi-darkness, Emma, feeling unaccountably restless, wandered over to the big windows. They opened like French windows into the room. The *persianas* were closed, and Emma stood looking down between the slats at the Rio Urumea. The blue haze of heat outside made it seem as though she was looking at everything through blue glasses. Presently her mind wandered, and though she remained still, looking down at the blue haze that hung over the river, it was Alphonse's face she saw, its strong lines, its ready sympathy and its kind eyes. Before lunch, Emma, wearing sunglasses, for the glare was blinding, and carrying a sunshade, slipped out of the hotel and walked along in the shade of the tamarisk trees to the *parc* in front of the Casino.

She sat for a while on the sun-blinded terrace in some degree of comfort, and looked about her at the Bay of the Concha. It was not a new sight for her, but it was always delightful. The scallop-shaped bay, smooth and green, was more like a lake, the flat side of the 'scallop' being the narrow exit to the Bay of Biscay. It was guarded on either side by rocky heights, with the Isla Santa Clara blocking the channel to all but small vessels.

The bay sparkled like emeralds in the brilliant sunshine. Many yachts with white sails moved slowly over the water. Gay flags fluttered from the Yacht Club. There was a white lace-like froth edging the water where gentle waves rippled, and hundreds of bathers played in the warm water. Ringing the yellow sands were the bathing tents, and behind these moved a rainbow-coloured throng of people.

Cars were parked in serried rows behind the *playa*, under the dark green band of tamarisk trees. On the other side of the road were the dazzling white hotels and *casa*s, all veiled in a shimmering blue-green haze of heat. Beyond the town and stabbing the sky was the undulating line of the purple and mauve Pyrenees, menacing against the perfection of the flawless blue sky. The scene was one of lightness and gaiety. The noise and confusion inseparable from an excitable happy throng did not reach Emma.

It was restful sitting here alone. Emma had not to exert herself to talk or listen, or to keep the peace between Arthur and Tim.

She sat with one hand in her lap and the other balancing the sunshade tilted to keep the sun off her face, for the awning above the terrace was there more for decoration than use, and looked at the colourful scene about her which was like a rich living tapestry, but not taking it in.

She was not conscious of thinking of anyone or anything. Her mind was quiet with the heat. She was probably half-asleep.

Then she was aware of Alphonse's presence beside her.

She turned her head to look at him and smiled, like a child who is waking from a sleep, for suddenly the world that had seemed a little empty was different, and she was happy again.

Without speaking she moved aside to let him sit beside her, and moved her sunshade to shield his face, too, from the sun.

He smiled his thanks. He was hatless, and had shed his jacket. The sleeves of his white cotton shirt were rolled up above the elbows, showing his strong tanned arms. He, too, was wearing tinted glasses.

"I saw you come out of the Maria Cristina and followed you. Are you crazy, Emma, to venture out in this heat?"

"I suppose so, but I wanted to get away for a while."

"Madame?"

"She is all right. I left her talking happily to Señora Huneues... You don't look too hot."

"I have changed my clothes. The others were covered in dust, and I have handed them to the steward at the hotel to clean and press."

Emma laughed at such fastidiousness, but it was sensible and made for comfort.

"Where is Pierre?" she inquired.

"I had to let him go. He has promised by all the saints he can think of that he will be at the turnstiles at the Plaza de Toros at four o'clock. I shall meet him there."

"Are you going to the bull-fight?"

"If I want to hold Pierre I must go with him, and he is determined to go."

"You don't like bull-fights?"

Alphonse shrugged. "I am not squeamish if that is what you mean. I am not interested in the noise and heat and blood inseparable from such a fight today, but I must hang on to Pierre. I cannot drive two cars home at the same time."

"I could drive the little one."

"No, it is unthinkable. I shall hold Pierre." Then Alphonse dismissed Pierre as something troublesome from his memory, and smiled. "Let us not speak of that one," he said, "I want to talk about you."

"Yes?"

"Something important. I want to tell you how much I have enjoyed your good temper with that impossible young man, M'sieur Crake."

It was too hot to exert herself much, and Emma agreed. "I don't think he means to be horrid, it is just that he can't help himself. Please don't judge all Englishmen by Mr. Crake's behaviour."

"Of course not. He must be a black sheep."

Emma's reply soothed Alphonse. He gathered from it that she had noticed Tim Crake's behaviour and disliked it.

Alphonse smoked a cigarette and relaxed. He held the sunshade over them and told Emma to rest her arm.

"This is an enchanting spot," Alphonse said. "What a fantastic blue it is over everything."

"The success of the season depends upon the sun."

"Is not that what we all should like — a place in the sun?"

They spoke in desultory fashion of the things they saw about them. There were long satisfying silences between them.

Emma felt more natural with him than she had ever been. It was pleasant sitting by him, listening to his melodious voice.

All fear of him went out of her suddenly. In the past Alphonse had been a mentor and teacher, and that alone instilled some fear into her. But all that was at an end, and they met as equals.

"My hat seems to be a great success with everybody," Emma told Alphonse.

"I knew it would be." He glanced at it critically. Yes, it suited her — even he could find no flaw in the line. He must have been inspired when he chose it.

"Both Mr. Arthur and Tim Crake like it, yet their tastes are as opposite as the poles."

"That shows it to be popular."

"I think it was very clever of you to choose such a good fit."

"Oh, not so clever from my point of view," Alphonse told her airily. "Though to me it is not so perfect as I should like."

"What is wrong?" Emma asked in some alarm.

Alphonse smiled softly.

"Only, *chérie*, that the seal is missing." Then he laughed because Emma had stiffened. "To anyone but you, Emma, that would have been an obvious remark. But you, with your head in the clouds, and your heart only half-awake, will nevaire guess."

Emma did not answer. She knew what Alphonse meant, and her heart began to flutter crazily. He was an adept at making such remarks, and Emma quickly took herself to task for reading a meaning of her own into it. Yet the fact remained, she did believe Alphonse. She was at once happy in a new kind of way, with a happiness greater than she had thought possible. She felt excited. Nothing else seemed to matter except Alphonse, her reactions to him, and what was far more important, his reactions to her. And she thought, 'I don't suppose I shall ever be lonely or depressed again, because Alphonse will always be there.'

After a while Alphonse looked at his two wrist-watches, both of which gave the same time, and started.

"*Bon Dieu*! I have been so happy and peaceful in Paradise I did not realize it was so late. What is the matter with us, Emma, sitting out here during the hottest part of the day? The sole reason Madame wanted to start early from Biarritz was to avoid this tropical heat. Let us go back or you will be late for your lunch."

Then he asked: "Are you tired? But of course you are."

"No, I feel rested."

"You have no headache?"

"Oh no." Wild horses would not have dragged it from Emma that she had a violent headache, brought on not so much by the heat as the excitement that was seething within her, a kind of joy, because she was with Alphonse, that seemed to make her feel delirious with delight.

They walked back unhurriedly through the fantastic blue haze that made them feel they were not in this world, but in some other light world of their own creating, a place where they walked in solitude and companionship and happiness.

Instinctively they kept to the shade of the green tamarisk trees, past soldiers in hot scarlet uniforms, and women whose tanned bodies were in the scantiest of bathing costumes, where everyone seemed to be laughing and light-hearted, and through side streets to the great hotel.

At the lift Alphonse said, "*Au 'voir*, Emma."

She smiled and replied, "*Au 'voir*, Alphonse."

She gave him her hand and Alphonse clicked his heel, bowed over her hand, and swept her knuckles with his lips. There was nothing in such a public salute. Alphonse had done the same to thousands of women. He thought nothing of it. Emma took it like that. But the little ceremony never failed to please her whoever did it, for it made her feel more important than she was, and gave her the confidence, so she said, of a princess.

Tim, coming onto the patio from the bar, saw it. He was dumbfounded. So there was something up between Emma and this Frenchie, something important to make her brave the midday heat of this place which seemed to Tim as hot as hell. He wondered if Olive knew about this. He must hint to her that there were strange goings-on about her. Then he grew angry with the Frenchman and himself and Emma, but most of all his anger was directed against Emma, who had lied to him and hoodwinked him into believing there was nothing between the Frenchman and herself.

Coming out of the blazing sunshine into the semi-darkness and comparative coolness of the reception-hall, with its mosaic-tiled floor and fluted marble columns wreathed in gilt acanthus leaves, Emma did not see Tim.

She had forgotten his existence, and unless he had hailed her she could not have noticed him. She went straight to the lift and was taken to the floor where Olive's room was. She opened the door quietly, not wanting to disturb Olive. It was fresh and dim and much cooler than downstairs.

Señora Huneues was still chatting to Olive. She came from a hot country and did not feel the heat. She was a pretty, dark-haired, small-boned girl, her skin smooth and bronzed by the southern sun. She had a vivacious manner when some of the shyness had worn off, as now, and Olive liked her because she was full of fun and had an apt sense of humour.

There was a tray with bottles and glasses on it standing on a table by the door, and Olive told Emma to help herself. Olive was sucking a piece of ice, but the señora was holding a glass of some green mixture which was half-full.

Over by the window was another dark girl with glorious velvet eyes. She was introduced as a friend of Señora Huneues' — the Señorita Carmen 'So-and-So'. Olive said the name, but it was both difficult to pronounce and to catch, and Emma never really knew it, but always referred to her as Señorita So-and-So. She was an actress making a film on location outside San Sebastian. Olive had already asked her to lunch with them, knowing how delighted and surprised the men would be at having such an acquisition to the party, for she was beautiful as an angel, and she could speak English.

Olive did not ask Emma where she had been, for the girl liked poking around streets in new places.

It was Emma who mixed a drink, put in a couple of lumps of fast-melting ice, and said, "I went on a sight-seeing trip, and met M'sieur Alphonse in the *parc* by the Casino."

"In this heat?" Olive exclaimed.

"I didn't especially notice the heat."

The Chileans laughed and Olive smiled. She looked better now. She had got rid of the dust and weariness of the hot journey, the pain in her leg was bearable, and when Emma asked if she were rested, Olive replied:

"I am ready for anything."

There was no hurry. The four women sat gossiping for twenty minutes. Then Olive retired behind a screen, and made up her face and redressed her hair. In the meantime, Señora Huneues had also made good the damage heat had caused to her make-up. Then they went downstairs, where Carmen was introduced to the men who were waiting for them.

Lunch was served at a big round flower-bedecked table in the centre of the restaurant. Olive asked Tim to sit on her left hand with Emma next to him. Clockwise around the table after Emma were Arthur, Señora Huneues, the Comte de la

Tremblay, Carmen, and Señor Huneues, who was on Olive's right.

The tablecloth was also strewn with scarlet poinsettias. There was a large paper fan by everyone's place, with a view of the Bay of the Concha, with its yachts and bathing tents, and shady tamarisk trees stamped on it. Olive de Witt had a marvellous collection of fans in cases at her villa at Versailles, but she was delighted as a child with this little paper souvenir of San Sebastian.

Everyone studied the gold-printed menu. It was some time before a clear order was given. They had iced cantaloupe, huevos, then partridges stewed in sharp red wine and served with truffles and an assortment of vegetables, and afterwards a marvellous *glacé Marquisita*, which was a speciality of the hotel.

It was too hot for much exertion, mental or physical, and from the beginning of lunch it was a light, frivolous party.

When Emma had passed him by in the reception-hall, Tim had been astounded to see her, then angry. That deepened to abject misery, for she was absolutely insensitive to his presence. It was bad enough that he who had so far managed to avoid falling in love had done so with Emma, without realizing what was happening to him. It was complete. Tim was whole-heartedly in love, not in a holiday fashion, which might be expected to die away in a short time when he was back at work, and life was a monotonous grind. This was for keeps.

Surely the least that should happen was for Emma to reciprocate the feeling. She had not done so. The first attraction, and Tim was sure she was attracted to him at one time, had worn off as their friendship progressed. Emma seemed no longer interested in him. He was sure that she had slyly crept out in the heat of the day to meet the Frenchman. It was obviously a prearranged thing. Tim was angrier than he had ever been, because no matter how he suffered in that he wanted Emma in spite of what she was, he could do nothing about it — at least, nothing that could be used to build up his own happiness. Of course, he could hurt her by spoiling her little game with Olive de Witt, something he meant to do as soon as possible.

Tim was subdued at lunch, partly because he was sitting by Olive de Witt, whom he had long ago dubbed 'high hat', which meant he would have to mind his p's and q's. It was a kind of honour he could have well done without; but also he was feeling too miserable about Emma to exert himself to be pleasant. The only satisfaction, if it could be called such, that he got out of this wretched business, was that Arthur also was out of the running. He, Tim, was in good company. That seemed odd to Tim because he could not get it out of his head that Emma, underneath, was practical where money was concerned. She could never mean serious business with the Frenchman, who was only a glorified chauffeur, while the American, with his dollar account, wanted to marry her.

Tim did not talk much at lunch until the waiter had filled his glass and he had emptied it several times. Then he found a sardonic amusement in talking to Olive de Witt about bulkheads in steamers, which he knew something about. She gave him more of her attention than she should, and seemed to encourage him to talk. Of course, he knew she was bored stiff, but that drove him into more technical detail, and caused him some inward laughter.

Towards the end of the meal, when Olive and the señor were busy talking 'nitrates' (the señor's father had made a fortune out of nitrates), for Olive had parcels of shares in various great nitrate concerns, Tim found himself listening to what the pretty film star was saying to the Comte de la Tremblay, whose little head and small bright eyes made him look exactly like a monkey.

Carmen was talking about the director of her film, who was a Frenchman named Roth.

The Comte said: "I once knew a man called Roth. I wonder if it is the same person. Is yours married?"

Carmen laughed and shrugged her shoulders. "Who knows? I only met him but yesterday. I have not asked him — yes?"

"Does it matter?" inquired Arthur indulgently.

"Not a bit," Tim interrupted unexpectedly. "All Frenchmen who can afford it seem to have a wife and mistress. I always understood the latter was the measure of a man's success."

There was a general murmur of disagreement, and Tim turned to Emma and said in a low voice: "I expect that Johnny Frenchman of yours — Alphonse, isn't it? — has a lover or two in his past — if not the present. I bet with his experience he could give us all a lesson or two in love." He tried to speak impersonally, but his voice trembled oddly. He was repaying Emma for some of the hurt she was causing him.

Emma was eating her last spoonful of the delicious iced pudding. She paused, and put the spoon back into the cut-glass dish. It was as though she had been struck. Then to hide the emotion that rose and burst so shatteringly within her, making her dizzy, she picked up her fan and, opening it with a sharp click, used it languidly as a screen to hide her face. Happily no one else had heard Tim, for they were all talking at once, Carmen's director forgotten.

Tim was staring at her. He saw that her face had gone white, and her blue eyes were staring above the fan straight in front of her. She did not speak, but he knew she had heard him. The shaft he had aimed had gone home, and Tim was delighted.

"Anything wrong?" he queried, determined that she should speak.

"You should know," Emma whispered.

"It is true then? Oh, that was just a guess on my part. Pretty good shot, eh?"

Emma did not answer him directly. She said quietly: "Years ago, when I was first employed by Mrs. de Witt, a rough sort of girl, with no idea how to dress or enjoy myself or get the best out of life, and scared to death of all the luxury and ceremony about me, M'sieur Alphonse took me in hand. One of the first things he taught me was how to treat impertinent young men — and that was to slap their faces."

"Oh! Is that what you are going to do to me, in public?" Tim asked lightly. "Why should you want to treat me like a naughty boy, because perhaps I have happened on the truth about Mrs. de Witt's chauffeur? If you do forget yourself so far then everyone will ask, and quite naturally, why do you of all people take up the cudgels on his behalf? They will think you are in love with him."

Tim spoke in an undertone. He felt a little anxious in case Emma should make a scene. He counted on his last warning to stop her doing anything rash.

Emma turned slightly to face him. There was hate in the lovely eyes that met Tim's for a fleeting moment. Her tongue was venomous.

"I despise myself for ever speaking to you," she said between her teeth. "Do not be afraid that I shall slap your face. I would rather die than touch you."

There was a momentary lull, and Olive glanced around the table. She noticed Emma's paleness.

"Have you a headache, Emma?"

"No, I am feeling very well, thank you, Mrs. de Witt."

"You look — strained."

"Do I?" Emma laughed. It sounded false to her ears. "I assure you I am all right."

Olive rose then. "We will have coffee on the patio," she said, and led the way slowly from the restaurant, passing through a lane of bowing waiters, and stopping to speak for a moment to an unctuous *maître d'hôtel*, commenting on the partridge dish which had tasted so delicious, and sending her compliments to the chef.

Emma touched Arthur's arm with her fan. He responded immediately.

"Yes, Emma?"

"I want to ask you a favour, Arthur."

He dropped back with her saying, "Go ahead," to the others generally. "We'll be there in a moment." To Emma, Arthur said, "It's yours, Emma." They stood facing each other outside the patio.

"Wait until you hear it."

Arthur looked at her in a puzzled kind of way, wondering what was on her mind.

She seemed pale, as though the heat were too much for her. He said with some concern, "I believe you have a touch of sun, Emma?"

Emma shook her head. She was feeling sick, but nothing short of actually being sick would make her admit it.

"I am just tired," she said with a smile.

"I knew there was something," replied Arthur kindly. He thought now that perhaps she wanted him to get her out of going to the Yacht Club with Aunt Olive. Well, he could do that. He would chuck the bull-fight and go off with her somewhere. He was in the mood to be alone with Emma. He said, "I'll do anything in the world for you, Emma, while you are wearing that wonderful hat."

"It is heavenly, isn't it?"

"I'll say it is. Well, out with this favour."

"You are taking Mr. Crake to the bull-fight?" she said diffidently.

"Mr. Crake!" echoed Arthur gaily. "He is Tim to you and me. What's cooking, Emma?" Then, as she made no response, Arthur knew he was not to take her out, and he said more quietly, "Yep, we are going."

"And after the fight you are meeting Mrs. de Witt at the Yacht Club?"

"Sure — so what?"

"Just this. Don't bring Mr. Crake to the Club. Take him home by train when the fight is over."

Arthur stared.

"I can't do that, honey," he said soberly. "Crake is Aunt Olive's guest. Say, Emma," as an idea illuminated his brain, "Crake hasn't been too fresh with you, has he? Because if so —" Arthur stopped, his expression pugnacious.

Emma shook her head. "No."

There was still a frown on Arthur's good-looking face.

"Then I don't get you, Emma."

"I did not think you would."

"What's it all about anyway? I hate riddles. You don't have to be secretive with me."

"It isn't that. It would take too long to tell you now. But I have a good reason. Promise me you'll take him back, Arthur?"

There was a short silence. So the two had quarrelled. Well, he was glad to hear it. The knowledge brought a kind of relief with it. Arthur had been more deeply troubled about this friendship between Emma and Tim than he would acknowledge even to himself. Common sense told him that even if Emma and Tim had squabbled, it would not necessarily improve his own relations with Emma — but it did lessen the field against him.

He said: "I don't know what to say. I guess if Aunt Olive knew I was even contemplating being rude to one of her guests she would be furious with me."

Emma said persuasively: "I can only say that if Mrs. de Witt knew all, she would agree with what I suggest. Of course, she might think up something better, but I don't want to bother her now."

"Okay. You are a silly egg, Emma. But you want something done, and it would take a stronger-minded guy than me to refuse you. What tale I shall concoct for Aunt Olive to swallow I don't know; or how I can persuade Tim to go with me when there is plenty of room in the car, I know even less. I suppose something will occur to me."

Emma heaved a sigh of relief. Arthur had a fertile mind, she knew. He would find it easier to work out a plan than most people.

"Mr. Crake will go without much bother, I think," she told him.

"You should know. I'm hanged if I do," said Arthur.

Having gained her point, Emma said: "Thank you, Arthur. I really am grateful. Then I will leave it all to you. We had better go onto the patio now, or Mrs. de Witt will wonder where we are."

CHAPTER 15

Sitting on the sun-blinded balcony of the Yacht Club, overlooking the Bay of the Concha, Emma thought the afternoon would never end. Yet ordinarily she would have been intensely interested in the racing, and in meeting the many friends who milled about Olive throughout the afternoon. Olive appeared to be enjoying herself, but then she always did, for she had an insatiable zest for life, and was able to pick out unerringly any fun that was going.

Emma sat in the background, away from the limelight, partly because it was shadier and cooler, but also because she wanted to have some time to herself to sort out in her mind the events of the day. The hat. Meeting Alphonse. The warm look in his eye. Tim's insult to Alphonse and her own violent reactions which had astonished herself. Above all, this new love for Alphonse that had grown up in her heart. Something she had only lately discovered existed, and what on earth she was going to do about it.

While the yachts raced over the green water Emma, behind the screen of her dark glasses, was able to close her eyes. Her head throbbed badly. She thought of her bedroom in Biarritz, which suddenly seemed a haven. It seemed a long while since she was there, and yet it was only this morning.

Arthur, the Comte de la Tremblay and Tim had gone off to the Plaza de Toros in a taxi at four o'clock. Tim said "*Au 'voir*" to Olive and Emma, waving his hand and shouting, "See you later."

Emma took no notice of him. She was looking at Arthur, who contrived to whisper in passing: "Bye-bye — see you at the Palais. I'll wait dinner for you."

Emma smiled brilliantly, because with Arthur's going it seemed as though things were on the move at last.

She saw Olive staring at her round-eyed, and asked, "Are you in pain?"

"A little."

That meant a lot. Olive would not admit a little pain.

"Shall I find Alphonse and tell him we will start home earlier?"

"Oh no. Anyway, you would not find him among the crowd at the bull-fight."

Emma returned to her chair. She had a queer feeling that there were more important events of her day to come.

There was a sense of unreality in the air. Of course she should have slapped Tim's face. Someone ought to make him behave. Her mind wandered. There was a moment when Emma, sick with love and longing for Alphonse, was jealous of the Rolls-Bentley that took so much of his time.

She was brought back to the present by Señora Huneues' soft voice telling her in pretty broken English that she and her husband had met some friends from Santiago at the Yacht Club. This was not surprising, for the Club was crowded with South Americans who adored yacht-racing. They were not returning to Biarritz, but staying overnight with their friends in San Sebastian.

"Does Madame de Witt know?" asked Emma.

"Of course: my husband he has told her already, yes."

Emma thought grimly: 'The Chileans are out. Arthur and Tim are not coming with us. We shall be a small party.'

Soon after six o'clock, the Comte de la Tremblay returned alone. He sat down beside Olive and put a large poster, the programme of the fight, and a big fan with pictures of an actual bull-fight on it, in her lap.

"I won't ask if you enjoyed your horrible afternoon," Olive said, glancing at the 'spoils' of the game in her lap.

"I saw four bulls despatched, and then I came away," replied the Comte.

"Where is Arthur?"

"He and his friend came away with me."

"I suppose they have gone to some bar."

"I do not think so. They took a taxi to the *gare*."

"Whatever for?"

"Arthur sent his love to you. I was to tell you that he and M'sieur Crake are returning to Biarritz by train."

Olive was not surprised, for Arthur did not always stick to Alphonse's programme.

She said in an intimate whisper to the Comte: "Between you and me, I am glad that Mr. Crake is not returning with us in the car. Except for a few moments at lunch when he grew lyrical over bulkheads for steamers, I found Mr. Crake a boring young man. I am sorry for Emma. She may feel herself slighted."

Olive went over to Emma, who was now leaning over the balcony rails, watching a yacht which had fouled someone's anchor chain.

"Emma…" she began.

Emma straightened herself to listen.

"I am sorry to have to tell you that Arthur and Mr. Crake have basely deserted us. They have gone to Biarritz by train. I think that long wait at the frontier this morning tired them."

Emma smiled. "Don't be sorry for me, Mrs. de Witt. I am glad. I like Arthur's company, but I cannot bear Mr. Crake."

Olive's expression was relieved.

"I thought he was your friend."

"So did I; and then I found that I had made a mistake."

Olive patted the girl's arm. "Good for you, Emma. I have never met a man I disliked more. I only welcomed him at all to please you." She thought: 'Thank goodness, Emma has decided to write *finis* to that affair. Now I can drop Mr. Crake.'

The Comte sat down with them and had a drink.

Emma said, "Now shall I go and find Alphonse?"

"Please do. Tell him about Arthur and the Chileans."

Emma turned to go, and just then Alphonse, smart and debonair, came out onto the balcony, and looked around for Madame.

Emma saw that he was disturbed, his manner distrait. He went up to Mrs. de Witt and saluted her smartly.

She asked in surprise, "What is it, Alphonse?"

"I have lost Pierre, Madame."

"Lost him! I have no doubt he will turn up presently."

"No. He has gone away with his relatives. It is an *au 'voir*, Pierre."

"You cannot get in touch with him?"

"But no, Madame. We must leave him in San Sebastian. Perhaps Mr. Arthur would be so kind as to drive the Chilean señor and señora in the little car. If he does not know the route, he must follow me."

Olive shook her head. She told Alphonse the news, adding, "It is a pity, but we shall have to garage the small car here and fetch it later."

Alphonse would not agree. "It will be much fuss if we leave the car this side of the frontier. I know the red tape we must cut to get it across later."

"What else can we do?"

Considering Alphonse had been so much against it earlier in the day, he said a strange thing. "It is arranged. Mees Ferrer shall drive the car. She shall keep behind me. It will be no trouble."

Olive demurred. "She is tired."

"Shall we ask Mees Ferrer?"

Emma had not heard this talk. She knew that something untoward had happened, but had no idea what it was.

Alphonse beckoned her to join them. "Shall you be too tired to drive the small car back to Biarritz, Mees Ferrer? I shall lead the way. Pierre, he has failed us."

"Of course," Emma replied simply. Anything Alphonse asked her to do in that soft musical voice she would do.

It was like asking a singer at a party to sing them a song.

"There, Madame. As I said, it is arranged," cried Alphonse triumphantly.

Olive agreed reluctantly. "I don't like the idea at all, Alphonse." And to Emma ruefully: "I told you not to be a 'yes' girl, Emma. You should have said 'no'."

Alphonse smiled. "It is not difficult, Madame."

"Then the sooner we start, the better," Olive said to Emma. "Promise me you will say if you are tired when we cross the frontier. We can garage the car and Alphonse can send for it tomorrow."

Emma promised.

On the long ride back, past Pasajes, where the endless row of dock lights were already on, pale against the glorious but unreal glow of a marigold twilight of orange and yellow; and through streets bordered with tall grey houses in Fuenterrabia, then to Irun to the Spanish Frontier guards where cars seemed to collect from nowhere and form a queue a mile long, the wait seemed interminable.

Emma had followed the big Rolls-Bentley. She could see Olive's hat through the back window, and sometimes the iron-grey head of the Comte de la Tremblay as he leaned over to speak to her; and occasionally she glimpsed the outline of Alphonse's sleek head. During the wait, at Madame's request, Alphonse got out of the big car and came back to Emma. She was not wearing glasses, and Alphonse thought her eyes looked strained. He stood by the open window smiling down softly at her, and his look was a warm caress that brought the blood swiftly to her cheeks, and a kind of vertigo came over her so that she closed her eyes to hide the confusion of her mind.

"Sleepy?" Alphonse asked.

Emma opened her eyes. "No, but I could do with a cigarette."

"There will be time to smoke one before we move on." Alphonse took out his cigarette-case, a slender gold affair with an ornate crest upon it and, opening it, offered Emma a cigarette. She was interested in crests, and knew this one to belong to one of the great families of France, whose estates were lost in the Revolution. As she took a cigarette, with his free hand Alphonse snapped his lighter to life. She had known Alphonse for five years, yet it had never happened before that she was able to see the delicate inscription on the inside of the lid. Tonight it was clear, as though she viewed it through a magnifying glass.

The crest on the outside was repeated in miniature, and underneath it said in French, 'To our dear son Alphonse, on his twenty-first birthday, from Maman et Papa' — and then the date. Emma's heart seemed to stand still. The Alphonse she knew was now dead to her.

So this was Alphonse's secret! It explained his charming manners, his poise, his 'live and let live' attitude towards all men. It explained, too, the Comte de la Tremblay's deference to Alphonse's wishes. He knew the truth, and so probably did Olive de Witt.

Emma lit her cigarette and sat back, her mind in a worse confusion than ever. Now Emma knew why Alphonse would not marry. Certainly he would never marry her, for his family would never approve.

Alphonse spoke and Emma answered at random. It could not have been important.

Presently he left her. "*Au 'voir*, Emma," he said gaily.

"*Au 'voir*, Alphonse." She continued to smile, but she was too miserable to feel happy. She watched Alphonse's back as he returned to the large car and took his seat at the wheel, and it was like looking at something that is over and done with.

She flung away the half-smoked cigarette. It had lost its savour anyway.

At last they crossed the bridge.

The French Customs were not so fussy, and they were soon on their way again.

Then a disturbing thing happened.

The Rolls went forward up the hill. A big powerful car, and several on its tail, which had been held up behind Emma's small car, swept past the latter. Emma had to slow down to let them pass. Everyone seemed impatient to get on, and cut in, forging ahead.

Emma tried to keep count of the tail-lights, for it was darker now, and the mist she had seen rising over the river had thickened into fog.

She came to a bend and kept a car's tail-light in view. Then there was a fork in the road, and Emma kept her eyes fixed on the big car's lights.

One after another, because her mind was busy on other things, Emma made two or three mistakes.

There was an acrid smell of burning, or perhaps it was the fog. Her eyes began to smart. It was a lonely road. All the cars had outpaced her. She was lost.

Emma realized the fact and accepted it philosophically.

She knew, too, that she was near the forests which had recently been on fire, for the smell was not fog, but the burning of trees and all kinds of vegetable matter.

She drew up at the side of the narrow road, while she decided what to do for the best.

She took off her hat and put it carefully on the seat beside her. She loved it because Alphonse had given it to her. The fact that she was lost did not worry Emma unduly, for her mind was occupied now by something far bigger than she had ever known. Looking back over the day it was as though a series of events had happened, each one not important in itself yet contributing to the end in such a way as to change the whole of her life. The Chileans, Tim and Pierre had all played a part.

She thought tiredly, 'It is all finished with Alphonse,' and she thought, too, 'How can I talk about finishing what was never begun?'

In the past she had tried to tempt Alphonse. There were times when she had fancied he was jealous of other men's attentions.

She recalled that time at Fontainebleau, when one evening Alphonse had stood beside her by the little grey stone bridge outside the Château, at the edge of the forest. She had tempted Alphonse to make love to her. It had nearly come off. Yet he had managed to draw back because he did not want to make love to her, for love meant marriage, and Alphonse had no wish to marry. She knew that now.

Alphonse liked the restless life of travel which being in Olive de Witt's service meant; and, above all, he was greatly attached to Olive, who had all the finest qualities a woman could have, but whose disability made it essential for her to have a man at the back of her.

Emma had taunted him once, saying, "You like ducks, don't you, M'sieur Alphonse?"

Unsuspecting, he had agreed, speaking in that melodious voice which enchanted Emma, though she told herself that thousands of men had resonant, musical voices.

Whereupon she had added hastily and with a spice of mischief, unthinkingly too, but not spitefully, "I mean lame ducklings."

He had misunderstood her, taking her literally. He had stared at her with grief in his nice brown eyes, too hurt even to feel angry, and she had felt a worm.

She had cried out in horror: "Please, don't take it like that. I wasn't being personal. I was only meaning people who need you."

"I see," he had replied gravely, but she knew that he had not seen at all.

Emma panicked when she thought of the lonely future. 'How long can I go on now, being near to him, hearing his voice daily, talking to him?' It could not be long. 'What shall I do with my life?'

It was something that would have to be faced, and soon.

A brief ray of hope came to her as she remembered Alphonse's recent outburst when she had asked him to help her choose a new hat and he had refused, thinking she wanted to wear it to please Arthur or Tim.

He had said with genuine anguish, "I am only human."

'So am I,' thought Emma wildly. 'And I haven't Alphonse's strength of character. It is easier for him than for me.'

A break, for her, meant breaking with Olive and Alphonse, and all those people who had made her life for five years. It meant starting again. For them, well, if she went away Olive de Witt would soon find someone else to take her place; thousands of girls were waiting, in imagination, to take on a dream job like this. What curious fate had made her fall in love with Alphonse? Leaning her arms on the steering-wheel, Emma pillowed her head on them and began to cry, quietly at first, and then noisily. It was as if all her frustrated hopes and crushing disappointment with love came pouring out of her in an uncontrollable, copious stream of grief. Nothing would ever matter again now.

Then, when it was all gone, and her mind was relieved and empty of all the torment, slowly she began to take hold of herself once more. She was conscious of the throbbing pain in her head which had been there all the day, but which she had forgotten for the last half-hour. She thought of the red Moroccan bag with regret. It was in the big car. She thought of Olive and her gift of making the most of life, and of the men she had known, some well — a few very well. Through the haze of pain, Emma was conscious of a closeness and stuffiness in the atmosphere which she had not before noticed. She raised her tired head and looked about her with swollen eyes, seeing only a grey haze in the reflected glow of the headlamps.

She opened the window to let in some fresh air, but all that billowed in like a dense white cloud was a suffocating smell of burning.

Emma closed it swiftly, choking a little.

She thought alertly, 'The forest is on fire again.' At the same moment she saw a tongue of flame leap up close by the car.

Several things happened at once.

Instinctively Emma backed the car to turn it. She saw flames licking greedily at the dark ground on either side of her. She went back down the road she had come. Fantastic shapes sped before her vision — a herd of deer, rabbits, their white scuts visible in the haze — a troop of soldiers in red-and-blue uniforms chased across the road, and were swallowed up in the darkness. Woodsmen, brandishing besoms, and looking like witches in their black hats, raced towards a long line of red and yellow flames, flickering like playful imps on the bank before her.

It was like an evil dream, and Emma wondered what was going to happen next. She sped down one road and then up another, having no idea where she was, always running away from a small fire that leaped from the smouldering undergrowth around her.

At last she came to a crossroads and stopped the car, and she thought:

'This must be where I went wrong.'

The acrid smell that had been with her now for what seemed hours was not so bad here. Emma thought: 'Alphonse will miss me. He will come to look for me.' She was sure of that.

She was not worried about being lost, only about that girl Emma Ferrer, who was crying for the moon which she was not going to have. Her heart and mind felt numb. She did not even bother anymore about being found and what was going to happen next.

It was dawn, and Emma was dozing when Alphonse opened the door of the car.

"Thank God you are safe, Emma," he cried. "I have been looking for you everywhere. I have died so many deaths tonight wondering if you were safe."

She awoke with a start, and there was such a look of ineffable sweetness on her drawn face that Alphonse felt a lump rise in his throat.

He took both her hands in his and carried them to his lips, exclaiming at their coldness, trying with his kisses to give them warmth. All the while he was murmuring little endearments, and punctuating them with his kisses.

The steely strength of his hands and his vehement words startled while they comforted her. But even then their full meaning was not understood by her.

Then Alphonse helped her out of the car, saying, "Come with me," and like a child she obeyed.

She saw the big Rolls-Bentley drawn up behind the car she had been driving. It was empty.

Alphonse saw the look and explained: "Madame is safe at the Palais. Mr. Arthur has hired a car and gone back to the Frontier. The Comte de la Tremblay has gone through the pine forests —"

"I was there. The forest is on fire," Emma told him hysterically.

Alphonse put his arm around her.

"There is an old Château near here. It is now an hotel. I have called in there on my way. They shall have a meal ready at any minute."

"You were so sure of finding me?" Emma asked tremulously.

"But, yes, *certainement*. Did you think you could lose Alphonse?" He laughed at the idea.

They went through great open gates and up a vast avenue of trees, and climbed many stone steps until they reached a great iron-studded open door, where they were welcomed by an old man in a bygone livery and a big white apron who led them inside. Alphonse telephoned Olive, who was waiting anxiously for news of Emma. That done, he devoted himself to Emma.

Sitting at a table drawn up by a pine-log fire, they were served with some potage which they ate with wooden spoons, and some silver trout which the old man said were caught last night in readiness for the guests' *déjeuner*. They drank glasses of red wine. Alphonse watched Emma eat. He insisted on her having the choicest morsels.

By that time, some of the numbness that had paralysed Emma's brain had worn off. She was still bewildered, not sure lest at any moment she would awake to find it all a dream.

The old man was garrulous, and suddenly Emma said to Alphonse:

"Tell him to go away."

"*Bien!*"

Alphonse gave the old man a bundle of notes, and told him to go to bed. After a little while, when he had seen the amount of money in his hand, the old man bade them 'goodnight' and went away shutting the door after him, leaving them alone in the huge room.

Emma sat back in her big chair, a half-smoked cigarette dangling between her fingers. She was drowsy with warmth and wine, but too excited by Alphonse's nearness to sleep.

"It is so cosy here. I could stay here like this forever, warm and secure," she confided in Alphonse.

She could speak like this to Alphonse: or could she? Emma caught herself up sharply, and suddenly her face crumpled up like a child's that is about to cry, for she had remembered that the Alphonse she knew was dead. He was as inaccessible as the moon.

"What is it, *chérie?*" Alphonse begged in alarm, not liking her reaction.

At first Emma could not say, and then it did not seem to matter, so she confessed brokenly, yet with a kind of relief: "I have come to the end, Alphonse. Somehow I just can't go on any longer. I can't."

He seemed to understand, for he said in a strong voice that was both comforting and reassuring:

"You could with me, Emma?"

"Please, don't tease. I can't bear it tonight."

"I am serious. It is not a question of if or how you will carry on: I shall not permit you to do so alone."

He rose and came round to her side of the table, and stood for a moment looking down at her in silence.

With her heart beating fast, Emma glanced up at him wonderingly.

Alphonse was smiling. He took out his pocket handkerchief and tenderly wiped her face, which was streaked and sticky with tears.

"Such a dirty face!"

There was that in his smile which was akin to tears, for tonight Alphonse had thought her lost to him forever in the forest fire. He had been down to the depths in hell. He was still shaken but thankful now, and determined that this kind of scare must never happen again.

He took the cigarette from her limp fingers and threw it among the pine logs in the fire. Then he knelt beside her, and put his arms shyly around her, and drew her head to rest on his shoulder.

"Dar-r-rling! Nevaire shall we part," he whispered tenderly. "Emma, my beautiful, *je t'adore*. You must have guessed the way it is with me. I am only human. How could I be near to you and not love you? Do you not know that life means nothing to me if you do not share it?"

Arrested by his loving words, Emma raised her head.

"You love me, Alphonse!" she breathed in wonderment.

"I have loved you ever since that evening, nearly five years ago, when I met you outside the Rochester in London, and you seemed to me so little and lovely and alone, so much in need of someone's love and care. I put my cloak about you. I longed but to cherish and protect you and serve you."

He held her close again and pressed his cheek on her hair. He whispered words of love in English and French. Emma had no idea there were such lovely words in either language, or that they could be said in such soft, loving and caressing tones.

"Why didn't you tell me, Alphonse? If only I'd known! It would have made all the difference."

"I do not know," he told her in a deep slurred voice, "unless it is that I had got it into my stupid head such a beautiful girl could not possibly love me, when there were others better than me around. You do love me, my Emma?"

She was silent for a moment, then she drew away from him a little, and with an exalted look in her lovely eyes she said:

"You are my life, Alphonse. But —" She had suddenly remembered Olive. How could they desert her — even though they loved each other?

Alphonse raised his hand quickly and held her face to him — over his heart.

"No 'buts' tonight, please. Tomorrow we shall talk with Madame. I am not worrying. She is so sweet, kind and understanding. Something will be arranged. But that is for tomorrow —" he glanced up at the windows where the daylight was showing, and corrected himself — "or rather, today."

Emma moved her head to look out of the window too. Alphonse blocked her view.

"Dar-r-rling!" He kissed her eyes tenderly and softly. "*Chérie.*" He kissed her little nose. "*M'petite.*" He kissed the dimple in her chin. Then with a great cry he gathered her close to him, and his lips sought her mouth.

Emma closed her eyes. She had reached for the moon — and got it! She was blissfully happy, for her heart was bright with laughter, love and happiness.

A NOTE TO THE READER

If you have enjoyed the novel enough to leave a review on **Amazon** and **Goodreads**, then we would be truly grateful.

Sapere Books is an exciting new publisher of brilliant fiction and popular history.

To find out more about our latest releases and our monthly bargain books visit our website:
saperebooks.com

Printed in Great Britain
by Amazon